Northern

Fire

BOOK TWO, TORN ASUNDER SERIES

TARA COWAN

Author's Note

DEAR READER,

I hope you are excited to continue Shannon and Adeline's journey. While the *Torn Asunder Series* was initially conceptualized as two books, the story arc eventually demanded three. Therefore, a third and final book will be available soon. Thanks so much for taking this journey with these characters. Buckle up for the ride!

With Love,
Tara

Chapter One

If she had ever pictured her wedding, ever dreamed of it, it hadn't been shotgun. It was June and hotter than blazes, as her grandpa would say, in the Holy City. The restoration of Ravenel-Thompson House hit the usual snags along the way, creating a series of crises to overcome. Adeline, trying to balance work, wedding-planning, and the awkward stares from the men in her crew about the wedding, found herself spread pretty thin.

Adrian was busy with work, and they saw each other little, although when they did it wasn't much of an improvement. There was generally some awkward tension in the air, like the night a couple of days after she had agreed to marry him when they had discussed how much to tell their parents.

He was standing in the kitchen, making something for his son's lunch the next day, and she summoned the courage to say, "Are you going to tell them?"

He looked up from what he was slicing. His eyes made a quick read of her face. "About the baby?"

She nodded. The crickets in the background sounded overly loud. Maybe Jude's nanny, Jane, had left one of the old windows cracked before she had headed home. You would think you could hear the ocean, but nope: Southern crickets were louder.

"Yeah," he said after a moment of thought, alarming her with his bravery. He brushed his hair back with his sleeve. "My mom will know within ten seconds anyway."

She felt him studying her again. His eyes flickered over her face in a disconcerting way. She'd had to stumble upon a psychiatrist. "You?" he asked after a minute.

"No," she said decidedly. "We'll tell them an appropriate three months after the wedding."

His brows drew together slightly, and he came around from behind the counter, crossing his arms and leaning against it. Gah, why did he have to roll up his sleeves after work? There was only so much a girl could take. "Are you sure?" he asked doubtfully. "They'll probably know anyway."

"They'll strongly suspect," she said, holding firm. "But they would prefer it this way. I promise."

He had ventured no further argument and must have told his parents within the next couple of days. How that conversation had gone down and what battles had been waged, she shuddered to think, but she had gotten a very stiff phone call from his mother the next day during which Mrs. Ravenel offered her congratulations and help with the wedding. Overpowered, Adeline had hung up the phone, realizing she needed to have some sort of real wedding.

Adrian had gotten married the first time in the Cathedral of St. John the Baptist in Savannah. She knew that because her historical research of the house had happened to take her to some very modern-looking photo albums. She hadn't been surprised that his wife had looked like Miss America, with long, silky blonde hair, a stunning body, and a beautiful face. What had surprised her, and intimidated her more than all the rest, was that Adrian had actually looked happy in those pictures.

But at least he seemed to be all-in for this wedding, offering both help and funds. Her dad had offered, when they had a rather uncomfortable conversation, to pay for the wedding. But letting the parents pay for the wedding when you were twenty-two was one thing. When you were twenty-eight with a decent job and marrying a man of means, it seemed a little different, especially when they would already be paying for her sister Annie's wedding in December.

Never mind. She needed, she thought, sitting at the kitchen table with a cup of juice while Jane took Jude out for a walk, to plan the wedding. Adeline was more of a beach wedding kind of gal, but she had a feeling the Ravenels would balk at that. She didn't know for sure, because she had only met her once, but she could picture Mrs. Ravenel's mouth turning down in disapproval as she thought about how far her son had fallen. She thought the woman halfway suspected Adeline had entrapped him anyway, so...there was no need for further ruffled feathers.

On a whim, she ran the problem by Adrian once he had gotten home. It was Thursday, but with summer term he wasn't teaching right now. He had put Jude to bed a couple of hours before and had ambled into the kitchen for a glass of tea. He sat down at the table when she asked him and said, "We'll get married at the beach if that's what you want, Adeline. It doesn't matter to me."

"I know, but…" She met his eyes and confessed, "I can't really picture your mom taking off her heels to walk through the sand to her chair, can you?"

A slight twinkle entered his eyes. "No, but on the bright side, Jude would love it."

She traced the rim of her cup. "Have you told him yet?"

He shook his head, expression sobering. "I'm going to this weekend. About the wedding. I thought we would go to the park and talk about it for awhile."

She bit her lip. "I hope it doesn't upset him."

"He'll be fine," he said. "Not much will change for him."

She hoped that was the case. "What park?" she asked, an idea forming.

"Hampton Park," he answered, the idea seeming to strike him, too. "It has a white gazebo and manicured gardens. Would that be respectable enough for you?"

"Yeah," she said, liking the idea, although it would be really hot, and she didn't want to get sick.

"We could have it in the evening," he said, "when it would be cooler."

"True," she said casually, pretending it didn't freak her out that he could read her mind.

And so the plans had been set in motion.

She endured a call from her sister, who expressed equal parts confusion and hurt and was not much assuaged by the idea of being the maid of honor. "Yes, but Addy, are you *sure*? You just met this man! Does it have to be so fast?"

The call from her grandmother was similar, though more reserved, and her parents were being strangely nonintrusive, which meant they were totally freaked out. Adeline laid her forehead in her hand, while mentally trying to prepare for the restoration team from Williamsburg who would assess the structural damage to the newly-discovered fireplace in the library.

Luckily, that took up the greater part of the next week as they assessed, gave figures, and set to work. Adrian had once given her carte blanche for the fireplace. Looking at the figures, she hoped he had really meant it.

Beyond that, she endured an awkward conversation with Jane, who, while smiling and expressing her delight, was probably judging her the whole time, thinking the younger generation abominably haphazard and wondering what the heck was going on.

In addition, she booked the park for the wedding and went to a bridal boutique, coming away with a breezy bohemian creation with Greek-style wrapping at the chest and bodice, a neat natural waist, a cascading skirt with light ruffles, and sleeves with the same shredded Greek feel. She wasn't sure how the groom would like it, but it was in her style and budget, and it was flowy in case she gained any weight. But she didn't think that would happen, since the wedding was only two weeks out, and she was only eight weeks. Though they were a hard-fought eight weeks, with sick bouts and headaches and soul-searching.

She attempted to keep her mind off the crazy turn her life had taken by throwing herself into work, trying not to think of all she and Adrian hadn't discussed, as if that were possible. They both carefully avoided *forever*. He had said that they would see how it went. That was fine, but they needed to talk about the guidelines to this relationship.

When she broached it with him, catching him at his desk one Saturday evening, he had looked up at her where she stood at the door. There was something about his posture that took her back to the General Longstreet Inn. Would the desire ever stop haunting her? It disturbed her that she maybe made him just an object in her mind. She had always thought substance should come first and that physical attraction was a bonus. Not that there wasn't substance to him. It was like a sudoku puzzle trying to figure him out. And that moment in the doctor's office parking garage when she had agreed to marry him hadn't been lacking in substance. Not by a long shot. Maybe she was freaking out for nothing.

"I'm not going to discuss guidelines with you, Adeline," he said. "You're carrying my child."

She flushed a little, as if some lingering 1950's wife-in-pearls within prodded her with the need to shield him from her interesting condition. "Well, that's...very gentlemanly," she said kindly. "But...wouldn't you advise your clients differently?"

"I don't do marriage counselling."

Don't be difficult. "I mean, if you did. Wouldn't you tell them to talk through things carefully, to learn what the expectations are?"

He shifted uncomfortably and finally admitted, "Yes."

So they had discussed a few things. He thought it would be better for Jude if he continued to split the work with Jane, and better for Adeline, too, who had a lot on her plate. She agreed but realized, for the first time, that her relationship with Jude would be a little delicate. Adrian didn't seem to be willing to relinquish much control, which would make it a little difficult to navigate.

They would give each other space, not forcing anything. She had told him, a little awkwardly, that she wasn't ready for a physical relationship, to which he had held up a hand and told her that he understood completely. That was a pretty easy hurdle. She'd been a little uncomfortable about it. It wasn't every man who serenely contemplated marriage in celibacy. But he seemed to take it in his stride. He was being *veeeery* accommodating. She wondered at what point he would snap. It was all getting very real, this marriage thing, diamond rings and legal name-changes real. She had a feeling he didn't like his world being thrown into disorder any more than the average perfectionist. It only remained to be seen how he would handle it.

Dr. Ravenel was sitting at the desk in his disordered library, enjoying a welcome reprieve from the crew's restoration of the fireplace. As he was wondering how to prevent Adeline from working on Saturdays, his brother strode in with little ceremony. Adrian lifted his brows, laying aside the accounts he was working on, and said with a little surprise, "Harris."

Harris was looking relaxed. One might almost think his brother didn't have a six-year-old son, a disaster zone for a house, and an impending wedding.

"Thought I'd come to see how you were holding up," Harris said, eyes scanning his face sharply.

Adrian lifted his brows a little haughtily. "I'm perfectly well. I'm glad to see you, but there was no need."

Harris rolled his eyes in a fashion he probably thought was unnoticeable, sighing.

"What?" Adrian demanded.

"Nothing," Harris said, inspecting the fireplace with repressed horror. It did, indeed, resemble a gaping hole in the wall. Turning back, he said, "I've been stalking Adeline."

Adrian scowled.

"On Facebook," Harris said, unchastened. He pulled out his phone and scrolled through it. "She seems pretty clean," said the attorney in him. "There was a boyfriend about seven years ago. It seems to have been fairly serious. Did she tell you about that?" he asked, looking up briefly.

"No, but considering I myself had a somewhat serious relationship in the past, I think I'll let it pass," Adrian said acidly.

Harris gave him a look. "If there was partying, she was smart enough not to put it on social media. Other than that, your interests don't align at all, but I'm guessing you already knew that."

"Stop! Why did—"

"We need to know what we're dealing with here," his brother responded, pocketing his phone in his blue shorts. He settled his gaze upon Adrian and said, after a moment, "We also need to talk about a prenup."

Adrian met his eyes. After a moment passed, he said, "No."

Harris studied him in a long-suffering manner. "Everyone always says this. I can't tell you how many people tell me there will be no divorce, and then they're crying in my office two years later, and we're trying to unfreeze bank accounts."

"I'm not saying that," Adrian said, feeling harassed. "Neither of us knows where this will lead. I'm saying I'm not going to offer her the insult."

"Legal formalities aren't an insult. It's just being careful."

Adrian clenched his jaw. "What would you have me say? Thank you for sacrificing your whole life for the sake of my child, but will you sign here? No. Even if I had no respect for her, I hope I respect myself more than that."

Harris's jaw clenched and unclenched. He looked like he was using some measure of restraint, but he did say, "Haven't you been through enough? You may not care to see her lawyers bleeding you dry, but your family does!"

Adrian studied him, thinking of several of Harris's relationships that had made him, perhaps, wary. And then his thoughts took another direction, and his eyes became more distant. It was awhile before he answered. When he did, he wasn't quite meeting his brother's eyes. "She isn't like that, Harris," he said quietly. "I couldn't tell you how I know. I just do."

He felt Harris studying him and then met his eyes. A long moment of silence passed. Finally, Harris sighed, saying, "All right." He looked away. "Do you need anything?"

"I told you I'm fine."

"And I told you one of these days you're going to snap," he said, apparently recharging.

Adrian smiled. "Not today."

"Whatever. I'm taking Jude out for ice cream. Where are your keys?"

Reaching into his pocket, Adrian said, "I didn't give you permission."

"I'm taking him anyway," he countered, taking the keys. "How is he taking it?" he asked, losing interest in the squabble.

Adrian hesitated. "It's hard to tell. He's...very contemplative and quiet. It's hard at his age to take in, but he'll process it. He only knows about the wedding, so don't mention anything else."

"I'm glad I came," Harris said forcefully, walking toward the door. "What a mess."

"Yes, we needed only you to set us back in order," Adrian retorted acidly.

The days passed amazingly rapidly, with Adeline working diligently and seeing little of Adrian. The heat was growing more stifling by day, and the tourism to Charleston was pretty intense during the summer, but Adeline wasn't troubled by either: she rarely left the house. She wasn't sure if summer was a busy time at work or if Adrian was trying to get ahead for the honeymoon, but he worked really long days. This left him only a couple of hours at night, at which time she usually tried to stay out of his hair so he could be with Jude. She tried not to dwell on the fact that he might be avoiding her.

She merely concentrated on the house. She was trying to stick to her extended seven-month deadline, both for professional and personal reasons.

It was a week before the wedding when they received a summons from Statesboro. Adrian, who usually went his own way on Saturdays, found her working on the fireplace and stopped inside the door.

"Hey," he said.

She jumped, turning around. "Hey," she breathed, touching her chest.

"Didn't mean to scare you," he said, surveying her work and then her. He came a little closer in, stopping a few feet from her, as he was always careful to do. She appreciated it and everything. She really did.

"No, I'm just jumpy," she said, taking her instrument away, removing the wood chips from it and looking at him.

He studied her features. "Are you tired? You've been going at it pretty hard," he said.

"No, I'm used to it," she said chipperly. "The crew's not here, and I can get so much done. And I really want to finish before...you know..."

"Yeah," he said, looking like he wanted to say something more but refraining. A slight silence developed. "So my mom called. They want us to come to dinner tomorrow."

"Oh." That was very familial and married. Strange that when she had longed, occasionally, for a relationship, that was one of the things she had wanted most. "Um, yeah, sure, that's good with me."

"I can't guarantee it'll be less tiring than working," he said grimly.

She smiled slightly. "I'm sure they just want to get to know me, and to see Jude."

"I'm sure," he agreed, sounding, however, less than convinced.

Adeline found herself riding in Adrian's SUV toward States-boro the next day. She felt like she was going to hurl the whole way there. She tried to chat with Jude, but he was a little quieter, even, than usual. Until she hit on a subject that interested him.

"Do you boys like football, Jude?"

His black eyes sparkled in the way that was so irre-sistible. It was a good thing he had a good nature, or he would be miserably spoiled. She couldn't think Adrian was able to deny him very much. He nodded, smiling his sweet little smile.

Adrian looked in the mirror. "Tell her your team, Jude."

"LSU," he said.

"Oh, yuck!" Adeline said with mock disgust. "Not LSU, Jude!"

Jude giggled. "And Georgia Southern," he added conscientiously.

Adeline gave Adrian a level look. "What an interesting coincidence that you happen to like those teams. I don't believe in indoctrination, Dr. Ravenel."

A smile hovered. "Jude liked those teams on his own."

"I'm sure!" she answered with deep sarcasm.

"Don't tell me you're a North Carolina fan," he said dryly.

"Of course I am," she responded defensively.

"Jude, we may have to get Adeline a separate house to live in."

Jude giggled, and Adeline wrinkled her nose playfully at him, making him bite his lip on a little smile. It made her feel better, too, and when they pulled up in front of his parents' stately Victorian, she was a little more composed than she had thought she would be.

"Daddy, carry me!" Jude pleaded softly as Adrian unbuckled him. Adrian did so without argument, something he wouldn't usually do.

Harris's Infiniti was parked in front of them, so they skirted it, and she let Adrian lead the way up to the back door. He held the door for her and followed her in. There was no need to announce their presence. Everyone was in the kitchen, looking like they'd been having a pretty intense conversation. She couldn't possibly guess what that had been about.

"Hey," Adrian said, looking around cautiously, and maybe a bit warningly.

"Hello, darling," his mother said, coming forward. It was soon to be revealed that she was addressing Jude, whom she took into her own arms, rather than her errant son. "Hello, Adeline."

"Hi!"

"Did you have a good drive?" the elder Dr. Ravenel asked, coming forward, lanky and handsome as ever.

"Yeah," Adrian said, apparently accepting his father's pat on the arm as the sum of affection he would receive from parental quarters.

"Hi, Adeline," Dr. Ravenel said, smiling vaguely. "Welcome to the family."

Adeline suddenly felt embarrassed. She couldn't really explain the sudden attack, except that it was the first time she had been with them alone as a family. And they all knew. "Thank you, Dr. Ravenel," she said, knowing the color was high on her cheeks.

"Call me James," he said, moving off upon his wife's peremptory command to carry the plates out to the patio.

Harris moved forward, obviously pitying her, and looking a little guilty for reasons she couldn't know. He reached for her hand. She gave it, and he pressed it. "We really are happy to have you, you know. And about other things, too," he said, smiling at her in a kind way that reminded her of his brother in his more open moments.

She returned the pressure. "Thanks," she said, releasing her breath and feeling a little of the tension leave her shoulders. At least she had guessed right with her outfit. She was wearing white pants and a lacy blue top, and his mom was wearing something similar.

"Come on, we'll go on out," Harris said, indicating the porch.

"Okay. Do you need help, Virginia?"

Mrs. Ravenel looked up from mincing chives. "Oh. No, I'm sure the smells are bothering you."

And the awkwardness was back. If anyone had forgotten for a split second, they remembered now. Adrian looked quickly at her, apparently worried for her, all lost in this lion's den. But she smiled, and said, "If you're sure," and followed Harris outside.

They talked about the progress on the house and the stuff she had been learning from the ill-fated family box until Adrian joined them, bringing the meat with him. He sat down next to her at the round table, looking like someone who had just had an argument. She wondered if Harris had wooed her outside so Adrian could call their mom to order. She didn't like to be the cause of familial disharmony, though. It kind of made her feel awful.

"So Adeline," Mrs. Ravenel said, in an attempt at friendliness once they had all settled, "what do your parents think about the...wedding?"

Adrian was stiff beside her, but he never looked up. She wiped her mouth. "Um, they were surprised. If you want the honest answer, they think it's kind of crazy."

"Hmm," she responded, apparently content with that. She turned to feed Jude a bite.

Harris brought up some political tidbit, steering them into safer waters. Adeline was just beginning to relax when she began to feel queasy. She told herself she wouldn't be sick, but the fact that she had waited too long to eat hovered in her mind.

Adrian was pretty much stonewalling beside her, obviously still put out by something. Harris was carrying the conversation, his dad responding in a distracted way that simultaneously seemed to amuse and frustrate Harris. Jude interposed now and then to ask what a word meant, and whether Uncle Harris would please cut him another piece of chicken.

Well if nothing else, she thought, trying desperately to keep her supper down, it was good for Jude to come here and be with his extended family. When they arrived, he hadn't even been able to detach himself from Adrian long enough to attack his favorite uncle.

Yep, she was going to have to get up. "Excuse me," she said, covering her lips and getting up. She walked quickly into the house and found a bathroom. Seeing no towels, she went into the kitchen once she was finished, which wasn't long. She had just put her hands on the paper towels when Adrian came through the door.

"Hey," he said softly, scanning her.

"Hey," she said, wetting the towels and dabbing her mouth. "Sorry."

He came forward, getting a glass and going to the fridge. When he had filled it halfway with water, he brought it to her, meeting her eyes as he handed it to her. "No, I'm sorry," he said in the same quiet tone, a soft smile in his eyes.

She smiled, taking the glass. "Not your fault—well, never mind."

He waited while she rinsed her mouth and then said, returning to his usual tone, "I thought only strong smells made you sick."

"I waited too long to eat," she answered, dabbing her mouth again.

He leaned against the counter, studying her. He was being very careful not to step on her toes, to give her space. He might've wanted to ask a question, but he didn't.

"They're probably wondering where I am," she said, filling the gap in conversation.

"They know where you are," he said. "You can stay in here if you don't feel like smelling the food. I'm kind of thinking you should try to eat something, though."

"Yeah," she said, fortifying herself. "Thanks for coming to check on me."

"Adeline," he said levelly.

"I know, but I was thinking that my sister's fiancé would probably say, 'You okay, babe?' when she got back outside," she said thoughtfully, arms crossed as she took another sip of water.

He lifted his brows, looking like he didn't want to touch that one. But he also looked kind of surprised, which boded well. "Feeling better now?"

"Yeah." She met his eyes. "We should probably go back out. Your mom will...something."

"Don't worry about my mom, Adeline. She's just protective. She'll accept you—eventually."

Great. "Yeah, okay," she said agreeably. But she kind of doubted it.

The next week floated along busily without much of a hitch. That was, until the day before the wedding, when the entire wedding party and their families were at the fancy hotel for the rehearsal dinner. They were having dinner on its iron-gated porch overlooking the harbor when Adeline got a call from Hampton Park. The park and the buildings on either side of it had a major sewer problem: the ground was muddy and everything smelled like poo.

Adeline, having left the table, stood off to the side in her light blue dress, blinking and saying, "Okay..." over and over, trying to tell herself not to freak out. She hung up with the promise of a full refund, but afterwards she just stood there, staring into space and wondering what on earth they were going to do. And if it were an omen.

After a few minutes had passed, she looked up and saw Adrian entering the portico where she was standing. Brows drawn together, he said, "Are you okay?"

"Yeah." He was probably thinking it was a repeat puke-fest, but she actually felt okay.

He studied her, hands in his pockets, dress pants and shirt on point but trouble in his eyes. He was about to back out or something. Tell her she could live with him, and he would be there for the birth. She didn't really blame him.

She would've run a long time ago if she hadn't worn her flats that rubbed.

"It wasn't your doctor, was it?"

Her shoulders relaxed. "No." That grounded her. The baby. "We are currently short one wedding venue. Sewer and flooding and…stink. But no biggie."

He smiled, and she felt her spirits lifting as she got lost, for just a moment, in his eyes, dark and inky as the ocean at night. "No. We'll be married at the beach, like you always wanted. Like we should've planned in the first place."

And so they were. They were married on Folly Beach, on the grass, the ocean visible just beyond the narrow dunes, and nobody had to walk through the sand. The pier was also visible in the background, and it was a beautiful wedding, if a little windy. They held the reception at night under the pavilion with lights strung elegantly, lightning bugs adding to the summer ambiance.

They had decided, after almost agreeing not to do a honeymoon, to get away for three days. It would be a long time for Jude, but not enough to traumatize him, especially not while being spoiled by his grandparents and uncle. And maybe she and Adrian could get to know each other a little better. Maybe.

In any event, they set out a little after ten for one of her favorite beaches in North Carolina.

Chapter Two

They ended up spending the night in a hotel along the way since they were both exhausted. She suspected Adrian's contacts were bothering him, too, though he hadn't said as much. And she did not want to ride with anyone at half visual capacity. So she had told him she was tired. It might, perhaps, have been a mistake. Not like stopping at the last hotel was a mistake. In different, and, she had to admit, less entertaining, ways.

The hotel was not up to par and had received a shady cleaning job at best. He came out of the bathroom in a pair of stylish glasses, confirming her suspicions, so at least she had that. But the room had two full beds, which made things awkward. She was almost wishing for a king bed, so no one got insulted, but no one had to touch, either. *Wedding night. Wedding night.* She immediately shut off that strain.

He offered to let her get a shower first, such that it was, but she needed to get caught up on her emails, so she ended up going last. Another big mistake. When she came out, he was already sitting on one of the beds, and she had to be the one who decided. Feeling awkward, she chose the empty bed, which may have insulted him. The beds were hard, the pillows flat, and the air conditioning weak. It was a restless night.

By the time he loaded their bags in the Land Rover (after a slight struggle to get her to relinquish control over her duffel), she was wondering whether they should've come at all. Doubts assailed her as she waited in the car. They didn't know each other well enough for exclusive company for three full days, they were in a stressful situation, and so far, everything had gone wrong. Even the orange juice had seemed gross at the hotel, but maybe that was just her.

He got in, and she studied him, thinking that he was a little quiet, and also that he was still in his glasses. He had probably pushed himself ridiculously to be able to take a couple of days off work. His eyes had been red at the wedding. Hopefully her family didn't think he had had to get drunk to go through with it. She smiled. No, she didn't think so. Her whole family had been stunned when they had seen him, especially Annie's fiancé, who had fancied himself a very handsome man before then. "Is he your *type*?" her brother Austen had demanded. *No,* her mind answered for her. Harris had saved her from that one, claiming her for a dance and being so nice that it went a long way towards putting her in charity with his whole family.

She was sick along the road, having to pull over because they hadn't eaten breakfast. Soon, Adrian found her a sandwich, and she began to feel better. The ride was longer than she expected, though, and she was wearing down. They were about thirty minutes away when he said, breaking an apparent vow of silence, "Feeling any better?"

"Yeah, I'll just be happy to get there, you know."

"Maybe we can get better sleep tonight."

"Yeah, hopefully," she agreed, the large diamond on her finger catching her eye. That had been a surprise. Their relationship felt a little more T.J. Maxx than Tiffany's. But he never made her feel cheap.

She stared moodily out the window, knowing that her thoughts were dark and not sure how to stop them. She knew it was the baby, but it was as if occasionally here lately she actually enjoyed wallowing in misery. The overcast sky and occasional thunder added to the somber mood.

But when they turned into the historic bed and breakfast they had booked, her spirits unaccountably lifted. The house oozed Southern charm and was secluded from much else. The foyer was pleasant, the staircase the stuff of dreams. A bellhop carried their bags up, and Adrian tipped him before turning back to survey the room. Very classy, coastal with an antique feel. And it had one large bed.

Adeline's eyes skittered over that, and she carefully skirted it, going to the bathroom. Once there, she washed her face, rearranged the bandeau in her hair, and came out, hands in her back pockets. Adrian was sitting in the chair by the fireplace, phone in hand, but he looked up when she came out. "Feeling okay?" he asked, looking at her closely. So disconcerting.

"Yeah, pretty good," she affirmed.

"Were you wanting to go out, or..?"

It was Sunday night... "I was kind of thinking to watch Masterpiece..."

He looked like he got a sinking feeling. "All right, but you have to eat. What do you want?"

She looked up at his tone. She was feeling a little tired and would've liked to have ordered in, but, in the interest of peace, she said sunnily instead, "Oh, whatever you want! It doesn't matter to me."

After a moment, his eyes narrowed in their continued survey of her. "You're tired, aren't you?"

"A little, but it doesn't matter. Like you said, we have to eat."

He studied her a moment, hesitating before saying, "We'll do takeout. You stay and get a shower, and I'll be back in a little while."

She smiled gratefully. "Thanks, that would be perfect."

He returned with wholesome food, not at all like the pizza she would've ordered, but then again, it didn't make her sick. Unable to get enough to eat, she popped the complimentary popcorn and sat on the bed just in time for the classy commercials before the show started.

Adrian stood nearby, looking like he wanted to do something but feeling, since it was their honeymoon, like he should stay with her. She looked up at him and lifted her brows in polite inquiry.

"I think I'm going to go down to the lobby and call my mom. Jude will be going to bed, so..."

"Oh, yeah, of course! He'll be missing you, poor little guy," she said.

"Yeah," he said, still wavering. "I'll be up in a minute, then."

She nodded, going back to her show.

Adrian walked around in the lobby, phone to his ear, contemplating the woman above stairs, waiting on his mom to answer.

"Hey, honey," she said on the fifth ring.

"Hey."

"Did you make it?"

"Yeah, we're here."

"I think the wedding went well."

He lifted his brows, surprised. But why question it? "Yeah, I think so."

"Adeline looked pretty."

He blinked. "Yeah, she did." He turned the subject, not sure how long the benevolent mood could last. "How's Jude?"

"He's fine. He wanted to watch something on PBS. Something British. Adrian, dear, you don't have to push him so hard."

He sighed, rubbing his forehead. "I don't make him watch that, Mom. He *likes* it."

"Hmm. Well, your father's watching it with him."

"Was he missing me?"

"Yes, last night a little. I thought he was going to cry, but Harris stayed with us. He did pretty well today, and Harris came to dinner. He just left, but he may have to come again tomorrow. I think Jude actually prefers him to me," she said, sounding baffled.

"He's used to getting his emotional needs from a man, Mom. And Harris probably reminds him of me. Don't be insulted."

"I'm not. It just breaks my heart, Adrian."

He swallowed. Drew his fingers through his hair. He didn't know what to say, so he didn't.

"I've been thinking that...I'll be nice to Adeline, if she's nice to Jude."

He exhaled, rubbing his eyes. "Mom. You have to be nice to her."

"Are you going to let her be a mother to him?"

He sighed. "We're just trying to get through right now. I don't know." Trying to cut off any further harassment, he said, "Can I talk to him, please?"

"Yes, I'll get him."

A few seconds passed. "Daddy?"

"Hey, buddy. Have you had a good day?"

"We went to mass, and then we went swimmin'. I'm watching TV right now," he said, by way of a hint.

Adrian smiled. He had been dismissed twice for this show. But it was good that Jude was a little absent from the conversation. His mind wouldn't start wandering to his cozy bed in Charleston. Adrian told him goodnight and then looked around the lobby for some tea to make for Adeline, guilt pinching him for his sharp tone earlier. She hadn't deserved that.

He made the tea and started for the stairs, using his key and entering. She looked up, tearing herself away. "Was he okay?"

"You have made a monster," he said, handing her the tea.

"I?" she questioned, lost. "Thanks," she said, securing the tea.

"He's watching this," he said, gesturing toward the TV, "and didn't have time to talk to me."

Her eyes lit. "Is he? Smart kid! There are worse things he could watch, you know."

"If you say so." He hesitated. "Well, I'll...get a shower, then."

"'Kay!"

He dragged a hand through his hair, going into the bathroom, taking a lukewarm shower, and coming back to sit on the edge of the bed, a good three feet between them.

Adeline sat beside Adrian on a towel, knees up, binder on her legs. The ocean spread out before them in a sweeping vista. She wore her black 1940's style suit and a healthy dose of sunscreen. He wore swim trunks. That was it. She had thought he was tanned from his daily runs, but as it turned out, he was just blessed with that olivey complexion. And the kind of physique that made it not even a thought to wear a shirt on the beach. And really good feet. She knew that was beside the point, but they deserved an honorable mention.

"What are you doing?" he asked, flecking some gray sand off the blanket and tossing a cautious portion of their snacks to a friendly seagull.

"I copied some of the documents from your dad's box before we left," she said. "It's better than touching them over and over." She wondered if Dr. Ravenel, the elder, would mind if she preserved them, but she didn't want to sound too pushy. He was already being very nice to let her borrow them indefinitely.

"Dad won't care what you do with them."

Adeline shifted. "I might work on them when we get back."

The water rolled in especially close, and she drew her toes in.

"Have you found anything interesting?"

"Yeah, but..." She readjusted her black headband. "Useful..? Not much. You wouldn't believe how negligent these people were in failing to talk about the colors of the walls or the grain of the wood on their floors."

He cracked a small smile.

"Do you know what your family's connection to Middleton Place would have been?"

He narrowed his eyes on a sailboat in the distance. "Maybe Frederick Ravenel's mother was a Middleton."

"No, she was a Shannon. I talked to Joe Kelly over at Middleton Place. He thinks the daughters were friends, but there seems to be a pretty strong connection between the families in the letters that I can't quite grasp. I was thinking that I might do better in their archives."

"You might. They couldn't have *less* than we do."

She smiled. "True."

"Are you hot?" he asked.

She was baking, but no biggie. "A little."

"Is it making you sick?"

She glanced at him. They rarely talked directly about the baby, but he was fairly solicitous in matters of her health. Which was, she thought, his way of showing he cared. Or maybe it was just the doctor within. "No, I'm fine."

"I'm going to go in the water. You'd be cooler if you did, too..."

She shifted, not meeting his eyes. "Oh, I'm fine."

She felt his eyes on her. *Stop that.*

"Are you afraid?" he asked gently, after a moment passed.

What was it about that particular tone of voice he used that made you want to confide all you ever felt to him, when in general, you wanted to hide everything? "Um. A little." She tucked her hair behind her ear, hoping he would leave her alone.

"Do you know how to swim?"

"I used to. I'm not sure now."

He studied her for a moment. "Well...we'll work on it over the summer."

Not likely, Dr. Ravenel. But he looked pretty determined, and she had a feeling he could be about as movable as a rock when he wanted to be. She went back to her underlining, trying not to glance up while he walked toward the ocean and started swimming.

Her eyes landed on a very old, handwritten deed. Her eyes skimmed down to the property description. *Beginning on the Northeast corner of Christian's farm, thence South 145 poles to an oak...* Her eyes skimmed some more, until the end. *Containing 932 acres, more or less.* Her eyes rapidly slipped up to the top. Jean Granger Ravenel had bought it from an Edmund Bellinger in 1700.

The wheels started spinning. Definitely French Huguenot. They had been hugely successful in everything they set out to do, from marrying well to planting. But more importantly, if she wasn't mistaken, she had a property description of Santarella. And a better impression of the Ravenel family's wealth. If they had had 932 acres in 1700, how much more in 1860, on the brink of war and at the height of the South's wealth? And how had it felt when, if she wasn't mistaken, their daughter had left her husband in defiance of rigid Victorian social rules?

Chapter Three

S he was running the moment her feet hit the cobblestones. Her breathing was labored, her emotions threatening to overcome her as she saw the house. The street was darkened around her. She could hear Phoebe calling to her, but she ran up the steps and plied the knocker without looking back. She gave an involuntary cry of gratitude when the door opened and she saw the Ravenel's butler standing on the other side, staring at her as though she were a ghost.

"John Tilman... Oh, John," she gasped, tears streaking down her face. "I prayed I might find you all at home!"

"Miss Shannon," he said softly, and then said it again in wonder, staring at her, blinking beneath his gray brows. He forgot to take her coat or to perform any of the duties of a butler, but Shannon barely noticed.

A deep tremble had overtaken her as she entered and looked around the foyer, dark save a few lamps. Her gaze was almost frantic as she appeared to take in Ravenel

House—the archway, the turned staircase, the handsome furniture—but her eyes were unseeing as her feet started to move forward. Swallowing, she followed the light beneath the door of the library, and, hearing no sound within, she slowly reached for the knob and turned it, staring down at her hand before opening the door.

There was some commotion behind her in the foyer as the servants caught on and word of her arrival spread. But Shannon merely stood in the doorway, looking through vision clouded with tears at her father, whose head was in his hands. He was wearing a black coat. Her father never wore black. That told her everything: her mother was dead.

Her intake of breath brought his head up. He first stared, unseeing, and then he looked as though he, too, were seeing a specter. "Shannon?" he breathed, pale.

"Papa," she whispered, starting toward the desk and sinking to the ground at his feet, the skirt of her travelling gown pooling around her.

"Shannon," he said, blinking and shaking his head. "How can this be? Am I dreaming?"

"Yes. It is I." She reached for his hands, tears blinding her, and, gripping them, said, "She is... My mother is dead?"

His expression changed almost instantly from desperately searching to something quite different—some faraway look she had never seen. He merely looked at her for a long time, letting her grip his hands, though such familiarity was not common to them. "Yes," he said finally. "It is three weeks now."

A whimper left her lips. She had missed it, missed her, missed one last chance.

"Shannon..." His gaze turned intense suddenly. "Is that why you have come? *How* did you accomplish it? My God, did you face two armies alone?"

She drew a hectic breath. "Phoebe was with me. I..." She couldn't think of the last two weeks now. She might go insane if she did.

He stared at her, aghast. "I cannot believe it. I haven't heard that any civilians have been able to pass the lines. Shannon, you could have been killed!

Her lip trembled. She lowered her head, looking at her skirt. Scenes returned to her. Tearful pleas at the Union lines—her mother's illness, her family, her need to return to them. Being held until the Colonel could decide. The terror of the land between. Facing the Confederates. The long journey from Virginia to South Carolina.

He groaned. "Shannon, it was impossibly unwise. I don't think I will be able to return you to him!" He stood, pacing. "Let me think." He plunged his hand through his silver hair, making turns on the carpet. "An appeal to the government, perhaps—"

"I have left him."

He stopped, looking back at her, brows drawing together for a long moment before he said, "What do you mean?"

She stared blindly at the grand white bookshelves. "Just that," she said very softly.

He slowly sank into a chair, not taking his eyes from her. "How? It is impossible!"

"Our differences, they were..." She swallowed, unable to finish.

"Speak plainly to me, girl, do you mean to imply that there will be a divorce?"

"If he wishes it. I said as much in my letter."

Her father was as pale as a ghost, so stunned he couldn't speak for several minutes. Standing, he paced toward a bookcase and dragged a hand that was not quite steady again through his hair. "Did he *ask* you to leave?" he demanded finally.

"No."

"Then you have made a foolish step. The most foolish step that could be imagined for a woman of your position! What do you mean by it, Shannon? What could possibly have been provocation enough to plunge yourself into such disgrace?"

"Believe me when I say there was provocation enough!" she said passionately, tears streaking down her face. "If it is a consolation to you, I don't believe he will divorce me, on religious grounds."

"Divorce or estrangement, it makes no difference to me! The world will know!"

"What do I care for the world?" she burst out. "It is at war! Young men are killing one another on battlefields, and I gather my marriage is to make a difference?"

"Shannon, why?" he demanded, his tone different, more mournful. "Why marry him against all odds, only to...to do this? I cannot understand it!"

She dashed her arm over her eyes. "Do you think I knew how it would be? Do you imagine for a moment I would've... Oh, I cannot explain it!" she exclaimed, running for the door and opening it, only to be brought up short in her mad dash by the sight of Marie on the stairs with one hand lifting her black skirts slightly, a bewildered look on her face.

"It *is* true," she whispered. "*Shannon*."

Shannon stayed where she was another moment, until, overcome, she began walking hurriedly toward her. Marie met her halfway, clasping Shannon against her, stroking her unkempt hair, tears in her eyes as she looked beyond Shannon to her father-in-law and held his eyes. "How..? Never mind that!" she said, feeling Shannon's trembling body.

"Take her upstairs, Marie," Mr. Ravenel said. "I'll see that Cook prepares her dinner. Shall I send Abigail up to you?"

Her mother's maid. The thought made her gasp on a sob against Marie's shoulder. Marie cupped her head as tenderly as though she were a child and said, "Yes, indeed, dear sir, and send word to my Rebecca to draw a bath for her, if you will."

He nodded, looking at Shannon a moment before leaving. Marie studied her another moment in worry before drawing Shannon's arm through hers and leading her gently up the stairs.

Shannon sat in her nightgown on the edge of the bed, the fireplace glowing, her wet hair hanging unheeded against her shoulders. She stared into the distance, so unaware of her surroundings that she may as well have been in a desert as her beloved home.

The door opened, jarring her to awareness, and she saw Marie, still fully dressed, entering with some linens draped over her arm. She had forced Shannon to drink soup and washed her hair with her own hands, but she had not questioned her then. Shannon only hoped her cousin's restraint continued.

"I have another blanket for you. You must be chilled to the bone. You haven't stopped trembling yet."

Shannon looked up, meeting her cousin's eyes. Marie came forward and draped the blanket along Shannon's shoulders. After placing it with care, she sat beside her and took her hand. Shannon could feel Marie's deep, worried study of her profile. There was a slight hesitation, and then Marie said with emotion, "Shannon, I've never seen you like this. Do not... Please do not tell me something has happened to John Thomas."

"No." Shannon blinked slowly. "No."

"Then explain to me... Make me understand what possible reason you can have for coming here, when it must mean your separation from him throughout the duration of the war, however long that may prove to be." Marie's face was a mask of pain, her eyes glassy with unshed tears.

Shannon swiped away a tear and looked toward the wall behind her bed stand, where shadows of the fire danced. "I have severed ties with him. I consider... I consider our marriage as at an end."

There was a long silence. "What?" Marie breathed.

"Don't ask me why—"

"Don't tell me not to ask you why, Shannon!" Marie exclaimed, horrified, squeezing her hand so tightly she thought it might shatter. "I *will* ask, and you will tell me!"

"He—the war—it became...much too difficult."

"Nothing is too difficult for two people who love one another!" her cousin exclaimed, a tear rolling down her cheek.

"You don't know of what you speak. Please. That is at an end. I— yes, I knew that coming here would separate me from him. That is why I did it."

Marie looked utterly startled. "Shannon, I..." Moisture glistened on her eyelashes. "No, I cannot believe it. You *were* resigned to waiting until the war should be finished. You had some argument, perhaps... Something that will seem not to be so very important in time—"

Shannon got down from the bed and walked to the fire, staring into its flames. "Yes, we argued."

"I knew it must be that. And with your longing to see your mother—"

"He accused me of spying for the Confederacy, Marie."

Marie flushed, a pink color spreading lightly to her cheekbones. "Shannon, don't tell me of private words spoken between you," she whispered. "He would not have dreamed they would be repeat—"

"Oh, when will you release this foolish loyalty you feel for him? You must believe me when I tell you that he has dishonored me, and that he will by now know that all ties between us are severed!" Hot tears streamed down her face, while Marie sat looking at her, white as a ghost. She was so shocked she could not speak for several minutes. "I...am certain once he has learned that he is mistaken he will—"

"Apologize? He already did, though whether he truly believed me, I know not and do not care. Don't you see that it was finished before ever that fatal argument occurred? It was impossible to go on. Impossible." Her cousin looked at her painfully, as though she couldn't understand. But how could she? She hadn't been there, hadn't witnessed the slow disintegration of bonds.

Finally, Marie got up slowly, going to her and reaching for her hand, taking it between both of hers. How long they stood there, both crying silently, neither knew. At long last, Marie said softly, "Shannon, it won't do. You cannot divorce. Your reputation will be in tatters. You will not recover from it."

Shannon looked at her numbly. "I have no choice," she whispered.

Marie drew a breath. "You...truly mean to stay here the length of the war?"

"I do."

Her cousin let go of her hand and walked to the bed, wrapping her arm around the bedpost while she looked faraway in thought. "Then we must have some sort of plan, Shannon."

"I see no need to concoct a story. As my father has pointed out," she said bitterly, "the world will know. But all may not be lost. The country is at war—times are difficult. Our neighbors will not disdain me for fleeing a Yankee stronghold, a husband who has taken up arms against my family. And I am a Ravenel, am I not? I hope I may have some credit in this society."

Marie continued to think for some time. "It is very bold, Shannon," she said finally, meeting her eyes. "To fly in the face of such deeply-held beliefs, to threaten the very fabric of society in such a way. We might say that you were summoned to your mother's deathbed, and naturally there would be whispers, but—"

"And when I don't return to the North?"

"It would be too dangerous to do so. No one could question *that*. Oh, we must discuss it with your fath—"

"My mind is quite made up, Marie. My marriage is at an end. I will live here. I will not hide the circumstances."

"But that's just it, Shannon. You *are* still married to him—"

"Only until it can be adjudicated otherwise—"

"Oh, hush, Shannon. He won't do it, and you know it! Marriage is sacred—to him."

Shannon met Marie's eyes and heard in her words a recrimination. Her lip trembled, and she looked away, a tear dropping from her chin to her hand, where her arms were crossed. She looked at the tear, and it seemed to magnify in her eyes, sound drowning, her mind receding. Her brain whirled until she could scarcely stand it, the room seeming as though it were spinning, and she was only brought to the present by Marie taking her arms gently. "Oh, Shannon—oh, no, no—as you say, I can't know... Can't truly know what another's marriage is. You are here now, and safe. That is all that matters. Oh, my dear, what you must have been through! Such a look in your eyes!" And then she was leading her to the bed and tucking her gently. "There, my sweet cousin," she said, kissing her brow. "You are our own. It will be as you say. I will make it so with your father."

Chapter Four

A breath of air like spring toyed with her as she lay on her side, her cheek against the fine fabric encasing the pillow. Shannon slowly blinked awake, the sounds of a city drifting to her. She wasn't still travelling, but she wasn't in Washington either. It was much too warm for December.

Her eyes landed on the red walls with their faint pattern, the soaring ceilings, the magnificent canopy bed, the sumptuous furniture. She hadn't known such luxury since…

She sat up, looking around her as her senses oriented to the time and place. She felt nothing, only numbness.

In a few moments, the door opened, bringing in Marie with Phoebe trailing behind her. One of the dresses Shannon had brought was freshly pressed and draped in her maid's arms. "Such fine weather you have brought with you, Shannon," Marie said, going to the open window, which looked out onto the bay, and closing it before drawing the shade. "Come now, we will dress you."

Shannon swallowed. "Phoebe, I... Were you comfortable last night? I didn't think..."

"Oh, yes, ma'am, I was just fine," she answered, assembling Shannon's hoops and laying all of her undergarments and trappings out. Once Shannon was in them and waiting for Phoebe to button her bodice, she gasped. "Oh, Marie—Frederick! How could I not—"

Marie smiled. "He is well. He was home for..." Her smile slipped. "For the funeral, you know."

Any animation in Shannon's face faded. "Yes," she whispered. "I daresay he must have been."

"He was furloughed for a week. I received a letter from him a few days after he left saying that he had made it to his ship, and that it may be some time before we hear from him. We have tried to accustom ourselves to that."

"He is in good spirits, then?" Shannon asked in worry.

"Oh, yes. And doing what he was meant to do, as I daresay you know."

"Yes. But he cannot like to be away from you and little Rose, *that* I know for certain—oh!" Her eyes grew round, and Marie laughed.

"I wondered when you would remember her."

"I have never forgotten her! To think she is under this roof! Oh, I must see her!"

Marie laughed again. "And so you shall! Just as soon as you are dressed."

Almost as soon as their conversation receded, the faraway look returned. Marie touched her arm, conveying, when Shannon looked at her, a look in her own eyes which said there was more to be discussed when they were alone.

When Phoebe finished fluffing the hem of the gown, she stood, and, asking her mistress to sit at the tigerwood vanity, she began to pin her hair. When that was finished, she withdrew with Shannon's nightclothes.

While Shannon was still sitting, Marie reached for a gold necklace she had brought in and fastened it around Shannon's neck, glancing down at Shannon's wedding ring. Shannon covered her hand with her other.

Marie pressed Shannon's shoulders comfortingly and then knelt beside her. "I meant what I said last night, Shannon. It will be as you say if you truly wish it."

"Papa—"

"Your father is in agreement. He says that you are his daughter and that you shall always have a home under his roof."

Shannon's eyes filled, a weight lifting from her shoulders. "*Marie*," she exclaimed, reaching for her cousin's hand. "How did you manage it? You must know witchcraft!"

Marie laughed. "Nothing so useful as that." She pressed Shannon's hand, look growing more serious. "We are family. We will support one another."

"Frederick will—"

"Leave Frederick to me," Marie said firmly.

Shannon sat still, finally nodding after a moment. They sat in silence for a time until Marie, standing, said, "Well, then, shall we meet your niece?"

The nursery at Ravenel House was just as Shannon remembered it. Nestled between two bedchambers, it was not a large room, but the ceilings were high enough that one didn't feel confined, and its tall window commanded a view of the small formal garden off the back of the house. The walls were white, but it seemed everything else was infused with color. The riding pony was a chestnut, the toy chest red, the rattle lying on the circular carpet blue, and the seat of the rocking chair a rich yellow.

Marie had said as they were walking, "Shannon, you must know that I cannot hold Mammy off from you any longer. I have done so until now, but I imagine she must question you soon."

Shannon fought an inner trembling. She would not be able to stop her from an interrogation of the harrowing journey from Washington. And Shannon had no desire whatsoever to think of its horrors. "I… Yes, well…" She motioned for Marie to continue, and her cousin did so, opening the door and preceding her into the sunny room.

Shannon watched Marie smile and bend down as a waif in a dress toddled toward her, hands outstretched. "Yes, my darling. Your Aunt Shannon has come to make your acquaintance."

Shannon's lips parted as she looked at the bundle in Marie's arms, not a small infant, but, instead, a one-year-old child with an undeniable likeness to herself. Shannon walked forward, filled with wonder for her niece. Rose Marie

Ravenel was as fair as a lily. Her little chin was determined, like Frederick's, and there was some hint of Marie in the eyes that her aunt could not quite discern. But her nose was flat and sloping, like Shannon's, her wispy hair which curled slightly a fine rust red. Shannon's trembling hand stroked over it. "I thought... I had thought it was dark."

Marie bounced her, smiling. "It was, when she was born." She laughed, seeing the wonder on Shannon's face. "I knew you would be pleased."

Shannon flushed. "Oh, no! That is, yes, I see the likeness—"

"Even her papa couldn't believe the resemblance when he saw her a few weeks ago," Marie said, kissing her daughter's cheek.

Shannon's throat burned from unshed tears. "Yes, but I am merely filled with wonder. Oh, Marie, I know it is nothing to yours, but I had not imagined I could love her so much!"

"You always did," Marie said sweetly, reaching for Shannon's hand. "You told me so, remember?"

Shannon's eyes misted, remembering that day at the train station. She could not cry. If she did, she might drown and never recover. She could barely see Marie, but she saw that her cousin was looking concerned and sympathetic.

"Miss Shannon, I've got some things to say to you, ma'am." Shannon knew that *ma'am*. It was not a word intended for respect.

She looked over her shoulder, seeing her old Mammy, who loved her but was not above pointing out the error of her ways. "Yes, I imagine you do, Mammy," Shannon said, gathering her courage. "But I am not your charge anymore, you know. And may we hope that your new one is more biddable."

The woman was of medium height, in her late fifties or early sixties, her frame thin and her arms strong from wrangling children. She had managed both of the Ravenel children to admiration and now exercised an authority over Frederick's child second only to Marie's. But surrender her authority over her former charges she would not, as Frederick could have warned Shannon. She made a noise. "She'd have to be. What were you thinking, putting yourself and Phoebe in that kind of danger? What if you'd been carted off by one of the Yankees? What would your mama say? You think she'd not tell you it's not ladylike? You think she'd stand for it? And how are we going to get you back to this Yankee husband you had to have? I'm not saying he's not a gentleman, because he always was. But— Well, enough of that—"

"Yes, indeed," Marie interrupted hastily, seeing Shannon receding, her eyes growing remote, her thin frame perhaps even trembling slightly. Her brows drew together, and she took Shannon's arm, handing the baby back to Mammy. "Miss Shannon was unable to bring most of her things, so we must see about her wardrobe," she said, drawing Shannon out into the hall and closing the door lightly behind her. When they were alone, she looked at Shannon for a long moment. The sunlight was muted in the upstairs landing, but there was enough light for Marie to make a thorough study of her features. Shannon turned her face away.

"Shannon, you weren't harmed on that awful journey, were you?"

Shannon looked up, lifting her brows. "On the journey? Oh, no."

Marie's brows drew together. "I still cannot believe you undertook it. It is unfathomable to me, what it must have been like. That you weren't caught in some terrible skirmish, we may only thank God."

"Yes." Shannon nodded. "Yes."

Marie studied her. "Well, then. I must go and speak with Cook about dinner. You will find your father in his library, I imagine. And we'll see about dyeing your dresses black this afternoon."

Shannon opened the door to the library, which was brightened by sunlight spilling in from the large bay windows and the white bookcases which soared up to the ceiling. Her father was standing at one of the windows, looking out onto the Battery, his hands clasped behind his back. Just beyond his vision was Fort Sumter, where the Confederates would be holding firm in their defense of the city. The day was so unseasonably warm that the windows had been opened to allow in a gentle breeze. She wondered briefly if the weather were a welcome reprieve for the men isolated on the island.

Shannon shut the door behind her, making her father aware of her presence. He turned. She stayed across the room from him, her green skirts pooling elegantly around her, her hands clasped. "Marie introduced me to Rose," she said softly.

He nodded, looking at her. He had always been regal and intimidating. Neither her marriage nor her time away had made him less so. "I hope I did not imply that you are unwelcome in this house, Shannon. You must always be so."

"Thank you, Papa. I know the circumstances are..."

"Regrettable, to put it lightly." He walked behind his desk. "But as you say, we are at war. Times are...uncertain. The world is not at rest. I must ensure first your safety, and that of Frederick's wife and child. All of the rest must be inferior." He lay his hand along the back of his desk chair. "I do believe Charleston society will do as you say and accept the circumstances. They know it could not be an easy thing to have a Yankee husband. We must ensure that they *do* accept the circumstances, in any event."

She swallowed, having only just considered the taint she might bring to the family. Her nails dug into her hands as she felt breathless for a moment. What had she done? Was there no where she could go?

Her father had seated himself, and, after a long time staring into the distance while Shannon was lost, away in another world, he looked at her. "Daughter, I cannot imagine it being so, but I suppose a father never truly can know." There was a pause. "Did your husband raise his hand to you?"

She looked at him quickly, recalled from the other place to which she had receded. "No," she whispered. "No."

He studied her closely. "I could not imagine it. I always thought...'*The best man who ever lived*,' I believe your brother once said to me. You may imagine the inward reflection such words might produce," he said with wry pugnacity. "But in God's truth, I did think that I was giving you away to a good man, and that I might rest easy in that knowledge, whatever else discomfited me about the life you would lead. And so I must ask: what has he done?"

She blinked, startled. She saw murder in her father's eyes, beneath his silver brows, beneath his calm demeanor. "We... we argued..."

"I knew there'd be lovers' quarrels, not aided by the youth of the groom and the mule-headedness of the bride," he said with annihilating honesty. "Don't speak to me of your arguments. They are not enough to sever a marriage, Shannon, however unhappy you may have been."

Her lip trembled.

"Speak, girl!"

"Do you have any idea what it was like, with a war between us?" she demanded. "With the knowledge that I might never see all of you again? With the awareness that his family barely tolerated my...my Southernness? That sometimes *he* did? Slavery, abolition—it was all we spoke of, it seemed! Every look was questioned, every action scrutinized. And then when the war began, we never saw one another, except to hear that my mother was dying, and for him to accuse me of being one of the young women who aided Mrs. Greenhow in her spying! I hadn't heard from all of you in months, didn't know if my mother had yet died, if Frederick had been killed, whether Santarella had fallen into Yankee hands, and yet I was still loyal...did the best I could to...to be a good wife to him. I didn't know how it would be—didn't imagine I couldn't. I had never felt so alone, so isolated. It was intolerable! When the last terrible quarrel happened, I knew. Had we had children, we might have had something to bind us together, but there was noth..." She caught herself up short in her strong emotion, aghast that she had been so indiscreet, and bit her lip so hard it was a wonder it didn't bleed.

All the same, her father's expression had changed subtly, somehow. His look was a bit distant as he sank slowly into his chair. At length, he said, "Shannon, a marriage is..." He shook his head, letting his words die on the wind. He sighed, and at length said, "You mentioned a letter. I take it you explained your intentions to him in this letter and posted it before you left?"

She stared at the carpet, letting her silence answer him.

He drew a long breath. After a time, he said, "I imagine that there may be a chance after the war that he will be willing to—"

"No, Papa. Please, don't imagine such a thing. I have done the unthinkable. I am aware of that. And I have no idea of a reconciliation, in any event."

He pursed his lips, a sign of anger, but he nodded once, sharply.

She took it as a sign that she was dismissed, and she left feeling mildly ill.

When three o'clock came, Mr. Ravenel, Marie, and Shannon sat down to dinner, and Shannon learned that Santarella was not one of the islands which had fallen into Federal hands. It was too close to Charleston. As yet, it was protected, despite what had happened at Port Royal and to some of the other Sea Islands.

Shannon's mind had been so fevered that she hadn't considered that it was December, and that her family was in Charleston to participate in the season. However, Marie reminded her that, although there was still something of a social season because there were so many officers stationed nearby at forts, the Ravenels were exempt from it, being in deep mourning.

"Of course," she said softly, eyes distant. "Of course."

Her father covered her hand, looking concerned, but saying nothing, only looking to Marie.

"Dearest," Marie said, reaching across the table for her other hand, her mouth set in lines of pain. "Won't you tell us about your journey? What you experienced, I shudder to think!"

Shannon looked at her and then at her father, both of whom were watching her intensely. She hesitated. "I left Washington and rode with Phoebe to the Union lines at Alexandria. They...were suspicious at first, and they took us...for questioning," she said hurriedly. "They held us three days at the barracks, questioning us intermittently. I...told them about my mother, pretending I had been in Washington visiting relatives and praying no one recognized me. Finally, the Colonel decided to let us go. We travelled six hours more before we came to the Confederate lines, and they..." She couldn't tell them that they had been convinced Shannon and Phoebe were prostitutes—they had looked quite haggard by then—and that only Shannon's wedding ring had saved them from being taken into the camp as camp followers, "returned" to the nearest brothel, or arrested as spies. "They questioned us, too. The worst of it was from then on. We encountered some skirmishes. Sometimes we had to flee from them. I had enough money that we were able to spend the nights at posting houses or inns." She didn't mention the harrowing night they had spent under the stars, terrified for their lives, or the difficulty in exchanging her money for Confederate currency. "We managed to take the train from Richmond to Petersburg, and on through North Carolina. After some travel by hired carriage, we boarded the train into Charleston, and...and were able to hire a carriage to Ravenel House from the station."

Her father sat, his jaw hard, staring at the soft yellow wall across from him. Indeed, for a father whose daughter had never travelled more than two miles without the accompaniment of a male, be it slave or family, it was a terrible revelation. A long silence passed. Marie looked at Shannon sympathetically and then stared at her plate.

Slowly, Shannon became aware of her father looking at her, regarding her in his usual way. Finally, the smallest smile flickered and he gave a wry shake to his head. "I believe never was a man cursed with such a bold, daring daughter," he said, laughing softly.

Marie smiled slightly. "Indeed, sir."

He was standing, preparing to retire to his study, but he stopped, pressing a kiss to the crown of her head. "And brave," he added. "Welcome home, Shannon."

Chapter Five

The wind was up, and it was misting rain when Adeline and Adrian crossed the bridge back into Charleston on Wednesday. The radio was playing in the background, the windshield wipers softly keeping tune.

If she were being honest, she didn't really know what the trip had accomplished. He said as little as ever and was as unknowable as the first day she had met him. He was a mystery to her, and their personalities were so different that sometimes, as she had lain beside him, knowing he wasn't asleep either, she had wondered whether he could even like someone like her.

That didn't stop her from being halfway obsessed with him. His mannerisms fascinated her, and even the way he drank his coffee was not small enough to be lost on her. Every detail of his past was contemplated, speculated upon, and pondered. He had grown up in Statesboro, gone to college at Georgia Southern, majored in biochemistry, minored in psychology, gone to medical school at LSU in New Orleans, completed his residency in Charleston, married, she suspected, his college girlfriend, had a son and an unhappy marriage, had a traumatizing experience, after which he had bought the house on Battery Street, maybe hoping to turn over a new leaf. Probably not expecting to father another child and get tied down to his preservationist. Beyond that very resume-like list, she knew nothing. It was amazing how little he let fall in the average conversation.

Adeline crossed her arms, watching the rain trickle down the window. Not even the gorgeous houses rolling by tempted her out of her solemn reverie. She felt him glance at her a time or two, but he didn't say anything. When they parked outside his house, she opened her door and got out on shaky legs. He was already around back with the bags, so she joined him there. He had let her carry her makeup bag on the trip, so she would get that and maybe make a bold move toward her shoes.

He handed her the makeup bag and then touched her arm, breaking his very strict no physical contact rule for the first time since the wedding. She hadn't precisely meant no touching at all. She had been referring to contact more of the General Longstreet Inn variety. But she appreciated it nonetheless.

"Are you okay?"

"Oh...yeah," she said, looking at him and tucking one of her Birkenstocks awkwardly behind the other.

He dropped his hand from her arm, crossing his and touching his chin before tucking his hand back in his other arm. "Adeline, I...wanted to tell you that I'll move all of my things to your room, and you can have mine. I don't want you to feel uncomfortable here."

She touched his arm briefly, to let him know that minor touching was allowed. "Adrian...no. I can't allow that."

His jaw became a little rigid. "Well, you'll have to. I'm not letting you stay up there in that closet."

"No, I meant... Why don't we just move my stuff down there, and...share your room. I didn't mean that I needed to, you know, live like a nun." She winced at the reference. Geez, that was probably offensive to him! "Just that..."

He looked like he was trying not to smile. "Yeah, I got it."

"Yeah, but...are you okay with that?"

He cleared his throat, said, "Of course," and looked away, reaching for another bag.

She glanced at him a few times as they walked up the sidewalk. They climbed the steps and entered the back door, and the smell of supper cooking hit them. It smelled like vegetables and maybe barbecue chicken.

There was running and then a voice said, "Daddy!" Jude appeared, pounding down the hall in his socks. Adrian put the bags down and knelt to accept his crushing hug, rising with him in his arm. "Where's your Nana?"

"Kitchen," he said. "Pa's in the living room. I threw up on the way home."

Adrian lifted his brows and continued to carry him as they made their way toward the kitchen.

"I did, too," Adeline said, eyes laughing. "I mean, on the way to North Carolina."

Jude looked back with interest. "Did you eat too many cookies, too?"

Adeline met Adrian's eyes and flushed. "Probably!" she said.

Adrian sighed, and the first thing he said when they entered the kitchen was, "Mom. You know he gets carsick."

She held up a hand, looking splendid in dress pants, a sweater of the same color tan, and pearls. "Your father gave him the cookies, not I." She transferred her eagle stare to Adeline and said, unenthusiastically, "Hello."

"Hi," Adeline said, shifting her makeup bag when she realized the woman was looking for evidence of her next grandchild. "It smells good."

"I didn't know whether you cooked," she said, "and thought you might be hungry after the drive."

Even though Adrian looked at the ceiling, Adeline said, "Thanks. That was thoughtful. Do I have time to go up and change?"

"I suppose."

Adeline wavered, wondering what that meant. Sighing, Adrian said, "Of course. We'll wait."

"Okay," she said, making good her escape and going down the hall to get her bag. She went up the stairs and into Adrian's room. She had never been in before and felt like she had crossed some forbidden threshold. She wondered if she should have waited to go in with him.

Looking around, she saw evidence that attested to the room's male occupant. The walls were a light gray, the comforter some sort of gray, too. The furniture was nice, and there was one of those old-fashioned valets with a tie flung over it. The bathroom was kind of small, probably carved out of a closet in the twenties. She saw razors and shaving cream and manly shampoo. She set her discordant light blue makeup bag on the counter and washed her face before applying more makeup.

In the bedroom, she stripped to her bra and panties and then looked through her bag, reaching to close the blinds when she realized they were open. Oops. She pulled out a loose black comfy dress, so that Virginia would be able to see no evidence, if there was any.

She stuck her bag into a closet lined with delicious-smelling man clothes and went downstairs to the kitchen, where it looked like Adrian had been having a terse conversation with his mom. He broke off when she entered, and so she would never know what words had been spoken. His dad came over and kissed her cheek. "Here is the bride. You looked lovely, my dear."

She smiled, liking him more each time she met him, even if he was generally too distracted to truly converse. Although he did occasionally back his wife down, which was always scary but beautiful. "Thank you. What smells so good?"

"Chicken," Jude said, sitting at a barstool, looking cute in tan shorts, a white button down, and black eyelashes so long he'd be breaking hearts before too long, if he weren't already. She was sure the drama was as strong at Blessed Sacrament School as any other kindergarten in everyday America.

"Sounds good!" she said, as the last dish was put on the table, and they sat down. Mrs. Ravenel said the blessing austerely, after which everyone except Adeline crossed themselves.

Adeline was sitting beside Adrian on one of the benches and across from his parents. Jude was practically glued to Adrian's side, and going for all of the healthiest things on his plate, like his daddy, who had taken out only broccoli and carrots. She hoped nobody minded, but she was going for the chicken.

"Did you enjoy yourselves?" the elder Dr. Ravenel asked.

"Yeah," Adrian answered.

"What is there to do at this beach you visited?" his mother asked.

"Well, we…went to the beach, and there are several good restaurants," Adeline said. "A couple of good boutiques, and we went sailing one day."

She lifted her brows. "You were able to do that?"

Adeline hesitated, glancing at Adrian, who was giving his mom a significant look toward Jude. "Yeah, it was scary at first, but it turned out to be fun," Adeline said.

"Have you found anything in the box?" Dr. Ravenel asked abruptly. Whether it was an attempt to turn the conversation or because he hadn't been listening to it, they would never know.

"A couple of things," she said. "A land description, which I'm going to give to Harris so he can give it to a title abstractor to trace it down—Santarella, I mean. And there was a mention of the color of the nursery here at Ravenel-Thompson. White. Shannon Ravenel—Haley—was discussing its merits over dark green with her sister-in-law right before the war, and they ended up choosing the white. She must have had children here. I mean her sister-in-law." Gah, her brain was disjointed tonight.

"Where would the nursery have been?" Virginia asked, displaying mild interest.

"I can't quite track it down. I'm wondering if it was a really small room that was absorbed to make those closets and Adrian's bathroom in the twentieth century. The only thing that makes me think otherwise is that one of those walls seems, at first glance, to have been put up in the mid-nineteenth."

"It could be that little guest bedroom," she said.

"Yeah, or even on the third floor, since this was a city house. Anyway, we'll incorporate the dark green somehow since it was a color they considered."

Conversation steered into safer waters then, and the Ravenels left in a timely fashion after. Adeline then went upstairs to take a shower. Adrian's shower was small, but larger than the "refrigerator" she had been using on the third floor. And she forgot to bring in her body wash, so she had to use his man stuff. It smelled great, but she wasn't sure ladies were supposed to smell like that. She ran her hands over her tummy as she was washing. Oh, there *was* a little something. But not something his mom could've seen, or anybody else could if she were wearing a shirt.

She smiled softly, placing her hand over it, her wedding ring catching her eye again. She stroked her thumb back and forth before snapping out of it and continuing with her hair. If Adrian noticed, as he climbed into bed, that she smelled like a man, he didn't say anything. In point of fact, neither said anything at all. But the tension in the room was as loud as ten voices.

Chapter Six

A deline spent the next morning, since the crew had plenty to do, moving her stuff down from the third floor. She smelled whatever Jane and Jude were having for breakfast, but since it threatened to make her a little nauseated, she steered clear of the kitchen.

Adrian had dressed and gone to work before Adeline had even awakened. How he had been so quiet, she didn't know. She hadn't even heard his alarm. But she had smelled traces of his cologne. Geez, what *was* that? She'd like to date that bottle.

She went downstairs to confer with Joe. They were on schedule to be completely finished with the balconies by next week, which was a huge win, and made her feel slightly less irresponsible than the norm here lately.

The man from Williamsburg was willing to send a crew, for a price, to restore the family crest and motto on the fireplace. She had asked for examples of their work, and the pictures she scrolled through on her laptop boded well, so she scheduled a time for them to come. Thinking she would wait until that was finished before she began on the woodwork, she walked through the downstairs.

They had painted the dining room, and she had fully restored its fireplace. So all that remained was purchasing the appropriate furniture and finding an antique medallion worthy of the gasolier, which had, at some point, been converted to electricity.

She scribbled some notes and went into the living room. Looking around, she realized this might be one of the biggest challenges. She didn't know whether to be hands-off with it, like she was with the modern kitchen, and leave the Ravenel men the comfort of their leather sofa and flat screen TV, or to make it into a proper parlor once more. She knew she needed to strike a balance, somehow letting them live in the twenty-first century and yet maintaining the ability to hide away more modern features for entertaining or something like a tour of homes. It would definitely exercise her design muscles, and that wasn't her strongest point.

She walked toward the stairs, thinking to go assess the situation up there since they had to let certain projects lie downstairs. The logical place to work now was the bedrooms, of which there were four plus a little one that might've been a governess's room or the nursery, as Virginia had speculated. She would leave one for Jude, as well as Adrian's for the near future. That left a guest bedroom, where she could start, and a room still filled with Adrian's boxes from where he had moved in a couple of years ago.

Her mind floated to a nursery for herself. They would need one, but... It was too far off, and things were so uncertain that the bolter within made her suppress that thought. That would be getting pretty cozy and settled.

"Okay," she said, standing in the guest room. If one of the rooms was going to be dark green, she was getting more feminine vibes than that from this one. The room was currently a kind of dank '80's cream. So she had no qualms going over to the light switch and (possibly illegally) flecking up some (possibly lead-based) paint nearby. She scratched past a plum color, thought it had covered a white, and got out her key to dig down deep. She saw a scarlet red and lifted her brows. Although she wasn't very well-acquainted with Shannon yet, something made her think maybe this was her.

Adeline was so caught up in restoring the high baseboards in the room, which she had never intended to do that day, that the next time she looked up, she saw Jane taking Jude's friends to their mother's SUV which had pulled up. She had met the cute brother and sister duo: Brynlyn, who was Jude's best friend, and Mira, who was Jude's "girlfriend."

She heard Adrian return home about two hours later. She didn't know exactly how this was supposed to work, but she had always, when she had just been a preservationist around here, left him some time with Jude. She would just make herself a taco later.

She was still scraping paint at seven o'clock, her mask on and ventilator running, as if it had become a fascination to her, or more like an obsession. She was getting pretty tired and thinking about her taco when the door opened. She looked over her shoulder, removing her mask. Adrian looked tired but refreshed from a run. His brows drew together. "Adeline?"

She stood, her knees cracking, and said, swiping back a curl, "Hey!"

He looked around the room in confusion, apparently not understanding strange historian fervor. It appeared he was about to say something, but he decided against it. He glanced back at her, brows still lowered. "Have you been working all day?"

"Yeah."

There was a slight hesitation and then, "You...should take it easy, Adeline."

She didn't know why she bristled. It was irrational, and she was over-sensitive and touchy. But she felt like he was judging her. She suddenly wondered what he thought about her eating habits, and whether he even wanted her to be working. "I know what I can handle, Adrian," she said softly, not wanting a brawl, despite her prickliness.

"I didn't mean it that way," he said quietly.

She met his eyes.

"I meant that I think it's in your nature to drive yourself hard, especially when you feel you've slacked a little, or done something irresponsible."

She glanced up at him, biting her lip. He was being more psychiatrist than husband, but that was all right. Especially when he was deadly accurate. "Yeah," she said softly, unsure why she was on the brink of tears.

She felt like a potato. She was wearing old shorts and a torn T-shirt, and she had plaster on her knees. She was kind of sweaty and really hungry.

He seemed to get that, at least the brink-of-tears part. Slipping out of diagnosis mode momentarily, he squeezed her arm. "I'm about to start cooking," he said softly, answering the hungry thought, too. "Is anything appealing to you?"

"Tacos," she said honestly. He lifted his brows in surprise. "But I know you don't... Whatever you make will be fine." By which time she hoped to have a shower and look a little more presentable.

He was looking a little overwhelmed. "No, no, if that's what you want... Yeah, I think I can do that," he said.

"I'm pretty sure if you could handle medical school, you can handle tacos," she said, smiling, breaking the slight tension in the room.

He smiled, scanning his eyes over her face. "Jude wants to help me," he said. "So that should set us back thirty minutes at least."

She laughed. "Duly noted. I'll see you in an hour."

Jude had wanted to eat on the upper balcony, so Adrian carried their stuff there. It still wasn't dark when they sat down at eight, and the sun was sinking behind the harbor elegantly. It was still warm enough that Adeline's hair dried almost immediately, but at least the mosquitoes hadn't found them yet.

She was pretty sure Adrian was half grossed-out by his delicious tacos, and Jude seemed to regard them as an interesting specimen. Both were quiet. She wondered if it was because it was their first meal alone as a family.

Jude kept glancing up at her, as if finally understanding. She was glad Adrian had made it plain, by finding her upstairs, that they were going to function more like a couple than roommates. But she couldn't think what to say to reassure a scared little boy.

Jude swallowed his bite and then said, a little too matter-of-factly to really cover his feelings, "We used to eat with my mama. I remember."

Adeline's eyes flew to Adrian's. His lips parted, and he had gone slightly pale. The moment stretched out, and finally Adrian looked from Jude to her, nodding discreetly.

Heart hammering, she said, "Do you? That's great, honey." She could feel Papa Bear's eyes going between them. She wondered why he wasn't interfering. And she needed to get this right. She handed Jude a napkin from the stack they had secured beneath the citronella candle, striving to give the appearance that it was just a casual conversation. "What else do you remember?"

Jude shrugged infinitesimally, his eyes unfocused now in the distance. His voice was locked away, down deep with the memories, not all of them as pleasant as eating surrounded by the love of his parents.

"Well, she would be glad that you remember, Jude," she said, touching his hand, glancing over at Adrian to make sure she was doing okay. He was still watching Jude. "I hope we can be good friends. I was thinking maybe we could go out for ice cream tomorrow."

Adrian's eyes snapped to hers. Oops.

Jude was enslaved to his favorite passion. "Okay," he agreed immediately.

A silence grew until Jude leapt up, yelling, "Daddy, *look!*"

They both followed his eyes quickly, Adrian reaching to grab him back from the railing until Adeline said, "They're safe now." She looked out on the horizon, where a splendid flurry of sails were grouped like seagulls.

"I see, buddy," Adrian said. He looked at Adeline. "Harris is competing in the open ocean regatta later in the summer. He may be one of them out there practicing. I think he has the week off."

Adeline lifted her brows. "Impressive. He has a sail-boat, then?"

Adrian looked at her a little narrowly. "Yeah." He gave his taco one last look before pushing it away with relief.

"And here he was griping about student loans," Adeline said, twirling one of her curls around her finger as she watched the sails catch the wind and pick up speed.

"Our grandpa left it to him," Adrian said, a little shortly. "He always competed. Usually took us out with him."

"You sail, too, then," she said, studying him, surprised. Had he let a detail slip?

"In another life." He pulled Jude away from the railing, standing and bringing him up with a few tickles. Jude giggled, asking if he could go out sailing with Uncle Harris, or, failing him, Uncle Richard?

"No," Adrian said definitively. "Time for your shower. I'll be up in a minute." Jude scurried off, leaving just the two of them on the balcony.

"Go on," Adeline said cheerfully, standing. "I'll clean this up."

"No, you won't," he said.

"Come on," she coaxed. "You're tired, too."

"But not pregnant."

She met his eyes, flushing. "Inarguable."

He laughed slightly. He had a good voice.

In the end, they both got a handful and then tag-teamed the dishwasher. He agreed to let her put up the cooking supplies while he went to check on Jude. She sprayed some Febreze out of courtesy to him and then went up to put her pajamas on.

When he knocked, she was already in bed with a book on the aristocracy of Charleston during the Victorian era. She'd found it in Drayton Hall's gift shop next to the cute biodegradable bags that had caught her eye.

She studied him while he pulled out his clothes for the next morning. He was always quiet. Tonight he was contemplative, draping his suit over a chair by rote, fingering a tie but not really looking at it. "Is he okay?" she asked softly.

He looked over his shoulder and then, putting down what he was holding, turned around. "He's never talked about her. I've never been sure how much he remembers."

She touched her forehead. "I've stirred it all up."

He was quiet for a moment, eyes touching her. "I think he's more traumatized from the wreck than her death, but he associates her with the wreck, so when he thinks of her, it...brings it all up." It was said clinically, and almost as soon as he had said it, he looked as though he wished he hadn't. "Anyway," he said, turning and grabbing his pajamas, "I'll get a shower."

"Sure," she said, eyes following him.

The smell of his soap drifted out, teasing her senses. He looked way too sexy when he came out with towel-dried hair. Life was so tough for her.

"I, um, have a doctor's appointment Monday," she said, tucking a curl behind her ear, and thinking to focus his mind back to the future. "If you want to go."

He leaned up from pulling something out of his still-packed suitcase. "Of course," he said, looking at her. "What time?"

"Three," she answered. "We'll need to get there a little early, to update my insurance and name."

He nodded, going toward his side of the bed. He looked at her when he sat down. "Has he or she been giving you much trouble?" he asked, a warm smile in his eyes.

"No, it has its mother's temperament," she said.

He smiled, fairly close, eyes roving her face. She didn't think he would respond, but then he said, just before turning out his light, "I hope so."

Chapter Seven

The carriage rolled through the streets of Charleston, away from the destruction. Shannon and Marie rode opposite one another, their eyes fixed on the devastation wrought by the fire. They were in travelling clothes, bound for Santarella, Rose bundled in with them and sitting on her mother's lap.

All of it, the terrible calamity and chaos, had begun three weeks ago when a shout had pierced the night, jolting Shannon awake only for her to have the added terror of her door being banged and rattled. "Shannon! Marie!" It was her father's voice, and just as that thought receded, she caught the smell of smoke. She leapt from the bed. Hands shaking, she reached hurriedly for her dressing gown and tied it tightly. She walked in her bare feet to the large door and threw it back.

It seemed half the household was running through the upstairs hall, servants half-dressed. They had come to wake the family, she realized. She must have been deep in sleep not to have heard. "Papa!" she said, seeing him shoulder his way through the servants in his dressing gown, silver hair askew, something she had never seen. "Is the house on fire?"

"No, but Charleston is."

Marie came out of the nursery with the baby bundled in her arms. "Has the city fallen?" she asked over the sound of Rose's wails.

"No, we are too well-fortified. I don't believe it has anything to do with the war. Marie, where are your mother and father—at Kinwood?"

Her face seemed to pale as realization struck. "No. Here, on East Bay Street."

"I must go to them," her father said definitively, but staying. "Shannon, Marie, you'll not stray from the house. The fire teams are at work. I can hear them even now. You'll stay here unless the flames come close. If they do, John Tilman and Coffey will escort you to safety. I will send word where that may be. You mustn't fret if I am gone long. I will help however may be possible." He stopped, eyes falling on Rose, and he reached out, touching her head where her cap had fallen, and kissed her rusty hair. And then he was gone.

Shannon and Marie dressed hastily and then went out onto the upper balcony. They looked out past the columns across the night, unnaturally brightened. They couldn't see much of the city since they faced the bay, and the air was so filled with smoke that they had to go inside. They did their best to stop up the windows and doors, sending for sheets from below stairs.

Marie couldn't leave Rose, who continuously and angrily wailed, but Shannon decided to wrap a scarf about her face and go up onto the roof to see what she might find. She felt as though she stepped into a scene of horror. Mansions just streets over were crashing to the ground, slave and master alike dashing back and forth with water. The city's steam fire engine tried what it could to help, but it must be dead low tide at this time of night, Shannon thought, and almost impossible to get water.

The streets teemed with thousands of people whom she quickly realized were not spectators, but residents who would be homeless in minutes. Tears streaming down her face, she dashed to the door and hurried down the stairs, finding Marie in the parlor below. "Marie! We have to offer them shelter! They're going to burn up!"

"Good heavens, I hadn't... Yes—Rebecca!" she said, calling to her slave, who was sitting across the room. "Find Coffey and tell him to send word that the doors of Ravenel House are open to its neighbors."

Rebecca was standing, lifting the black skirt of her gown, ready to leave, when Mammy, holding Rose, interrupted, "That riff-raff? We're in *mourning*, child!"

"It is what my mother would've done," Shannon said defiantly.

Marie agreed, signaling to her maid.

"Yes, ma'am," Rebecca said, leaving.

Very few, apparently, were willing to tread on the hospitality of so dignified a household, especially one in mourning. But a handful of their neighbors, all genteel, did seek shelter with them, and Marie and Shannon saw that they had refreshments and were kept warm. A few were stunned to see Shannon, but the horror of the night seemed to place her situation in an easier perspective. One elderly lady touched Shannon's black sleeve as she poured her tea and said, "Bless you, dear child. And you in mourning. It is against nature that we should tread upon your hospitality."

"That is nonsense, ma'am. Are you quite comfortable?"

Rose, whom Marie had kept with them for fear they would have to flee, was the only thing, Shannon thought, which helped them retain their sanity as they waited in the cauldron of Charleston. It wasn't until close on midnight that Marie, looking toward the door, leapt up, a cry leaving her lips at the sight of her mother. Shannon stood back while they embraced but moved closer while her Aunt Coraline told her daughter that, while all were safe, their mansion was in ruins, utterly lost.

"Oh, Mother!" Tears streamed down Marie's face. "But what is that, when you are safe?" she said, attempting a smile as she held her arms.

Shannon waited until her Aunt Coraline spotted her. They had not seen one another since Marie and Frederick's wedding day, certainly not since Louisa Ravenel's death. She must have heard the whispers, for Shannon had been in Charleston two days. However, her aunt still seemed startled, as though in the rush of things she had forgotten. "Shannon," she said faintly, looking the picture of quiet dignity in the arched doorway which led into the parlor, her lace wrap around her shoulders. She studied Shannon for a long moment, her light eyes taking her in.

Shannon felt the gaze of the entire room upon them, while only moments before there had been endless chatter about the fire and its implications. "Aunt." She moved forward, extending her hand.

After a stiff moment, her aunt took the hand she offered. "My dear, it is good to see you," she said softly.

"And you, ma'am."

Her aunt looked around the room, seeming to meet every eye. "And I must say, your courage and bravery know no bounds, my dear. To do what you did... Oh, my dear, I must admit myself a lesser woman than you."

"Here, here!" an elderly gentleman, perhaps a trifle senile, exclaimed.

And then, as Shannon stood holding her aunt's eyes, the entire room chanted the same endorsement in chorus with hearty Charlestonian spirit, which could not be broken. After a long moment, she gave the slightest nod to her aunt, inclining her head. Though that could scarcely express her appreciation.

"Thus you became the heroine of Charleston rather than the pariah," Marie said, sitting in the peaceful nursery at Santarella while Rose played on the carpet. They were encircled by the light blue paneling which characterized Santarella, and sunlight spilled in from two windows, though it was too cold to be out of doors.

Shannon, sitting next to her cousin in a ladder-back chair, looked up from her embroidery, glancing at Marie before looking down again, concentrating on the flower pattern. "For leaving my husband?" she asked softly, glancing at the nursemaid who sat in the corner across the room.

"Your Yankee husband," Marie corrected in equally quiet tones. After a moment, she added, "You are apparently the talk of Charleston. Your kindness on the night of the fire proves what they had suspected: you are a woman of virtue and are faithful to your country."

"Equally they had suspected that I was fast, you must ad—"

"Very likely, but there is no question of that now, according to my mother, Mrs. Hill, Elizabeth Middleton, and countless others who have informed me of the victory of your saved reputation. Apparently when Mr. Pinckney said, 'Here, here!' he spoke for the entirety of Charleston. He may be an old man, but his words still hold weight. It would seem you have almost assumed the qualities and sainthood of a virgin goddess, Shannon, for all of the honor and epitaphs being bestowed upon you."

Shannon cut her eyes toward Marie, giving her a darkling look. After a while, she said, "Frederick's letter was… less than welcoming."

There was a pause of silence. "What did you expect, Shannon?" Marie asked softly, continuing with her sewing.

"I expected my brother to support me. My…husband and he may have been *like* brothers, but they weren't, and they are on the opposite sides of a war. Surely he must see the position that I was in."

"Indeed, he does see that, and he speaks of it with sadness. But you have challenged the very foundation of society, Shannon. Imagine Frederick's position for a moment: he has a daughter. He has the family name to think of. And moreover, he doesn't see that it can have been so very bad in Washington between the two of you—"

Shannon started to get up, but almost as quickly, Marie caught her arm. "Shannon, forgive me!" she said penitently. "Why am I raking you over the coals, when you *have* been welcomed and accepted back?"

"Because you have had a letter from Frederick, and he has not," Shannon said. "And let me tell you, Marie, that if you intend to become one of those women who quote back their husbands, as though they were the words of Jesus, which I never thought of you—"

Marie was almost laughing, her eyes twinkling, and it caught Shannon off guard, making her pause. "I won't do that," Marie said softly, only removing her hand from Shannon's arm when the tension eased from her shoulders. "We won't speak of it anymore. I promise."

Shannon nodded, and they sat in silence for a time. Slowly, it began to be borne upon her that something was between them, something Marie wanted to say but over which she was hesitating. Shannon glanced up at the nursemaid, and finally, Marie, after pressing her lips together, said, "Emma, leave Miss Rose on the carpet with her toys, and run down to see Cook, if you will, and ask if you may be of use."

"Yes, ma'am," the young girl said, doing as she was told and placing a blanket with little Rose, which was destined to be thrown off soon.

Shannon continued serenely with her sewing until the maid had left, reflecting that Cook would find something for her to do, poor girl. They had left behind some of the staff in Charleston since her father intended to stay a few more weeks. Marie's mother and father had already left for Kinwood, Aunt Coraline's family plantation which was situated near Columbia. Someone must stay, though, to look after their interests and to see what must be done about the fire, the property insurance, and the possibility of rebuilding. Such a prospect was a terrible thought during a war, especially with the economy struggling so.

Shannon worried for her father in the city, for the smoke was still thick, but he would merely shrug when it was mentioned to him, and, indeed, he did seem to have a constitution of iron. On the other hand, Shannon and Rose had both developed a cough, which had disturbed him so much that he had sent them packing as soon as possible after sending for Dr. Travers to examine them both.

When Marie still didn't speak, Shannon said, "And Frederick is well? I couldn't make much of his letter, for there was little but recrimination."

"Yes, he is well," Marie said softly. "And, indeed, Shannon, it seems frivolous to talk of these social things we have been talking of, when a war is claiming lives of so many young men every day. Only life does go on, doesn't it? For heaven sakes, half of Charleston burned, and..." She broke off, tears seeming to choke her, and Shannon, her brows drawing together, reached for her arm. "Dear Marie, I know it is all very bad, but this isn't like you!"

Marie bit her lip and hesitated another moment, collecting herself before saying softly, "Shannon, I am with child."

Shannon's lips parted, her eyes sweeping Marie's face. She saw all of her features, her dimpled chin, her hazel-green eyes, her auburn hair. She felt a little light-headed and couldn't immediately grasp what she had said. What was more, Marie was looking at her with something akin to apology. Shannon turned the ring on her finger. "How... How far along?"

"He...was home when your mother died," she whispered, flushing. "It has been nearly two months now."

"Oh. Yes, of course," she said. "Did you only just realize?"

"No, I knew a little while before Christmas. That is, I suspected before then, but I was certain of it then."

Shannon nodded slowly, pressing her arm. Finally, she said emotionally, "Marie, this is wonderful news, amidst so much pain. Does Frederick know?"

"Yes, I fancy my letter will have reached him by now," Marie answered, laying her sewing aside, brushing little threads from her black skirt. "I have not told your father or my parents yet, but I wanted to tell you."

Shannon smiled, and then tried to keep it steady. "Thank you, dearest. My niece or nephew will surely be a blessing to us all."

Marie studied her for a long moment, not speaking, seeming to gather her thoughts. "Yes. And I know... That is,

I can scarcely imagine how it must feel not to..." Her eyes strayed to Rose. "And I am so very grateful. But I do feel as though I should mention to you, since no other woman will, that... It *is* a blessing. But it is a mixed blessing, Shannon, as very few blessings in life are *un*-mixed. Even in marriage, we lose our homes and parents and former way of life. And that is a sacrifice we are willing to make, but it would be silly to pretend this is any different." Shannon watched intently, her eyes not leaving her face.

Marie continued, "Your figure changes, and there is little you can do to stop it." She smiled briefly before returning to seriousness. "Your husband is worried for you, and, while other women may like that, I do not. I do not like to give others anxiety, or cause a stir, or feel helpless, but...there are occasions where you simply do and are. And then you are forever altered, or, at least, your life is. In many good ways, and yes, I know *that* is what you must have desired so strongly, and I won't lie and say that it isn't breath-taking, and as close to a glimpse of heaven as I have yet seen. But it isn't easy, Shannon," she said, glancing at Rose, who was on the edge of her rug, clacking her wooden pony's hooves against the wood floor, "knowing that anything might happen to them. I sometimes feel as though I might go mad with worry, and that, when coupled with the expectations which society places upon me, makes me feel as though I might be mad altogether. But I won't, of course, for in the end, I play the part which is expected of me. And I always will, for that is who I am."

Shannon was too surprised to speak, for she had never heard this version of events. Or imagined that she would, or could, be anything but a mother. Only just now it struck her that, with her recent choices, she wouldn't even be a wife. And the realization hit her with such intensity, and she felt so adrift, that she nearly forgot how to breathe. What *was* she to do with her life? What other options were offered to her? Would she live out a life akin to spinsterhood under her father's roof? For she suddenly realized that she *never* played the part which was expected of her, which was her best glory and her greatest downfall, all at once. But the simple truth of it was that she had no notion what she would do and could make no plans until the war was finished.

When finally she could speak, she said, with a rasp that surprised her, "No, I know it was a blessing, my inability to bear children. I see that now, as I couldn't before." She stared into nothingness outside the window, across the sweeping lawn and down to the river.

Marie looked at her sympathetically. "Oh, Shannon. Forgive me, but you know that isn't true either." She added, more softly, "If the two of you had a child, you would still be in the North today, together, for you wouldn't have left in such circumstances."

"And ought we to be?" Shannon asked, tears starting to her eyes. "*That* is the question, Marie, and you *know* the answer to it."

Marie's eyes misted, and she let the silence grow. "Oh, Shannon..." she whispered. "Don't you miss him...think of him...wonder what his life is?"

Shannon pulled her hand away sharply. "Of course I—How can you ask me—?" Emotions overwhelmed her voice. She stood, nearly toppling her chair. She started for the door and opened it, flying from the room with tears streaming down her face.

Chapter Eight

John Thomas had been granted a three-day furlough before he was to be transferred from the coast of North Carolina to the Mississippi River Squadron. He stayed with Adams in his rooms in Washington, but he saw little of his brother since his duties for the War Department claimed all of his days and most of his nights. Adams was tasked with supplying the Western armies with sufficient rations and munitions, no small undertaking.

John Thomas, sitting in his brother's small sitting room, stared out the window across the evening until the shadows faded and night consumed the city. The occasional snowflake glistened by the light of the full moon. He didn't hear the carriage outside the building or Adams's tread on the stairwell, but he looked up when the door opened. His brother entered and took off his greatcoat. John Thomas had kept the fire stoked, and he now transferred his gaze to its flames.

Adams studied his brother in concern. John Thomas was steady. He would never rage or tear apart at the seams. But that he was hurting, no one who knew him could long miss. He was quiet, always polite, but almost never speaking unless spoken to.

It was not in Adams Haley's nature to pry into his brother's private affairs, but he had been charged rather strictly in letters from his family, who was still reeling from the news that Shannon had fled, to find answers. And such a shocking thing did sometimes seem unfathomable. Laying his long coat neatly across the back of a wing chair, he said softly, "Did your last letter from home mention that Father was unwell?"

John Thomas looked up quickly. "No, not a word. What is the matter?"

"I'm not sure," he murmured, sinking into a wing chair. "That is, they are not certain. He has no strength, and suffers from bouts of light-headedness."

His brother's brows drew together. "I hope it is not his heart. Why would Mother and Father keep this from me?" he demanded.

After a hesitation, Adams said quietly, studying the stem of the glass he had picked up, "I rather fancy they felt you had enough to think of."

John Thomas looked away, seemingly surprised that he had broached the subject. He didn't return his gaze, and his cheekbones tinged the slightest bit red. He looked into the fire again, into another world. "I wish I might have something else to think of," he said softly. After a moment, he looked up, chagrined, his blonde brows drawing together again. "Oh, not that. You know I—"

"Of course not," Adams said. Any one of his sisters could have dragged the whole story out of him by now, he reflected. "Have you...heard from her?" he asked.

After a long moment, John Thomas said, "No."

Adams blinked. "Then you have no notion whether she made it to Charleston? And whether, if she did, she survived the fire?"

John Thomas studied him for a moment as though he were hesitating. Then, finally, he got up and walked to the desk where Adams had let him keep his papers locked, opening its larger drawer and pulling out a newspaper. "I know she is alive," he said very quietly. "And I know she made it—though God knows how—to her father's house."

Adams was looking up at him in confusion when John Thomas handed him the paper, which he immediately saw was a copy of the *Charleston Courier.* He didn't ask how he had obtained it: the War Department had been collecting smuggled newspapers from Southern cities for months, and it would've been simple enough for him to obtain one. His eyes rested momentarily on an article detailing how the community had come together in Christian charity, and her name was mentioned, although it mistakenly, or perhaps boldly, listed her surname as "Ravenel." He scanned the paper, his eyes falling briefly on the article next to it, which appeared to be one of a series of memoriams to notable mansions which had been burned.

Adams sat in silence for a moment before he had the courage to meet his brother's eyes. After a long moment, he said quietly, "I cannot fathom what can have possessed her. I won't speak of her ill or good, but only what all of your family must think: it was an infamous thing to have done to you."

John Thomas sat down, not answering.

"Will you...divorce her?" he asked tentatively.

John Thomas finally said softly, "I cannot. You know that I cannot."

"When you are able?"

His brother looked at him. "I wasn't speaking of the war."

"If you feel loyalty to her, Brother, I must tell you that it is misplaced." He was surprised to find his voice rabid, but to have exposed John Thomas and their entire family to such a thing... It was unheard-of.

"I was speaking of religious...qualms," he said remotely. "I...don't believe it would be... In any event, it is against my conscience," he finished.

Adams nodded slowly, seeing a shadow cross his brother's face at the realization that such a discussion was taking place. "I won't ask you what happened—"

"I...accused her of something I never should have..." His voice trailed off. "We had strong words. I suppose that might be enough to have caused her to resort to flight. I don't know. I have wracked my brains—endured sleepless nights—" He broke off, tightening his jaw. "That is to say, I couldn't enlighten you. I must come to the conclusion that there was always a part of Shannon that I never knew." His words were clipped, hinting at repressed anger, and not at Adams, he would wager.

A silence grew and lingered.

John Thomas sat lost in his thoughts for a time before rising and saying, "Well. I suppose I will go to bed."

Adams looked at him, coming to his feet, staring at him awkwardly and hesitantly. "John Thomas... I need to tell you something."

He lifted his brows. "Yes?"

He drew a breath before saying, "I am courting a lady. Miss Renley. Senator Renley's daughter."

John Thomas blinked, stunned. "I had no notion. Would I know her?"

He hesitated. "She believes she met you last year some time, at a ball."

John Thomas realized his brother was watching him, nervous of his reaction, although perhaps he hesitated to speak of the bloom of courtship given the circumstances. John Thomas wondered if he loved her, as he had loved Emma Rawlins, before being separated from her. He couldn't ask, but one thing was certain: coming to Washington, and, perhaps, courting Miss Renley, had wrought subtle changes in Adams. He was a man independent from their father now. And so John Thomas gave a genuine smile, and said, "I will look forward to being introduced to her again. And this time under happy circumstances."

Adams nodded, still looking at him. The silence descended once more. Shannon's desertion rose between them again. There was a brief hesitance. "You will...take her back, should the circumstances and her wishes ever permit it?" he asked softly.

John Thomas's eyes dimmed. "I am given to understand that I have two options," he said. "Divorce, or eternal estrangement."

Chapter Nine

The ladies of Santarella walked its extensive gardens in the first blush of spring. The day was warm despite chilly nights, and all around them birds sang, flowers budded, and breezes teased the senses. Little Rose toddled ahead with one of her young nurses, collecting a posy of flowers in her hand. She was delighted with her new skill in walking, and with the responsibility of keeping her baby hand clenched on the stems, a little smile dawning on her usually-serious features.

Shannon and Marie followed more sedately in their black gowns, Marie's hand resting on her middle. "But for all the fanfare, for all the damage we inflicted, we cannot claim a victory, it seems," Marie said. They had been discussing the recent naval battle at Hampton Roads, Virginia, in which Frederick had participated. As they dwelled on it, the thought of whether John Thomas had been there flitted through Shannon's mind. She pushed it away, anger making her recoil.

She cleared her throat. "How *could* we claim such? The blockade has not been lifted, no matter how many ships we sank, how many...lives were lost."

Marie glanced at her and, looking ahead, Shannon said, "I still think it is infamous, the blockade, and I always shall. They know perfectly well most of the strain falls on the civilians. *We* cannot obtain sugar, or medicines, or anything which we can't produce ourselves."

"I suppose, in fairness, the same could be used to supply the Army, and our infrastructure. Were there no blockade, we might stockpile munitions from Europe, and gain materiel to use in battle." She paused and then said, "Did I tell you that Frederick is to be moved again?"

Shannon looked at her. "No. And he still will not write to me, of course. Where?"

"To Savannah, or at least the seas surrounding. Apparently, they feel there is little use in staying in the James River anymore," Marie answered.

Fear spilled into Shannon. "Little use? They are abandoning it?"

"Yes. Oh, don't look as though the whole cause were lost. It is only one seaport, over which there is no reason to lose more lives and ships."

Shannon sighed, looking ahead of her at the beautifully trimmed ornamental trees, to the fountain where Rose was stretching out her hands, unconcerned when cold water splashed them. She seriously regarded the horse statue, similar to the ones at Versailles, and seemed to find it unsatisfactory, for she grunted to her nurse and pointed at the summer house.

"I fear she will be strong-willed, like her father," Marie said softly.

"I believe there is little question that she shall be," Shannon agreed. "But as to whether the trait derives entirely from paternal quarters is another question."

"Indeed, some of it must come from her aunt," Marie said blithely, smiling at Shannon's scathing look and twining her hands around her arm, pressing it lovingly.

Shannon covered her hands. "Well, what does Frederick say to the notion of two children?"

"He is pleased, naturally," Marie said, taking up Shannon's invitation to sit on one of the stone benches. She added as Shannon sat beside her, "He has been thinking of names." Shannon smiled. "If it is a boy, I am to name it for your father—John Winder. And if a girl, however I choose. Magnanimous, is it not?"

"Oh, men are odious! I hope you will name it however you choose, either way, without regard to anyone's father. You will certainly have earned the right."

Marie smiled, watching the sunlight glint off Rose's hair as she bent to pick a weed, which she bestowed upon Alice. "I don't mind naming him for your father, if it does prove to be a boy. I do hope it may be, for I want the Ravenel name to continue, but I confess I wouldn't mind another girl."

Shannon smiled but couldn't think what to say. She could scarcely fathom what had been the delight of the entire family upon learning of Marie's condition. It was, she thought, even more dear a circumstance given the daily peril Frederick was in, and Marie's consequence had increased even more with family and slave alike.

"That child," Marie said, breaking into Shannon's thoughts, and looking toward Rose. She had planted herself in the grass and was now experiencing the freedom of a marvelous roll, which was staining her little beige gown. Shannon laid a hand on her arm as Marie started to rise, saying, "Oh, let her play."

Marie sat down, smiling and shaking her head, but said, "She will soon be spoilt past all repair."

"Nonsense."

"Yes! Only think of it: already she has three servants devoted entirely to her care. Mammy, Emma, and Alice, not to mention her mother, whom she seems to look upon certainly as a member of the serving class if not an especially devoted slave. She has no whim which is not instantly met, and nothing can be too good for her where all of us are concerned."

"She is merely well-loved. But if you refer to the pony my father has already begun training for her use, I must say that I *am* quite jealous, for I am sure he never thought of purchasing *my* pony until I was every bit of eight years old. By then I was already at school and could only make use of her on my holidays!"

Marie laughed. "Oh, Shannon. He does dote upon her wildly. And Frederick! I wish you might hear his plans for her! I believe he will not be satisfied with her marriage to any suitor less eminent than a royal prince of blood. And the terrifying truth is that if she *is* one day the very image of her Aunt Shannon, and the South wins the war, and all is as it should be, she *might*," she said in chagrin.

Shannon laughed, shaking her head. "Time enough for that."

Marie looked at her, her brow clearing as her thoughts turned to Shannon. She took her hand. "Dearest, we are to leave for Charleston soon, you know. Have you thought what you are to do with yourself?"

Shannon's fair brows drew together. "Do?"

Marie hesitated, studying her. "My dear Cousin, you cannot go on as you are. You will gain a reputation soon as the Ghost of Santarella, for you are as thin as a reed, and as soon as I leave you, you become enslaved to your thoughts, your gaze as distant as the sea. You wander the grounds on your walks, but I do not believe you derive any benefit from such excursions. Your father worries for your health and your mental state. We talk of it often and are in agreement that it simply won't do, Shannon."

Shannon swallowed, removing her hand from beneath Marie's and looking away. "What would you have me to do?" she asked coldly.

Marie waited in patience, as though Shannon were a recalcitrant child, until Shannon finally looked at her. "When we return to Charleston, I believe you must have something to occupy your time and thoughts. My mother writes to me of something—"

"You have discussed this with—"

Marie lifted a hand. "She is your aunt, Shannon, and she cares for you. You needn't forget that she saved your reputation."

"And yours. *You* needn't pretend as though she would have lifted a finger had it not been for you. She could not have her son-in-law's family reputation stained."

Marie kept her counsel, too wise to acknowledge the truth of this. But neither could she deny it. Her mother had never particularly liked Shannon, whose glow had far eclipsed her own daughter's. "In any event, she writes that the Roper Hospital—it is run by the Medical College, you see—is now accepting wounded soldiers. Obviously men are in short supply, and they are in need of nurses. Married nurses."

Shannon blinked. "But Marie, I wouldn't even know how to bandage my finger if I snagged it!" she exclaimed.

"You would learn quickly. You always did."

"Papa would never allow it. It would be unseemly. To... To see men in such a state—"

"No, he wouldn't allow it. But it wouldn't be unseemly, for you are not a maiden. And I believe my mother and I might convince him, if it is what you want, that it will be a good thing for you, and necessary to continue your reputation as a virtuous daughter of the South."

"Naturally, I...I want to help, but—"

"No, you don't, Shannon, for you haven't thought of anyone or anything but yourself since November," Marie snapped sharply. Shannon's mouth opened, and she was still reeling from the accusation when her eyes filled. Not daunted, Marie continued, "If I can get you to talk of the war, it is only briefly. Now, I know you are in misery, and shocked, and hurt, and frightened, and I am sorry for you, Shannon, but I love you too dearly not to tell you that you *must* move on from this, and make yourself useful. There, my darling, don't cry," she said, encircling Shannon in an embrace, her tone changing from the strident to the penitent and caressing in moments. After Shannon had wept against her, and had stilled, Marie whispered, "Will you consider it, Cousin?"

"Yes," she whispered back. "I will consider it."

Shannon crossed the threshold between twin doors at the foyer of Roper Hospital. It was a grand building, white and Italianate in style with piazzas gracing all three of its stories. There were at least six towers, one at every corner and two at the main entrance. Colonel Roper, a one-time mayor of Charleston, had bequeathed money for its foundation in the hopes of bringing medical care to Charleston's poor. Before the war, it had been used as a teaching hospital. Now it was an unofficial hospital for wounded Confederate soldiers, over the strong protestation of the trustees.

Shannon was met in the foyer by a gushing Mr. Drake, the director, who was thrilled, he told her, to entertain one of the daughters of Charleston's elite, especially one so highly regarded as herself. "Sir," she asked, fearing he thought she was merely present for a tour, "you did understand by my letter that I am eager to nurse the sick and injured?"

"Yes! Of course!" the man said in a high voice, stroking his mustache.

Shannon glanced at Phoebe, who was standing beside her, and then back at Mr. Drake.

At once, he said in an accommodating voice. "Naturally, your father wished for you to have an escort. Would you like for her to be kept with the other servants? We can ensure that she is returned to you once you have toured the hospital."

Shannon felt herself flush. Good heavens, to think she had once said similar... She drew in a breath, looking down her nose. "Phoebe is my free servant. She was manumitted in 1859 by papers signed by my father, here in Charleston. She will accompany me and act as a nurse also, if you please. She is willing to do so."

"But I...don't..."

Shannon smiled charmingly. "It was a condition of my father's allowing me to come at all, sir. Surely you must see that he wished me to be escorted at all times."

"Yes, certainly, but... There are other matrons in the building..."

"Indeed? I am glad to hear it. But Phoebe stays with me nonetheless."

His lips parted. "Indeed." He cleared his throat. "Indeed." Bolstering himself with a deep breath, he extended an arm, saying, "Shall we?"

Shannon inclined her head, letting him lead her through the hospital. He used throughout the tour the utmost courtesy and deference, treating her as delicately as a fresh flower.

While she was very used to such treatment, she did wonder if he realized she intended to be more than a ministering angel who brought baskets, cheered the men, and penned letters for them. His conversation revealed, quite soon, that he did not.

She stewed over how to enlighten him as he first showed her the amphitheater which had been used for lectures, and then the library and living quarters for the physicians. Shannon's father had not consented to allow her to live on the premises, despite the assurances of the trustees, who were fellow members of the Jockey Club, that she would be quite safe. A carriage would be sent to her and Phoebe at night to bring them back to Battery Street.

She was still shocked that he had consented at all. But after being closeted with Marie and Aunt Coraline at Ravenel House for close on an hour, he had emerged where she was waiting beneath the arch in the hallway and had kissed her forehead. *"My darling, if it will remove the cloud from your brow, give you a purpose, a direction—yes. That is, if you are certain."*

She had ceased questioning whether Marie indeed knew witchcraft, but she *was* feeling rather less certain about her decision once she had seen from afar the rooms full of wounded and sick men. In truth, she wondered that she had consented at all. She was no ministering angel. She had no training. She did wish to help, but it was almost as though she had acquiesced in a fog, and when the ultimate decision had been made, Marie had asked her whether she had been listening.

But now, though Mr. Drake tried to hold her at a distance, Shannon was drawn into one of the sick rooms. The ceilings were soaring, the walls white, the windows long enough to let in cheerful sunlight. But it was the men, moaning, or sometimes eerily quiet, bandaged and bruised and disfigured, who drew her in like a fly to honey. They mesmerized her in terrible fashion, and she walked in as though removed from the scene, turning a full circle, almost certain no one could see her, although that was impossible. Noise faded, and she could hear nothing, could only see the beds and the many, many wounded men in ragged uniforms.

"Miss Ravenel. Miss Ravenel?" She blinked, her consciousness returning along with her hearing. She swallowed. "Yes, Mr. Drake?"

She looked around her to realize she had created a stir. Those who were able were sitting up, gaping at her, and the room had gone entirely silent.

"Dear me, ma'am, I never meant to bring you into *this* room! I hope your dear father will forgive me! This is no place for a lady."

Moistening her lips and glancing once more at Phoebe, who nodded encouragingly, Shannon said, "Mr. Drake, if I may have a word with you?"

His brows lifted. "Yes, ma'am. Certainly," he said, indicating the door.

He took her into a small office while Phoebe waited outside and poured her a glass of wine and offered her teacakes, as though she could stomach them. She held up a hand, and he took the tray away. "Mr. Drake, you seem to be under a misimpression. I wish to serve here as a nurse."

"Yes, indeed," he said amiably, "and something befitting your station and gentility will be arr—"

"I saw women in that room," she said. "They were tending the men."

"Matrons, my dear lady, all of them. Or nuns."

She stared at him, drew a long breath, and then said, "You have called me Miss Ravenel, so I gather that you may not be aware of my marriage."

"Oh, yes, forgive me! An oversight! A slip of the tongue!"

"And you will no doubt be aware of…the misfortune of an…estrangement in my marriage."

"Yes, *indeed*," he said, all kind sympathy. "Dear me, so brave! So noble! Such a flight was yours! My dear ma'am, I hope you know that we, the citizens of Charleston, honor you for it! To have been forced to live with a Yankee man, to have…" He shook his head. "It doesn't bear thinking of. And I have heard, too, of your kindness to your neighbors on the night of our late, terrible fire—"

She interjected, "Then you must acknowledge that I, too, am a matron."

He lifted his brows. "Indeed, indeed, but with the freshness, the virtue, of a maiden, my dear lady."

Shannon sighed. "Mr. Drake, I intend to come every day, to do what those matrons I saw were doing, and to serve my country to the fullest degree possible in this hospital. Is that understood, or must I speak with the doctors?"

He blinked and said weakly, "Y...Yes. Quite understood, Mrs. Haley."

"Very well. I will start tomorrow."

It was as though the horror of that day awakened her. Her heart was still restless, still beat unnaturally fast within her, and her mind was still plagued. But she knew one thing: no longer could she think only of herself. She had never seen such suffering in her twenty-two years, and finally she understood that the war was something much larger than her troubles, and that she must contribute. But her loyalties at first gave her pause. She had struggled in Washington, naturally. Could she support the war effort wholeheartedly, even here, among the people who had been raised as she had? Did she believe as they did anymore, enough to throw herself passionately behind the cause? But it didn't matter in the end, she came to realize. She would be attempting to save lives, to alleviate human suffering. That could not be wrong, whatever one's inner turmoil.

She always wore to the hospital a simple black gown, and she donned, upon arrival, a white apron and white sleeve covers. Her first days were overwhelming in their demands and calls for mental fortitude, but they did give her thoughts another direction. That was, they occupied her so fully that she didn't have time for thinking of the crisis of her own life until she fell into her bed at night, and by then she was too exhausted to think. Sleep always claimed her within minutes, a welcome relief when compared to night after night of staring at the canopy of her bed until sleep was only a vague hope.

Now she sat at the bedside of a wounded corporal, a scrawny boy far from home. He had neither looks nor personality to recommend him, only the reputation that he fought bravely and with valor. All of the Southern men she knew fought with valor. But for what, she sometimes wondered? This thought flitted into her head only to be banished thoroughly as traitorous to a cause she had supported so long she remembered nothing else.

She gingerly redressed a wound on his hand, careful of the places the blood had seeped. In her first hours, the task would have repulsed her, but repetition banished such qualms speedily.

"And you are...from Virginia," she said, trying to be kind.

It seemed her reputation preceded her even with these men, many of whom weren't from Charleston. She was a brave daughter of the South, and all that such an image encompassed: nurturing, tenderly spoken but firmly resolved, utterly devoted, always respectable. And beautiful.

It was a lovely image, and one which she didn't know how to overcome, especially when they spoke to her so reverently. It amused and often irritated Marie. And indeed, a more unworthy subject could scarcely have been found.

"Yes, ma'am, Botetourt County," he answered, gritting his teeth as she pulled the last bit. "Town of Fincastle."

She had learned it was better not to acknowledge when the men showed signs of pain. So she said, "That is in the Shenandoah, is it not? I don't believe I have been to that part of Virginia, but I hear that the Valley is very beautiful in the autumn."

"Oh, yes, ma'am. Nothin' like it." He coughed and winced from a stomach injury.

Shannon bit her lip and began to wrap his hand in the new bandage. Dr. Eisley, the senior physician present, stopped by the Corporal's bed and examined him with his customary lack of grace. "Dried out," he said. "Aren't you drinking, son?"

"Hurts, sir."

"Well, do it anyway!" he ordered.

"Yes, sir," the Corporal agreed before coughing again.

Shannon sighed and said, "Dr. Eisley, as it happens, there was something I wished to discuss with you. Would you mind stepping into the hall with me?"

"Certainly," he said succinctly, motioning for her to lead the way. Their shoes made clacks on the wooden floors until they were in the hall. Standing there and watching other nurses, as well as a few of the patients returning from their constitutionals, flit by, she changed her mind and asked if he wouldn't mind going to the library.

He agreed to it, opening the door for her almost as an afterthought. Then they entered the room whose walls were lined with shelves full of medical books. Shannon brushed her black skirt to the side to manage the doorway and then stood in the middle of the room facing the doctor. He was perhaps fifty-five, perhaps sixty. He did not tend to corpulency, but his silver hair was thinning, and his clipped beard had even gone white in some places. Likely, he would have been a handsome man in other circumstances; instead, he simply looked weary. Columbia, where he had possessed a thriving practice before being asked to lead the efforts at Roper Hospital, was his home, not Charleston. He was sacrificing a great deal to tend these men, and he had earned Shannon's respect.

"Dr. Eisley, some of the men simply aren't getting enough to eat. I am aware that Mr. Drake says—"

"Drake is a fool. Never repeat anything he says to me. There may be parts of the South which are going hungry, but this hospital is well-endowed. There is no cause for it. Which men? None have mentioned it to me."

"Several. I might give you names, but there is no need: the kitchen staff hasn't enough supplies."

"If you speak of sugar..."

"No, no, I realize there must be some shortages, but I speak of things which we have no trouble obtaining, like corn, and chickens, and—"

"Say no more. Drake is too busy securing donors, it would seem, to remember to perform the duties of quartermaster. Well, I will light a fire under him. There should be no trouble in that."

Despite herself, Shannon almost smiled. "Yes, thank you."

"Was there anything else, Mrs. Haley?"

She studied him. "Yes." She swallowed, knowing better than to waste his time in foolish hesitations. "That is to say... Dr. Travers is my family's doctor. Do you know him?"

He nodded sharply.

"He assisted my sister-in-law in child-bed, where she had great difficulty. Is there any reason to suppose we ought to bring in a different doctor when she gives birth for a second time?"

"I don't like Travers, but he's a good doctor, if that's what you're asking. His reputation is well-established in the profession. No need to fret yourself, leaving her in his hands."

She nodded, relieved. "Thank you."

"If that is all, Mrs. Haley," he said with grim pleasure, "I find I must speak with Mr. Drake."

A teacup clanked as it was placed in its saucer. The china, delicate with pink and blue roses, had been a gift to Louisa Ravenel upon her marriage. Looking at it, Shannon remembered how her mother had treasured the set but always shared it with the ladies who called upon her.

It was too soon after Mrs. Ravenel's death for the Ravenels to host, for the ladies of the house still wore unrelieved black. But they did not think it would be amiss to entertain Elizabeth Middleton to tea after church. Shannon had missed her friend and had seen little of her since her return to South Carolina, something Elizabeth informed her was her own fault. "Imagine doing good at the hospital instead of calling upon me," she said, sipping her tea.

Shannon and Marie smiled, and Elizabeth added more seriously, "Shannon, is there anything with which I help? I feel so useless sitting at home, mending or helping to teach my brother and sister. And with Arthur in daily peril, sometimes I feel I must have something to occupy me or run mad with worry.

Marie looked sympathetically at her, but Shannon said, "I believe they would not have you, dearest. You are too unmarried."

Elizabeth sighed. "Doomed by spinsterhood."

"I wouldn't say doomed," Shannon retorted. "I heard you were never without a partner at the charity ball, where the cadets and officers were present, and no fewer than six gentlemen have asked if they might write to you from the front."

"Alas," Elizabeth sighed.

This made the other ladies laugh, but Shannon said while Marie sat quietly, "Do none of them strike your fancy, my dear friend?"

"The terrible truth is: no. But enough about me... Marie, how are you feeling?"

Marie was now three months away from August, when her child would be born, and she had felt more or less poorly throughout. She was round and rosy and now looked to be in good health, so that must mean *something*, Shannon thought. "Oh, quite unwell mostly," she said, "but today quite *well*." She looked at Shannon quickly. "And if you tell—never mind."

"Tell Frederick? Indeed, how should I?" She looked at Elizabeth with flaming eyes. "My dear brother does not deign to correspond with me, Elizabeth."

Her friend's eyes widened as she looked to Marie for corroboration. Marie looked down at her hands, always uncomfortable when this subject was broached. Finally, Elizabeth reached for Shannon's hand, and, glancing once at Marie, said softly, "I'm sorry, my dear friend. But I am certain your brother loves you, and that you will be once more reconciled."

"Yes," Marie agreed. "That is what I keep telling her. Frederick would do anything for Shannon, and he will soon forgive her."

Nonetheless, it was difficult when, as happened yesterday morning, the mail was brought into the dining room and Shannon watched her father and Marie's countenances light when they found letters addressed to them from sea, and nothing was given to her. His silence was as much a rebuke as any lashing whip. Taking a breath, she said, "Speaking of brothers: tell us of Arthur."

Elizabeth read her last letter from him, which they raptly listened to as he detailed life in the Army of Northern Virginia. "And can you imagine?" she asked, coming to the end and looking up. "In his letter to my mother and father, he mentions that Seymour Christian was lately transferred to his regiment, and that you would not know him. He has apparently seen a great deal of combat with his former regiment, which is now, more or less, all captured, dead, or wounded from a series of hard luck, and that he is quite *bearable*."

"Poor man," Marie said softly. "His mother was telling me about his experiences when she visited at Santarella. I told her not to think of that, but how blessed they were that he was alive."

Elizabeth nodded, wiping a stray tear, obviously thinking of her own brother. Shannon reached for her hand and pressed it, wiping a tear of her own. Marie was soon reaching for her handkerchief and lamenting, "Oh, what a morose trio we are! I shall send for Rose; she is just what we need."

Chapter Ten

Captain Haley climbed aboard the USS *Ohio* to the salutes of his men. He had made as much of the journey as was possible by train and the rest by horse or steamer. He was now on the Mighty Mississippi, where the terrain was difficult and the days hotter and more humid than he had ever known. Before he had left Washington, the President had invited him to the Executive Mansion, which presently resembled a headquarters more than a private residence.

"I tell you, Haley, I have been most impressed with the Western Armies, and the coordination between the Army and the Navy," Lincoln had said. "Now, the blockade is more or less secured over here, and Secretary Welles tells me that the *Maryland* is in the able hands of Richard Jay, who was promoted to Captain after his excellent performance at Hampton Roads."

"Yes, he is a very talented officer, sir."

"I am glad to hear it. Secretary Welles feels that to leave you in the Atlantic would be a waste. We are in need of talented and inventive men if we are ever to overcome these Mississippi River forts—Vicksburg particularly. Have you ever seen the Mississippi River, Captain Haley?" Lincoln had asked.

"I...have been to New Orleans, sir."

"Then you know the terrain!" Lincoln had said, joking that most officers would have been hard-pressed to point Mississippi out on a map before the war.

Certainly, it was a wild country. Alligators farther south, strange plants, overgrown vegetation which seemed to hide worlds beneath... And yet, beautiful. He had met and liked Admiral Porter last night at a dinner aboard his ship, and the men seemed to be in tolerably good spirits. As the introductions were made aboard his own ship, he wondered how far this would take him from everything he had ever known. He wondered how he would go on. And yet, he had no choice.

In the Union Army's quest to regain control of the Mississippi River, there were many obstacles. One was a chain near Memphis, which the Confederates had thrown across the entirety of the river, making it necessary to send divers to deconstruct it. As Captain Haley was finding, many of his sailors didn't even know how to swim.

He had spent three weeks carrying troops on gunboat flotillas near Northern Mississippi. This treacherous process was made all the more so by Confederate guns on steep bluffs, mines, and infernal machines buried in the riverbeds or bobbing just below the surface. Progress was tediously slow, but the lives of many regiments—some thirty-two thousand men—could not be risked in an explosion. Therefore, slow it must be. And in the end, they had delivered the armies safely to drive further into the South's interior. Now, after the fall of Forts Henry and Donelson, Memphis was in their sights.

Frustrated with the slow work of the chain, he had sent a scout out to see if there was any Union sentiment in the area. If there was, it was his hope that manpower and machines might be brought to the scene where thousands of Army and Navy personnel were spending more time than they had to spare.

John Thomas was examining a detonated infernal machine and forming a decent notion of its Southern engineering techniques when his winded and breathless quartermaster ran up to him. He looked up, lifting a brow and trying not to smile. Haynes had been an office clerk in Indiana before the war and had difficulty adjusting to the Southern heat and physical demands of his duties. He saluted. "Captain. Jones has returned."

"Yes?"

He took a deep breath. "He wishes me to tell you..." He breathed. "That there is not sufficiency of Union sentiment in this portion of the state to save Sodom."

His brows lifted. "Not one, I see. I hope he was not...injured?"

"No, sir, but a tarring and feathering was threatened."

"I see. Well, I suppose it was worth a try. Haynes, how many do you have on your sick rolls today?"

"Sixty-one."

John Thomas stared across the river, looking upon the beautiful shores of Memphis. Distant, but not so very far.

"How many is it, Captain, before we must go into quarantine?" Haynes asked.

"Between seventy and eighty, it is the Captain's discretion. Once the number strikes eighty, we have no choice," John Thomas murmured. "Let me know at once if we tally seventy."

"Yes, sir," Haynes said before striding off.

John Thomas considered what ought to be done. The men were not accustomed to river fevers which developed in the summer, with the mosquitoes, the heat, and odd strains. He wished to quarantine them now to contain the spread, but with Commodore Davis seeing Memphis in his sights, he knew such a decision would not be happily received.

He sent out feelers to neighboring ships, asking for their sick numbers. While all were suffering, his ship was more afflicted than any other. He thought this was likely because he had mostly boys from New England and immigrants from Germany.

He sent Davis a message asking if a quarantine were possible, and, if so, how it should be accomplished. Davis's reply was decidedly negative. He informed Captain Haley that, as his crew had been one of his most instrumental, they could not be spared from the assault on Memphis.

Having his dinner, the Captain stewed on this, and anybody, including his lieutenant and all the other junior officers, might have believed he meant to accept the order. But when he was awakened in the night by Haynes, who knocked on his door to tell him that the number of those taken ill had soared to seventy-five, he jumped up, dressing hurriedly. He followed Haynes down to the hull where dozens of men were lying, deathly ill, the stench and misery breath-taking.

"Captain...do come up. We cannot risk you—"

"If I catch it and die, you have an able commander in Lieutenant Rice," he said, standing a moment before mounting the stairs, his decision made. When he was again on deck, he said to Rice and Haynes, "We will dock on the west side of the river at a safe distance. Then all of the sailors—the entire crew—will be off-loaded."

"What?" Rice shook his head. The Captain looked at him. "Forgive me. I mean, of course."

John Thomas said kindly, "Ship quarantines are, I believe, for emergencies at sea. In this case, the men will stand a better chance if we take them to tents, and those who are not yet ill will have a better chance of maintaining health in the open air. Are all of the doctors below?"

"Yes, sir."

"Relay the news to them. I will be in coordination with the Army, whose help we will need. If they can find a crew, our ship may still be used in case of battle."

Haynes wrung his hands. "Sir... Forgive me. Commodore Davis... He was most insistent that we drive on to Memphis, that you not..."

"I will speak with the Commodore."

Haynes shook his head and burst forth, "You haven't understood: you will be disobeying a director order! I shudder to think what will become of your career. Davis—"

"To hell with Davis, and to hell with my career! I am following naval law, and if anyone takes issue with me doing that, saving dying men, or preventing this disease from taking the entire Mississippi River Squadron to its grave, he may take it up with me. Now run along, and don't fear for yourselves. You were bound to follow my orders, you know. *Your* careers are still salvageable."

"Typhoid?"

The surgeon nodded, standing with Captain Haley outside of the large makeshift tent for the ill. "Along with a few cases of Yellow Fever. But mostly Typhoid. The evidence is plain from the red markings on the men. Davis may thank the Father above that you quarantined when you did. Half of those healthy men still might be infected, and we wouldn't know for two weeks. It seems rather rampant."

John Thomas's brows drew together. "But I haven't caught it. None of my officers have."

"You would've had your own cabins, not been in close contact…"

"But how is it transmitted?"

"We are unsure. By contact, possibly. Certainly by impure air and poisonous miasmas." The doctor removed his spectacles, cleaning them with his handkerchief.

John Thomas glanced at him. "There is a physician—I can't remember his name—who argues that perhaps it is caused by contaminated water? I read of it in the newspaper back in Boston."

The surgeon lifted a shoulder. "Sounds like a great bunch of Eastern tripe to me," he said in an unheated fashion.

John Thomas looked out over the hills where white tents dotted the land for miles. The sick tents were naturally at a distance, and the healthy quarantined men were high upon one of the bluffs. "How may I be of service? What do you need?"

"Nurses, but we haven't enough."

"Put me to use," he said softly.

The doctor stared at him. "You cannot be serious. You are an officer. It is beneath you."

"Beneath me?"

"Well, yes. And it would be unwise to risk yourself. There is a possibility that you could take the disease."

John Thomas shrugged.

"You... You may be needed."

"No, I shan't be. I am given to understand that I am in the utmost disgrace with Commodore Davis," he said in his customarily calm voice, seemingly entirely unshaken by that fact. "I have been informed that a report of my conduct will likely be sent to Washington." He smiled in his charming, yet sweet way, and even the doctor could scarcely resist him. "So you see that I am quite at your leisure."

Captain Haley lifted the head of a man who vomited and then carefully wiped his mouth, asking him, because he knew he was dying, to tell him of his home in Ohio, and of his sweetheart.

"She has blonde hair."

"Does she?" he asked softly.

"And blue eyes."

"She sounds lovely."

"There's nothing prettier than blue eyes, is there?"

John Thomas fingered the fresh rag in his hands. "No," he agreed softly.

"You'll tell her, won't you?"

John Thomas met his eyes, holding them for a moment, before nodding. "Yes. Of course," he whispered. "That you love her? Is that what you wish me to say?"

The man nodded, tears in his eyes as he met John Thomas's, a moment of clarity amidst his fevered state. "Yes," he whispered.

He died minutes later, and John Thomas continued to sit beside him on the floor, with his arm upon his knee and his eyes against his arm. *God, is it worth it?* How long he sat there, he had no notion. The next thing he knew was his name being called by a brusque voice. "Haley? Captain Haley?"

He looked up, dragging the back of his hand against his eyes. He saw, towering above him, Admiral Porter. Blinking as though the man were a mirage, he finally came to his wits, standing and removing his cap. "Yes, sir."

The Admiral looked around the room, the two aides behind him doing likewise. "Haley, have you been treating these men?"

"Yes, sir."

The Admiral exchanged glances with one of his aides. "All of this time? How long have you been here?"

"It is four days now, sir," he answered.

"Hmm." He looked around the room again at the scene of misery, and his face flickered with sympathy for the men. "Well. I thought I might see how things stood here."

John Thomas nodded. "Not well," he answered softly, eyes skittering away from a nurse who tried to meet his eyes. "Sir."

Porter nodded and then went to speak briefly with a few of the men, glancing back at John Thomas from time to time. Once he withdrew, John Thomas became lost in his work again, and it wasn't until nightfall that he heard the sound of his old friend from the Naval Academy, Paul Harrell, calling to him. "Come out, Haley, you need fresh air."

"Yes," he said, absently scrubbing his hands and then following the Lieutenant outside the white tent. He looked up, seeing a clear night and a blanket of stars over the Mississippi. When he looked down, the glow of campfires dotted the scene.

"Haley, listen..." John Thomas looked up at him, for, though he was tall himself, Harrell was the tallest man he had ever known. He was broad, too, his skin tanned from the beating sun. John Thomas gathered since Harrell hadn't used his rank that he was coming to him as a friend. "Davis sent me to fetch you. More to the point, Porter as well. They want you to captain an ironclad for the assault on Memphis."

"But I ought to be quarantined."

"The sick are all around us, Haley. None of us are immune."

"Which ship? They all have captains."

"One has been removed, and he will be your second in command. They see something in you Haley, and I think they want to see how far you will go."

He blinked, trying to weigh his words.

Harrell laughed. "Congratulations, my friend. Porter has taken a liking to you. I don't believe it will be a *rebuke* sent down from Washington, if all goes well. Do you take my meaning?"

"Yes." He nodded, drawing a hand through his hair. "Yes."

"Come, you're dead on your feet," he said, drawing him away from the tent. "You must have rest, or you'll embarrass us all." The Lieutenant laughed, a deep chuckle which could cause one to forget, if only for a moment, that a war was in progress. "Now, beat the Rebs!" he called over his shoulder as he left him.

Chapter Eleven

Adeline set her alarm for early the next morning. Adrian was always the first to get up, but at least he wasn't gone yet, and he very sweetly left her a smoothie in the fridge. She spent the entire morning on the balconies with an inspector and an engineer.

Then, her stomach growling, she went into the kitchen. Jane was there making lunch for Jude, who was perched on a stool coloring.

"Hey," Adeline said, going to the pantry.

"Hello," Jane answered. "I made enough for you to have some, too," she added, looking at Adeline over her glasses. They had a jeweled chain going from either side, and her hair was clipped so short the sparkling jewels really stood out.

"Oh, you don't have to do that, Jane!" she said, hesitating.

"My guess is you'll be needing it," she responded, giving Adeline a pointed look.

Adeline was surprised to find herself flushing. She looked down at her invisible middle, making matters worse. She swallowed. How embarrassing.

"I went to school in the sixties," Jane said. "Nothing shocks me." Adeline's flush receded slightly. She glanced at Jude, who was oblivious. "And I was a secretary, so I know how to be discreet."

Adeline bit the side of her lip. "Thanks," she said, accepting the plate. An awkward moment passed.

"It's none of my business," Jane said, pouring Jude's drink. "But he's quite a catch."

"Yeah... We're...taking it one day at a time."

"Are we getting ice cream?" Jude asked.

Adeline looked at Jane, who said, "Your father mentioned you might."

Adeline smiled at the boy. "Then yes. Right after we eat!"

"Good," he said, eating his sweet potato fries with relish.

When he finished and Jane told Jude to go up and get his shoes on, Adeline looked at her and said, "So, did everything go okay with Jude's friends?"

"Oh, yes. they come over occasionally. His father thinks it's good for him to be with other children during the summer."

"Yeah, of course, that makes sense. Well, I better get going. I need to stop by an antique store on the way home, so it may be a little while."

"Well, don't let him touch anything," Jane said, looking worried at the prospect.

Adeline had been a little apprehensive that she had over-stepped when she'd asked Jude without Adrian's permission. But when she opened the backseat of her Rav-4, Jude's booster seat was there. She hadn't even thought about that. Great. She was going to be an awesome mother. And Adrian probably knew it.

"Buckled in?" she asked.

"Did I do it right?" he asked, little brow furrowed as he eyed the seatbelt.

Double great. Jude was more conscientious than she. She checked it. "Looks good," she approved, and then she went to buckle herself in.

They went to his favorite place—he was able to navigate her there himself—and by the time they left, he was so much in charity with her that he didn't complain about the antique store.

She had been ogling a dining table at Palmetto Antiques for about three weeks. It would be perfect since it was walnut and massive enough to fill the large room. It still had all of its original chairs, although she would probably have them re-covered with something that would complement the character of the room and not crumble on guests as they sat down.

She stroked it for about twenty minutes, walking around and around it, Jude growing more bored by the moment. "Are you Eighteenth Century?" she asked softly, kneeling and trying to look at its underbelly. She ran her hand across the bottom, falling more in love by the moment with everything but the price tag.

She couldn't make a purchase like that without calling Adrian.

"Just a minute, buddy," she said. "Let me call your daddy, and then we'll get out of here."

"Okay," he said long-sufferingly, no different from the typical male. She smiled as she dialed Adrian, wondering how best to present the price. He answered on the third ring.

"Adeline?" There was concern in his voice. She hadn't thought about the fact that she never called him at work, that the one time she had she'd kind of scared him. She also had a feeling he'd feel more comfortable when she reached twelve weeks. "What's wrong?"

"Nothing—sorry."

"Are you sure?"

"Yeah. Sorry. Am I bothering you?"

"I'm...with a client."

"Whoops. Sorry. We'll talk later."

A pause. "That...would probably be best."

She winced. "Yeah, okay. Talk to you later."

She pocketed her phone and then turned, looking back at the table. She traced her fingers on its beautiful grains. "I hope you're still here tomorrow," she whispered.

She heard a giggle and looked over her shoulder. She smiled at Jude, whose eyes were glittering. "What, young man?" she asked.

"You were talking to the table."

She smiled. "You're just going to have to get used to it, Mister," she said, tickling his belly before reaching for his hand. "Let's go."

Adrian stepped out of the hospital into the sweltering heat, already working on his tie as he walked toward the parking garage. He clenched his jaw, thinking about the phone conversation earlier. *Way to get things started off right.* She'd probably never call him again.

He sighed, getting into his SUV, slinging the tie into the passenger seat, and heading toward home. The sun was going down, but there was still plenty of light, and there were plenty of tourists near the City Market and on the Battery.

He turned at his house, parking and going in the back door, taking off his coat and draping the tie over it. The smell of spaghetti hit him immediately. He walked down the hall and into the kitchen, where Jane sat at the table with Jude, apparently working on handwriting, which would be necessary if he were anything like his father. Adeline was standing at the counter in a T-shirt and headband, her curls springing at random. She looked up, meeting his eyes. There was a slight, awkward silence.

"Hey," he said, searching her face.

"Hey," she returned, with a smile.

He blinked. He was only pulled from his reverie by Jude catching sight of him, jumping up, and saying softly, "Daddy!"

He turned, putting his hand on Jude's head when he attached himself to his leg. "Hey, buddy. Have a good day?"

"We got ice cream," he said.

He looked over at Adeline, chopping away at the onion, and she smiled, winking at Jude. Jane got up, looking between them, and said, "Come along, young man. There's time for your bath before supper."

Adrian looked at Jane. She didn't usually stay for Jude's bath in the summer, but he didn't question it. She gave him a look, which he couldn't interpret. "Thanks, Jane."

"Mmm hmm," she said, herding Jude out.

He looked over at Adeline while she was dumping the onions from the cutting board into the skillet. "You don't have to cook," he said softly, taking a step closer as he laid a hand on the counter.

"This is more about hunger than self-sacrifice," she admitted, chopping the pepper now, glancing up at him once.

He smiled fleetingly, still studying her. "About earlier…"

"Sorry. Brain lapse. Won't happen again," she said. She couldn't make eye contact now. She was biting her lip and chopping away.

"No," he said earnestly, reaching to cover her hand. She paused, meeting his eyes. She was looking a little vulnerable. Maybe it was because she had no idea where the boundaries were. "I want you to call any time you want. I…speak and then remember to be human sometimes. Most of the time," he admitted belatedly, after giving the matter some thought.

She smiled, her eyes softening, looking almost tender. "You were with someone, Adrian. No biggie."

He studied her face. She was an odd creature. And intriguing. "This particular person gets upset at interruptions, but it isn't usually like that. What did you need? I felt like such a jerk."

She exhaled a slight laugh. "Well, Jude and I were out—" She paused, seeing concern flicker in his eyes, and said, "No, no, everything went fine. We went to this antique store..."

"What did he break?" he asked in a monotone, shoulders relaxing.

"I don't know why everyone says that. It's incredibly unjust. I told him not to touch anything, and he didn't."

Adrian flicked his brows.

She sighed. "There's this table..." He must have looked lost, because she added, "For the dining room."

"Oh." He was surprised they were even having this conversation. "Well, go for it."

"Are you sure?" she asked.

"Yep."

"Twelve-thousand dollars sure?"

His brows lifted slightly. There was a slight pause. He waited another moment before saying, "Is it worth it?"

"Every penny."

"Is it the one?"

She made a decent impression of the wincing emoji. "Yes?"

"Then, yeah. I trust you. It's what I'm paying you for." Now he was wincing, only a little more grimly.

"What was that, Adrian?" she asked, eyes twinkling.

He clenched his jaw. "Just...get the table, Adeline," he said, before looking apologetic and walking out of the room.

Adeline was standing at the counter a week later, going over her accounting, thinking about her awkward conversation with her foreman, Joe, that morning. They had been discussing the paint color for the library ceiling when he suddenly said in his low, masculine fashion, "He being good to you?"

It had taken a moment for the comment to even register. She turned her head to look at him. "Adrian?"

He nodded once, looking uncomfortable. They weren't terribly close, but he had a tendency, randomly, occasionally, to get over-protective in a fatherly sort of way.

"Yeah. Yeah, he's good to me, Joe," she answered.

He sniffed, nodding. "Just that these rich ones tend to want what they want. You know the type. We always work for them."

"No, he...he isn't like that," she said. She didn't know what to say. She thought, by the way he was looking at her, and the way there seemed to be more he wanted to say, that he suspected about the baby. He'd seen her on the verge of being sick several times. That was probably why he was worried, too. But she couldn't be certain, and she certainly wasn't bringing it up. "We're good, Joe," she said, trying to exude confidence.

"Well, you know where to find me if you need me," he said, sniffing again and moving on, half-threatening with his carpenter's belt rattling.

She winced now, thinking about it as she made up the report to give Adrian. They were on budget, their amended budget, that was, taking the fireplace in the library into account. She was circling the bottom line when there was a knock at the back door and then shoes in the hall. She peered around the corner as Harris materialized.

She set down her papers. "Harris! Why are you here? Did you get fired?"

"Ha," he said, hands in his pockets, looking sleek and cool, and slightly sunburned. "I have the week off." His hair looked a little whipped, like he'd been out on the ocean.

"Oh! Adrian thought you had *last* week off," she said, leaning against the counter, crossing her arms as she smiled. "Sorry, he's not home yet."

"I know. I was in Charleston and thought I'd stop by. How's Jude?" he asked, picking up an apple from the fruit bowl and crunching into it. She hoped it had been washed. She couldn't guarantee it, though. It wasn't officially her kitchen—not that it would necessarily be washed if it were.

"Okay, I think," she said. "That's pretty much Adrian's realm, though." Her eyes skittered away before he looked at her too closely. She thought he was about to speak, and said, "Oh, hey! There was something I wanted to ask you about. Do you mind coming upstairs?"

He was agreeable, and they started up, stepping over random piles of building and restoration materials. She took him into the room she'd been calling Shannon's room, which she was soon to return to its crimson glory, and went over to the brick fireplace. She slid out the loose brick and retrieved what she'd been surprised to find inside.

She lowered it into his hand, and he fingered it: a Star of David on a gold chain.

"I'd put it at WWII era, but you're the Modern Britain guy. I thought maybe you could help me out."

He looked up, meeting her eyes, and then back down. He seemed almost struck. "My grandpa used to talk about a little Jewish girl they took in during the war. She was Polish, very possibly his first crush. She eventually went back to an aunt after the war, and they moved to England. I think they always kept in touch."

Adeline blinked away tears. Vicious hormones. "But...I thought your family sold the house in the 1890's."

He looked up, holding the necklace like it was precious. Perhaps it had been to someone. "Oh." He shook his head. "Duh. I guess other families took kids in, too."

"Yeah. I guess so." But it was curious.

"I wonder what other secrets that room holds," Harris said when they were back in the kitchen, he seated on a barstool, she tossing a salad across from him. Adrian should like that. If she could only think of something else vegan to put with it. "Shannon's room."

She looked up. "Do you know Shannon? We may have talked about her before—I couldn't remember."

"I've been reading some of the letters you sent me. Her life was kind of a whirlwind after the war, wasn't it?"

"Seems to have been," she agreed, noting that the sun was finally going down. "But she talks so little about the house. And that's what I'm really interested in, you know."

"Oh, boo. You're not a true historian if you don't love scandal."

"I do," she promised. "But I want to get this right for your brother."

She felt Harris studying her and looked up, meeting his eyes. He looked like he might say something but changed it. "Adrian said you had an appointment last week," he said. "Everything go okay?"

"Yep. Fit as a fiddle. I have a picture, if you want to see."

He nodded and watched as she went toward the drawer where she kept it. "Shouldn't that be on display on the fridge?"

"I have to keep it away from Adrian."

He frowned, but she said quickly, "He kind of gets emotional, you know?"

Harris smiled. "Aww."

"Yeah." She felt warm from the inside out, just thinking of his eyes going the slightest bit glassy when they saw how much the baby had progressed in six weeks. He never said anything about it, though, only laughing and swatting her arm out of the way when she tried to wave the picture under his nose in the Land Rover. He had looked at her, though, afterwards, and reached for her hand, bringing it to his lips briefly. She would've swooned if she hadn't been sitting down. He kept doing that, catching her off her guard. Scaring the living daylights out of her. "*It's perfect, Adeline.*"

She'd had a good, hearty cry over that one in the shower when they'd gotten home. They hadn't talked about the baby in so long, not really, that she hadn't been able to ascertain his feelings. Oh, sure, he'd done the right thing, had gotten all teary when he'd seen the baby for the first time, claiming it as fully as if they'd been married and planning it carefully.

Actually, she didn't know why she'd doubted his feelings, now that she thought about it. Only, six weeks without having a real conversation about it was enough to scare a girl. He had been a little out of sorts, and she wondered if he had bitten off more than he'd bargained for. Well, maybe he had, with her. But as long as they were on the same page about the baby, they were okay.

Adrian heard laughter as he walked in, having gotten off work early for once. He'd seen Harris's car outside and heard him now, talking with Adeline in the kitchen. It didn't take him long, walking down the hall and standing in the kitchen doorway, to figure out they were looking at the sonogram, Adeline pointing out proudly the newly developed fingers and toes, Harris asking if he, or she, had an abnormally large head. Adeline socked him, and he laughed, hastily apologizing.

They had such chemistry. Conversation was never lacking, and they had always been at ease together, right from the get-go. He wouldn't say they were precisely the same personality type, but there were glimmers of similarity.

She looked up, seeing him come through the door, still smiling with pleasure. "Well, hey!" she said. "You're home early."

The glitter in her eyes was enough to make a man sit up and take notice. It wasn't that he didn't trust Harris. He did. Implicitly. But they were polar opposites, he and Adeline.

And he didn't make her laugh like that. Didn't know her well enough to know how, or if she even wanted to.

"Yeah, we had a cancellation," he said, coming to stand by her.

"For once," Harris said, smiling.

He bent, kissing Adeline's cheek, touching her arm gently. Her look registered surprise as he stood back up, but she didn't slap him or discuss boundaries or anything. She even smiled a little after the surprise wore off, meeting his eyes. He studied her.

Harris cleared his throat, and Adrian looked at him to see his eyes twinkling. He shot Harris a look. The last thing he needed was to scare Adeline any further away. She was more or less a frightened doe, afraid of him, afraid of herself. That he understood perfectly. How to proceed was less clear. He knew all of the inner workings of the human brain, but psychology could only go so far towards grasping the mysteries of a woman's soul.

"Harris thinks it looks like me," Adeline said, hands in her back pockets. "The baby."

"He's trying to flatter you," he said. "It has a Ravenel forehead."

She looked back at the picture. "Does it?" she asked, looking at it and then his forehead and Harris's, and then back. "Oh, you're right."

They laughed, and she shook her head. "Whatever. We'll see who it's like soon enough."

Chapter Twelve

Having gotten her morning sickness more or less under control, Adeline spent the next week with Jake and José in the drawing room. They stripped the walls carefully down to the light blue silk she'd found before her life had taken its most recent crazy turn. They were going to try to save it with the chemicals and tools she'd carefully purchased.

The guys were great, easy to work with and always joking. They seemed to have gotten over their initial awkwardness about the marriage, or at least these two had.

She kind of underestimated how tired the physical labor would make her, and when Jake suggested ordering a pizza for lunch, she was more than happy to sit at the kitchen table with them for a little longer than usual.

"Does this mean you're staying in Charleston, then?" Jake asked. "After the job's over, I mean."

Adeline glanced up to find the two of them looking at her. She hadn't thought about the fact that they and the rest of the crew might be worried about how this would affect their jobs. They still had a few more months left here, but they needed more security than that. She would, anyway, if it were her.

"I... Everything's a little uncertain right now. I'm sorry to say that, but..."

José studied her. "It's just that we'll be needing to find different jobs if..."

She looked between them, her stomach clenching. Why was this so hard? Everything was turned on its head. She was supposed to leave here at the end of her seven months, going on to whatever job her secretary in Charlotte had decided would be the most lucrative, her men packing up and moving with her. How would that even work out now? What was her career path? And what was she supposed to tell them? "Guys, I..." She moistened her lips. Time to fess up. These two and Joe had been with her the longest. They deserved to know where this was heading. "You should know that Dr. Ravenel and I recently found out that we're...expecting a baby."

She saw surprise register in their eyes.

"Congratulations," José said, smiling.

"Yeah," Jake added, nodding. "That's great."

"Thank you," she said, trying to be regal. "So you see that complicates things a little. If you could just tell the crew, and also tell them that I'll make sure you have a job, one way or another, I would appreciate it."

"Are you thinking about directing things remotely?" Jake asked.

"It's a possibility," she said, nodding. "We haven't talked things out completely yet, but there'll be a job for you somehow."

They nodded, seemingly content with that for now.

The silk preservation went less than ideally. The whole week was taken up with it, and the main problem was the layer of wallpaper right over it, which kept sticking to it or leaving a thick residue of nasty glue. It was tedious work, too, and she began to have grave fears about saving it. Silk was delicate even if it weren't a hundred and fifty years old and badly abused. But she couldn't help picturing it just as it would've been for the wedding of the daughter of the house, or during a ladies' tea with soft chatter and hoop skirts pooling on the expensive carpet, the sunlight catching the silk and turning it a sort of ice color. It would've been magnificent to behold and would've left no one in any doubt of the family's wealth, which she imagined had been the point.

Adeline was determined. She would save it.

She took a hiatus down into the basement where the kitchens and servants' quarters would've once been. There were great stone pillars down there that she was interested in architecturally. She'd need to have them checked out before the house's final inspection, which just now seemed so far away that she couldn't imagine it.

There were also vestiges of the old pulley bell system that the family would've signaled from their various rooms to call slaves. When she'd broached the subject with Adrian, he'd seemed less than interested about restoring it, and she guessed she couldn't blame him.

Her mind whirled down that avenue—the avenue of Adrian, that was. She hadn't seen much of him since the doctor's appointment. He'd been working late or putting in double time with Jude since Jane was off on vacation. Adeline had offered to watch him during the days, but Adrian had made other provisions, not wanting to weigh her down with too much, or so he said. She tried not to let that thought bother her.

She did see him at nights when they got a quick bite to eat together or when he finally came to bed, usually long after he thought she was asleep. He never went to sleep quickly. She didn't know if he had always been that way, or if something else was bothering him. But the air was usually sliceable, and she always had a feeling he knew she wasn't asleep either.

On Saturday, her table was supposed to be delivered, so she had the crew there to help manage it. When the person from the antique store showed up in their truck, it turned out to be a woman, and of course, the entire crew thought she needed assistance backing into the narrow driveway, which in turn made her nervous and made it take twice as long.

Adrian had come outside somewhere during the chaos, and Adeline, with crazy eyes, she was sure, had demanded, "Why do men think they need—or have the right—to direct women in the operation of anything with a motor?"

He started to speak, and she held up a hand. "I suppose you know. But if you answer that, I'll murder you."

He had closed his lips and signed the check, which was all that was required of him. As she was directing the crew with the proper placement and helping them figure out the ancient leaves of the table, she wondered if Adrian thought she was crazy. He probably set it down to hormones, which enraged her for a minute before she realized she did, in fact, need to get her hormones under control.

So she went up and took a shower when the men left, putting on comfy clothes and going downstairs to see what the boys were into. She found Adrian in the kitchen, making lunch, Jude sitting on a stool chatting him up.

"Hey," she said at the door, feeling kind of awkward and embarrassed.

Adrian looked up from filleting a fish, fresh from the market, she assumed. "Hey," he said, with a fleeting smile. "You might want to keep your distance."

She looked down at the fish, two slices of it, and there was something else still packaged beside it, presumably for her. "You guys are going to turn into fish," she said.

Jude giggled, and Adrian smiled, looking at him. Transferring his gaze to Adeline, he said, "Lunch in about forty-five minutes?"

"Sounds good," she answered, stepping more fully into the room. "Need help?"

He looked at her, must have seen she was wary around the fish, and said, "Let me get this cleaned up first."

Once he had put it on the grill and eradicated the kitchen of the smell, she helped him slice carrots, and boiled some fresh corn. Jude had scampered off, an important date with Disney apparently on his schedule. She glanced at Adrian, at his attractive arms as he made slices in the sweet potatoes.

He looked over at her, lifting his brows enquiringly.

"When are you going to tell him?" she asked softly.

He offered her a different knife when hers made little headway. "I'm not sure. I kind of wanted to take it slow. He's been an only child for a long time."

She nodded. "I get that. I was just thinking it might be better for him to hear it from you and maybe me than for someone to slip. The crew knows it now, and—"

He looked up, black eyes narrowing. "The crew knows it?"

She laid down her knife. "They were asking about their jobs. I couldn't explain the uncertainty without..." She drew her brows together. "Sorry, I didn't know we were keeping it a secret from anyone, except Jude." And her parents.

He shook his head. "Never mind. Doesn't matter."

She had a feeling it did, but she couldn't think why. She studied his back for a minute, found herself dwelling on the way his button down hung, and ended up severely chiding herself. She had to stop getting distracted. Maybe she should just change the subject.

"So I...have this problem I've been needing to talk to you about."

He turned, concern in his eyes. "Oh, sorry," she said. "A house problem, not an actual problem." He pulled a bottle of water from the fridge, walking toward her where she now sat on the barstool and handing it to her. "Thanks."

"Adeline, if we need to extend the date, or wait until—"

"No, not this time," she promised. He studied her. "I need to get paint on the walls in Shannon's room and a couple of the downstairs rooms, but I really shouldn't be here for a couple of days after they do it..."

"Oh," he said, thinking.

"Should I get a hotel, or..?"

"No, don't do that." He leaned against the counter, thinking. "I have a friend who has a cottage on Sullivan's Island. John. Do you remember him from the wedding?"

"Yeah. Blonde, three kids."

He nodded. "We could go toward the end of August for a weekend. You'll need the break anyway, and he won't mind after tourist season fizzles out."

Could she postpone it another few weeks? Yeah, she guessed so, although nothing made a house look more finished than a fresh coat of paint, and she knew Adrian was probably beginning to wonder when they were ever going to see progress.

"Does that work?"

She looked up, meeting his eyes. "Yeah, if you'll go, too. You need a break, too, Adrian. Your eyes are all bloodshot all the time, and..." *Jude needs you. I'd like to get to know you.* "You can't expect me to learn how to swim if you never try to teach me."

The corner of his mouth tipped up. "Yeah, I'll go." He slowly reached across the counter for her hand. "And we'll tell him then. Together."

She smiled, reaching to press his hand.

Big mistake. She'd forgotten you couldn't touch his hands without getting a zinger, or without being swept back to a rainy night in the spring. She brought her hand away quickly, suddenly remembering that her restriction on all physical contact had been for a reason. But she wouldn't forget it again anytime soon.

Chapter Thirteen

"Shannon, there is something we must tell you."

Shannon was sitting in her father's library, staring into nothingness after an exhausting day at the hospital. To anyone watching, though, she was staring at the fireplace, where the Ravenel crest had once stood above a European mantel. Shannon's father had decided it was too precious to leave to the destructive hands of the Federals and had ordered, without consulting the ladies, to have the entirety of it covered over with new plaster and to install a new mantle, though it had nearly broken his heart. He decided they would not operate it anymore but would instead have the chimney lined with shelves upon which they would hide their valuables from Ravenel House and Santarella. Even if the house was eventually burned, he reasoned, the fireplace ought to stand.

Upon hearing the voice, Shannon slowly looked across the candlelit room to see Marie entering, Mr. Ravenel beside her. Marie was holding what appeared to be a newspaper clipping in her hand. For a moment, Shannon's heart stuttered, and then she felt as though it stopped utterly.

"Do sit, Marie," her father said gently, and Marie did so, crossing the rich carpet which graced the wood floors, and taking one of the ladies' chairs. Her father, too, sat just across, and they both hesitated. Hand against her bodice, Shannon drew a shaking breath, waited another moment, and then burst forth, "For God's sake, tell me!"

Her father looked most displeased at this unfilial outburst, but Marie intervened quickly saying, "Did we frighten you? Forgive us, it was not our intention, for...no one is harmed." She rested her hand against her middle, hesitating and looking at her father-in-law.

Shannon's eyes transferred to him, deeply hungering, and he said, "Frederick has sent us a newspaper clipping that he obtained—he doesn't say how—from Boston. It seems that your...husband has become something of a sensation in the North."

Shannon did not move an inch, and the blood seemed to rush in her ears. She continued looking at her father, searching.

He continued, "He was sent out to the Mississippi River, and, just as they were drawing in on Memphis, all of his men were laid low with..." He glanced at Marie when he couldn't remember.

"Typhoid Fever," she said apologetically to Shannon.

Shannon looked from Marie back to her father, who continued, "He had orders from his commanding officer,

Commodore Davis, not to take them into quarantine, but he disobeyed them and is now quoted as saying..." He got up and went to Marie, taking the clipping from her and reading, "'To hell with Davis, and to hell with my career.'"

Shannon watched, still not moving. "Apparently, it became one of those phrases which the public takes up. Of course, half the populace thinks he was talking about President Davis. But the article reads that even Commodore Davis doesn't take the quote in bad part. It seems the young man took the men into quarantine and stayed with them even when the disease was rampant, helping to care for them." He glanced at the article again. "He took Admiral Porter's fancy—he 'liked the spirit of the comment and the compassion'—and Haley was chosen to lead the flotilla which ultimately defeated the Confederate forces near Memphis on the river, regaining for the Union access to the entirety of the Mississippi River, excepting Vicksburg, of course. And he was promoted to the rank of Commodore."

Shannon blinked, turning away her face, her hand still pressed against her bodice, where her corset seemed to cut off any chance at a breath. She swallowed. "Why do you tell me this?" she asked softly. Her voice sounded weak, like a child's.

Marie got up, coming to sit beside Shannon on the sofa, reaching for her hand. "Because, my dear cousin, he is now very much in the public's mind. Perhaps it will be short-lived, perhaps not. And the Northern populace is eager to learn details of his personal life, according to the article. They request information from his family and friends. I do not think it will be long before you become a subject for their eagerness as well. Everything that can be known about you very shortly will *be* known. And we simply thought you ought to know. And Frederick did, too. Our hope is that their speculation will be kind, but..." She broke off, pressing her lips together.

They both looked up as Mr. Ravenel said, "Whether your fame, or infamy as it may be, will pour over into the South remains, I suppose, to be seen."

"It shan't be infamy," Marie said quickly. "Not here. Her story is known. And I believe there will be an outpouring of support for her. There can be no sympathy here for the man who caused Memphis to fall."

Shannon and Marie passed outside of the small garden at Ravenel House through the back entrance and went to the formal drawing room where tea and fresh fruit awaited them. The room had been hung in an ice blue silk upon Shannon's mother and father's marriage, and it created so much light in the room and provided such a cheerful respite, that it was one of the ladies' favorite haunts during the day, despite the room's grand size and formal mien. The ceiling was molded with white carvings, the fireplaces exquisitely wrought. Mirrors faced one another, and treasures collected from around the world were on display.

"I do wonder what is keeping them about Rose," Marie said, sipping her tea.

"I daresay Miss Ravenel was a trifle testy after her nap."

Marie laughed, saying innocently, "*My* daughter?"

Shannon had begun to look tired, which her father attributed to her work at the hospital. He had asked (commanded) her to stay home Saturday as well as Sunday. But he had no notion that there was no rest from the weariness she faced.

"By the by, did I tell you of Mrs. Drewry's invitation to us when she and her daughter-in-law called?"

Shannon shook her head, taking a sip of her tea, and hoping it would enliven her.

"She invites us to a ball, of all things."

Shannon placed her cup on her saucer. "A ball? Doesn't she remember that we are in mourning?"

"Indeed. She has thought it all out and believes, if you please, that we would not do wrong to come and dance one or two dances, given that we are more than six months from your mother's death. She also reminds us that we must keep up the spirits of the young men from the forts."

Shannon stared at her, dumbfounded. "In *your* condition?"

Marie laughed. "*I* shan't dance, but you know, it would not be wrong if it were to be a charity ball, which I believe she intends it to be."

"I should not dream of dancing until my mother has been dead a year," Shannon said firmly, and then, as another thought occurred to her, her eyes narrowed.

Marie regarded her warily. "What is it?"

"She does not for a moment dream it would be proper! She doesn't care if we are the talk of Charleston, as long as I am there to provide the entertainment!"

Since Charleston had heard of Shannon's estranged husband's successes, she had indeed become quite an object of speculation. Not only had she been virtuous and fled to her rightful Southern home and family, but she had also, as they had suspected in 1859, achieved a very interesting alliance. It was plain that the Ravenels were to be ranked with the best families, who might choose as they wished for their daughters, however odd a choice a New England Quaker. Or was it Unitarian? *Something* of that nature. Was his mother in truth an Adams? Well-connected and pious, *that* was what they had heard. And rich.

And since Marie had already suspected what Shannon said blatantly, she said, quite calmly, "Do you think so? Well, in any event, I had rather not go."

Just then, the doors opened, and the nursery maid Emma entered holding the hand of the nineteen-month-old Rose. The little beauty was quite capable of walking, and even running, without assistance, as she communicated through a series of grunts and forceful gestures to her maid.

Laughing, Shannon got up since Marie could not lift her easily and took her to sit between them. Marie kissed her and stroked her rusty hair, twirling a slight curl around her finger and looking at her lovingly. "Yes, my dear girl, have you had your dinner?"

"Yes, ma'am," Emma replied, head bowed.

Marie inclined her head and told Emma that she might go have hers. When Rose wiggled and wanted to get down on the imported carpet, which neither her mama's nor her aunt's skirts and hoops would allow, Shannon entrapped her, placing her on her lap and giving the child her brace-let to play with. She watched her, and felt, as she always did, wonder as her young mind learned something new every moment. Finally, Rose turned suddenly and offered it back. Shannon laughed, giving her wrist to Marie for her to re-clasp it. "Your Papa is going to be so proud of you," Shannon said.

"Pa-pa."

Marie smiled, wiping a tear. "Yes," she said, lovingly, offering Rose one of the toys Emma had left. "I wish I might have a portrait of the two of you."

"Of Rose and her Aunt Shannon?" Shannon asked. "Why on earth?"

"Purely aesthetic reasons. Your hair matches so pre-cisely. It would be very pleasing."

"Rose, I believe your mother does not appreciate the fullness of our qualities."

"No-no-no," Rose babbled, chewing her toy.

Shannon stroked her hair, feeling its softness, and, though she had tried to keep it at bay, an ache spread in her chest. Quickly, she said, "Did my Aunt Coraline make it safely from Kinwood?"

"Yes, yesterday," Marie answered. Her mother was com-ing to Charleston to stay with her aunt, ostensibly to shop, but, of course, so that she would be at hand when Marie's time came. "I suppose we must have her to dinner."

"What a thing to say!"

"She can be very infuriating when I am in a delicate condition, Shannon. Indeed, the walk we took this morning would have been thought too arduous, the food I consume not enough, or too much, the activities I undertake not conducive to—"

"Then by all means *don't* invite her!" Shannon declared.

"Well, perhaps I shan't. We shall see. Come Rose, a pagoda sleeve is *not* for chewing."

Shannon had begun to wonder at the wisdom of bringing Phoebe to the hospital, for she had heard one of the soldiers speaking disrespectfully to her earlier in the day. That had led Shannon to a rather stern discussion with Mr. Drake (and Dr. Eisley for good measure) that the men were to be told that Mrs. Haley would be appreciative if they would show her respect by extending the same courtesy to her maid.

"It's nothing to fuss about, ma'am," Phoebe said as they both reached for fresh bowls and cloths in the storerooms. "They're just hot and miserable, and they want to go home."

Still angry, Shannon snapped, "He would not have said such a thing if not for the color of your skin." She looked up, meeting Phoebe's eyes, her lips parting. It was such an odd thing to say here, in Charleston. And both knew its source. Phoebe dropped her eyes, seemingly uncomfortable, and said, "Thank you for talking to them, Miss Shannon," before leaving the room quickly.

Shannon stayed another moment to collect herself and slow her pounding heart. When she left, lips pressed together, she walked with a quick stride to one of the sick rooms where cots were laid out. She washed a man's face and dressed his wound before turning to another, still scarcely able to keep her mind from the news her father and Marie had brought her last week.

She had purloined the article from her father's desk, realizing afresh that they hadn't exaggerated. And certainly the newspaper hadn't. Yankees didn't exaggerate, in her experience at least. According to the newspaper, morale was very low in the North after Shiloh's death toll in April. It had shocked the nation to its very foundations, and, for the first time, the Northern populace seemed to doubt whether the war could be won at all. It seemed the people, with bruised hearts, had found solace and hope in a compassionate and capable officer, not to mention a brave one.

"You're right pretty, ma'am," a soldier said.

"Thank you," she said, washing his forehead.

"Don't see red hair like that much."

"It is an odd color," she agreed. She felt something trailing up her arm and realized with a start that it was his finger. The hair on her neck rose, and she jerked her arm away, giving him a startled look.

"Come, now. I've heard tell of you. High an' mighty, but I know about yer kind. Heard tell about yer husband up North. They might think yer respectable here, but *I'm* not from these parts, and *I* know that no woman who leaves her husband is a pretty picture of virtue. I just wonder what you would be willing—"

"If you touch me just one more time, I will report you to your commanding officer," came a low growl from Shannon's throat.

She jumped up, leaving the bowl and rag on the bed, and continued to stare at him, unable to remove her eyes from him. She could hear no sound and see nothing but him, and she felt so trapped that she wished to run. Slowly, her senses returned, and she rushed from the room, returning to the storeroom, where she dry-heaved for at least a full minute. Then she heard the door open and saw Phoebe's concerned eyes. "Miss Shannon! What did he say to you?" She helped her to straighten, and Shannon covered her eyes with shaking hands. "Whatever it was, he was just looking for vengeance, ma'am. Don't you remember that he's the one who spoke to me this morning? There, now, stop shaking, ma'am."

Shannon breathed deeply, slowly regaining her wits, and said, "Was he? One bearded, filthy man looks much like another, I'm afraid."

"What did he say to you, ma'am?"

"He...He thinks I am a...whore."

Phoebe's eyes flamed, but Shannon shook her head. "It was probably just as you say. Have the men...most of them... been kinder to you today?"

"Yes, ma'am."

"I...I'm glad." She took a shaky breath, knowing the man's opinion was isolated here but that there would be many men and women who accused her of such. Perhaps the entire Union did.

She covered her roiling stomach and tried to steady herself. But before she could do so, the door opened, and Mr. Drake entered, his face wreathed in smiles. "Mrs. Haley. I am so very sorry to disturb you in your Nightingale efforts, but your father is in the foyer: your sister-in-law, it seems, has begun the long labor of bringing into the world another child for your brave and noble brother."

It took a moment to comprehend his words, and then Shannon's heart dropped. She stood silent for a moment, and then she took her servant's hand, saying softly, "Come, Phoebe." Phoebe nodded, and they both left and got up in the carriage with her father, the tension palpable among them all.

Chapter Fourteen

S hannon sat in the library with her father the next day, unable to discern the length of time that had elapsed. Her Aunt Coraline was with Marie, and Shannon hadn't been invited to assist, for which she was frankly grateful. The house by now pulsating with servants running to do the bidding of the doctor and midwife, and hours elapsed as they heard intermittently Marie's screams and moans.

"Was it so terrible last time?" Shannon asked softly, staring out the long windows onto the Battery. Her hands were clasped against her black skirts, her eyes slipping closed every time a new cry of agony wafted to them.

"Yes." Her father sat behind his desk, his forehead in his hands. "I think it was worse, but your mother was..."

He broke off, but Shannon knew the last word. *Here.*

"She always did take command of a situation, didn't she?" Shannon's voice was constricted.

He nodded, looking away. Finally, he said, as though continuing their conversation, "We were at Santarella last time, which your brother later blamed himself for. He thought that if we had been in Charleston, she would've had access to better care, though how... And she wanted the child to be born there, in any event."

Shannon moistened her lips. After a time, she said, "It is a little early, don't you think? The baby."

He seemed to do calculations and then, standing, pulled a medical book from high on a shelf. After a moment, he said, "Yes." He read on for another moment. "Surely, though, not so early that..." He didn't finish the sentence, merely sat again, and they diverted one another's thoughts with predictions on the rice crop at Santarella.

He once again became confident and composed while discussing his kingdom, and Shannon insensibly found comfort in such confidence. She asked him how the rice trunks had faired, and whether he was hearing anything to cause him worry from his overseer regarding the slaves. There was no question, they agreed, that the Federal armies were close to the surrounding islands, or that their bondsmen might know freedom was only a stone's throw away.

But it was no good. Finally, they stopped talking altogether, and, when they took their supper in the dining room, Shannon could only force herself to swallow the most meager bites. They had not bothered to change out of their day wear, and it was the first time she could ever remember doing so.

A servant came down once they were on the point of rising, but Shannon stayed fixed in her chair, her eyes fixed on the woman's face.

"There's no news, ma'am, sir," the girl said, her hands clasped at her homespun skirts. "Dr. Travers wanted me to tell you that she is struggling."

"What do you mean?" her father asked, face sharp with an eagle stare.

She said, not meeting his eyes, of course, "That it's been real difficult for her, Mr. Ravenel. Said he wishes he could tell you more, but we're just waiting now."

There was a long silence, and finally, while Shannon's heart beat a fast staccato, her father said, "Yes, very well. I imagine you are needed."

They once more took refuge in the library, and Shannon sat, ostensibly reading. But her eyes fixated on the same words again and again. Her father worked on his ledgers, and slowly, agonizingly slowly, the night advanced again into the small hours of the morning.

And then, gradually, it began to dawn on each of them that the house had grown quiet. Impossibly quiet. Not a servant stirred. And it had been long, too long, since they had heard screams. Shannon jumped up, swallowing, her hands gripping her black skirts, and it struck her that this silence changed nothing. There was still nothing they could do until a messenger was sent to them. They must wait. And Shannon thought that must be crueler than any torment.

She burst forth, nearly in tears, "Papa..."

He looked up, eyes weary. "Yes, Shannon?"

She turned in the room, looking for something to say, trying to hush the voices of fear, to regain her equilibrium. "This fireplace... T-Tell me its story again?"

He hesitated but then looked at her compassionately. He told her the story he had told her and Frederick as children sitting on the rug in his library when they had been brought down, very occasionally, to see their parents after supper. She listened to the tale of their ancestors, Huguenots, who had fled France to escape persecution and death, and how a similar mantel had hung in their salon in Nantes. And how this one had been imported once the family began to prosper in America. And that her father had installed it in the home he had built so that he would never forget their suffering or their commitment to God. She clung to his words, as though, if she did not give them her full concentration, she would shatter into a million pieces. The thought almost made her laugh hysterically.

When he finished, she found herself breathless, and he got up, coming to her and causing her to sit on one of the sofas. He sat beside her and seemed to find comfort in diverting her mind, an endeavor in which he achieved moderate success.

And then, when it was nearly dawn, the door handle rattled, and Dr. Travers walked in, looking weary and old. They shot to their feet, Shannon holding to her father's arm for support, waiting with bated breath. She looked at him more closely and could see that all was not well. "The... baby?" she asked.

He hesitated a moment before shaking his head slowly, sadly. As his meaning dawned on them and fell like the weight of heavy bricks, Shannon could see nothing except the doctor raising a shaking hand to his mouth. And yet, it were as though, at the same time, she could see everything, hear everything, smell everything with sharper clarity. She could see, in her peripheral vision, her father bow his head and cover his eyes with his hand. She could hear the night noises of insects which she hadn't previously noticed. And she could smell blood. "Marie?"

He hesitated so long that her father regained awareness and looked up, paling. The doctor's chin trembled. "She wants to see you, Miss Ravenel," he said. He took a long, shaking breath and said in a constricted voice, "Come, my child, there isn't long."

Shannon gave a crazed cry of anguish, and stayed rooted where she was, feeling as though she had only a very thin hold on sanity and that she could scream in horror throughout all eternity. And then her feet began moving her blindly forward. She heard her father say painfully, "Shannon!" as though he wished to spare her this. She saw his face, tears flowing not of his own volition. But he did not stop her, and she continued to walk, not, it seemed, of her own will. When she came to the top of the stairs, she stood outside the door, her head shaking, her voice whispering like a madwoman, over and over, "No. No. No."

And then there was Phoebe coming down the hall. When she made it to her, she took Shannon's upper arms in her hands tightly. "Miss Shannon," she said, voice shaking, but *she* still was sane. "Miss Shannon, look at me. Look at me, ma'am." Shannon finally obeyed. "You've got to be strong. I'm so sorry, ma'am. So sorry. But you've got to do this. Do you understand, Miss Shannon? She wants you, and you must be brave."

Shannon stared at the door handle, feeling as though she would heave, wishing to bend over double and scream in terror. But instead she walked forward toward the bed, where Marie lay, looking so altered that Shannon at first did not recognize her.

The midwife motioned for Shannon to come to the side of the bed toward which her head was turned, and Shannon did so, taking only a moment to collect herself. Her cousin. Her cousin. No, her sister. How could it be… No, it could not happen! She walked up to the bed and tentatively reached for her hand. "Marie?" she said softly.

Her cousin's eyes fluttered open, and she said weakly, so weakly, her eyes hooded, "Shannon."

Shannon stroked her hand. "You must not talk, dearest," she said, voice shaking miserably. "You must conserve your strength."

Marie looked at her, and strangely, she smiled weakly. "So beautiful. I could never…hold a candle to you."

Shannon didn't know what to say, only shook her head.

"Shannon… I want you to…care for Rose. Until her father can. I have…told my mother…that this is my wish. Will you?"

Shannon held her eyes. And she realized all at once that the time for pretense was gone. Marie was fading. "Yes," she whispered. "As if she were my own."

Marie's eyes grew tender. "I wish that she might be Catholic. But..." She seemed to try to recruit her strength. "Tell Frederick that he isn't to blame. And Shannon..." Suddenly Marie's hand closed over her wrist, and she held Shannon's eyes.

"Yes, dearest," Shannon whispered, a tear rolling down her cheek. "Anything."

Marie studied her. "Promise me... If God ever grants you a second chance, that you will return to John Thomas."

Shannon stared at her, shocked, her lips trembling. She couldn't tell Marie that she asked too much. She wouldn't tell her. *Oh, dear God.* "Yes," she whispered. "I promise."

She could see that Marie was slipping away, and Shannon looked around the room frantically, seeing the eyes of the midwife, the doctor, her Aunt Coraline, and five servants, all of whom stood where they were, resigned, tears flowing down their faces freely. "And tell Elizabeth..."

Shannon looked back down at Marie quickly, but her eyes had closed. "What?" she breathed. "Tell her what? Marie!" she cried. "Tell her what? Marie! Marie!" And then someone's hands where gently on her arms, drawing her back as she screamed, meeting her Aunt Coraline's eyes. Her aunt stood curiously still, as though her spirit were elsewhere, gone from this room to endure the pain.

Shannon freed her arms from the hands that held them and looked around the room, finding only one destination: the heavy wooden door. She fled for it and out into the hall, down the stairs, and outside into the garden where she was momentarily blinded by the sun.

She ran as far as she could in the solitude and dropped to her knees, cradling her bodice, heaving and weeping insensibly. "I can't... I can't. I cannot *live* like this anymore. Oh, God! Take me, too! Please, I cannot live like this!"

She wept and wept, scarcely able to hear the voice over her own cries.

No.

Shannon looked up and around her. *No, my child.* She stood, frightened for a moment, still breathing hectically. Until the author of the voice was fully realized by her. She stared around her, shaken, turning a slow circle in the garden until the circle was full. The earth seemed a strange place, not quite as she had thought it, and she turned in another circle, trying to understand, to discern, to grasp the meaning.

Chapter Fifteen

Their father had been the one to pen the words to tell Frederick of his double loss. He had written back with what feelings they could not imagine that he was being transported back to the coast and would be escorted by the Army into Charleston.

When he walked through the door of Ravenel House, he looked so pale and thin and haggard that Shannon did not at first, standing in the foyer in the deepest black, recognize her own brother. Her aunt and uncle were elsewhere in the house, hidden away in grief. Only she and her father were there. They did not know what to say or do, Shannon especially, given that her brother wasn't speaking to her.

But it had been Shannon's shoulder he had collapsed against after taking one empty look around the beautiful foyer, weeping silently and whispering, "How shall we go on? How shall we go on without her?"

Shannon had no notion. She merely let him weep, and wept along with him. It was not difficult to see that he had been a prey to the same shocked grief which had wracked the entire household. And yet, for all of her grief, Shannon had been able to do what she must, to take burdens off the shoulders of others. She put that odd, almost troubling, thought aside, and told him, her eyes still wet and voice thick, that he ought to go up and bathe and that his dinner would be waiting for him.

Now she sat with her brother in the large parlor, handkerchiefs not far from either of them. They were alone, and silence reigned in the candlelit elegance of the room after dinner. What on earth was such wealth, such beauty for, Shannon wondered inconsequentially. Did it save them from troubles? Make them easier to bear?

In the silence of the room, she looked tentatively across at Frederick. His uniform had been cleaned, his face shaven, but he still looked older than his twenty-six years. The heat was stifling, even at the late hour, until it pulled even Frederick from his grief, making him jump up and angrily thrust up a window. When he sat back down, it wasn't long until his look grew faraway. At length, he said the words that she had been dreading: "Tell me everything that happened."

She bit her lip, feeling the fresh prick of tears, the raw strain of her nose and throat that was unending. She closed her eyes, still trying to fathom it. Marie had been alive, and then she was dead. However concerned they had been for her, it was still utterly shocking. All of Charleston was in shock. Those who hadn't known her were even asking one another whether they had heard about Mrs. Frederick Ravenel. Some of the servants could be heard night and day weeping, and Shannon experienced deep, soul-wracking grief, an agonizing, endless pain. But Frederick... It must be the very worst pain a man could suffer, she thought.

"Brother..." she croaked, staring at the blue-gray sleeve of his uniform. "Please don't ask me."

His jaw clenched and unclenched, his eyes brimming. "The funeral is tomorrow. I cannot be the least knowledgeable person present as my...wife and child are buried."

Shannon's lip trembled, and she fished for a fresh handkerchief, pressing it to both of her eyes in turn, taking a moment to compose herself. She told him everything Dr. Travers had meticulously explained to them about what had happened. Focusing on the medical details must be easier, or so she had thought. Every time she told him a fresh detail, his eyes would close as though he could not bear it.

Finally, she said, "She told me to tell you not to blame yourself, when I went to her."

His lip trembled. "We had thought it was merely because it was her first," he said, and it took her a moment to follow his meaning. "We were...encouraged to think there would be no trouble with a second."

She caught his hand, pressing it between both of her own. "Frederick..." she said, her voice failing her. "Of course not, dearest. How could you have known?" she mourned.

"Was it a boy or a girl?"

The question caught her off-guard, and Shannon shook her head, unwilling, knowing it didn't matter what she said.

Either would pierce his heart, for the child would be real to him, tangible.

"Please, Shannon," he said earnestly, holding her eyes, his own damp.

She swallowed. "A girl," she rasped.

His eyes closed, and twin tears snaked down his cheeks. "How long did she live?" he whispered.

A sob emanated from Shannon before she could contain it. She pressed her fingers to her lips, trying to contain her grief. "Only a few minutes," she whispered in return.

Frederick covered his temples, elbows on his knees, and sat silently a long while. Finally, he said, "What else did she say?"

"She..." Shannon swallowed with difficulty. "She was concerned for Rose, of course—"

"When did she know she was dying?" he interrupted.

"I..." She bit her trembling lip. "Do you want me to find Aunt Coraline? I don't know, Frederick, she had already accepted it when I came to her, though we had not."

He swallowed and sat silently for a moment. "What were you saying about Rose? I'm sorry."

She looked at him with earnest sympathy. "She wished..." Her voice broke over the past tense. A fresh wave of disbelief stole over her. For a moment, grief threatened to choke her. She couldn't seem to go a moment without thinking of her childhood, when Marie had been such a solace. And, their girlhood behind them, they had stepped into womanhood together. They had laughed together, wept together, been brides together. She pressed her eyes closed, more tears seeping out. "She wished for me to care for Rose until the war is over. But of course, Frederick, she is your daughter, and—"

"That is what I wish, too," he said. Shannon looked up suddenly, seeing that he was holding her eyes with more clarity than she had yet seen.

"Aunt Coraline said she accepted it, but, indeed, Frederick, I think she is already beginning to—"

"She is *my* daughter, and she will be raised in my home," he said defiantly, his jaw rigid.

She nodded, agreeing and yet feeling sorry for her aunt and uncle. Nothing could ease their pain just now.

"I will make my wishes known," he said, and she didn't doubt it. "And Shannon, Marie was...so proud of your work at the hospital. But the baby..." He choked. "Rose, I mean... She is motherless now. And fatherless until the war is through. Will you stay at home and care for her?"

"Yes," she said, nodding. "I know my duty." As her words floated into the air, she flushed, turning her face away until he could only see her profile.

He covered her hand quickly and said thickly, "No, Shannon. I won't heap any more incriminations upon you. That is in the past." He swallowed, looking away. As though making concessions, he added, "I know it must have been difficult, living in the North, and..." He looked at her again, with sympathy. "Only I was so bitterly disappointed," he said softly. "I had wanted you to be happy. And he... Well, we are on opposite sides of a war now, I suppose. And you are here, for which I can only be grateful, especially now." As his loss returned to him, his countenance crumbled. "And she was glad you were here, too. She loved you so, Shannon."

"And I, her," she croaked. She moistened her lips. When some time had passed, she thought she ought to convey one last detail of their conversation. "Frederick…" she said hesitantly. "Marie said something… It wasn't a request, but she expressed a wish that Rose might have been raised Catholic."

"What?"

"She seemed to accept that she would not."

"She said that she wanted Rose to be Catholic?" he asked, watching her intently.

"I believe her faith was close to her in that moment. That is, it was on her mind, as it would be."

He shook his head in misery. "I ought never to have asked her to have given it up."

"She was resigned to it, Frederick. You were her husband, and she desired to follow your wishes."

"Would that I could have deserved her," he said, lip trembling before he looked away.

She took his hand, causing him to meet her eyes. "You did," she said. "She was entirely devoted to you, and that could only spring from true affection and respect. You gave her happiness, and I do not believe she ever regretted for a moment marrying you or bearing your children."

He seemed to find comfort in those words, his face softening, and she was always glad that she had said them.

It rained the day of the funeral when they stood in the Magnolia Cemetery just outside the city. Shannon could not help thinking that they were not even out of mourning for her mother, whose grave still appeared fresh. She stood in her black gown and mourning jewelry, looking at the barren dirt before turning her face away.

It was difficult to get through the day, to lay Marie to rest. Frederick had named the baby, Marguerite, for the grandmother he and Marie shared, stating that she was a Ravenel, and deserved at least that.

It seemed as though all of Charleston attended. Even some male cousins on their mother's side had managed to come in their gray uniforms. Shannon could not see the hundreds of people through her tears, and she was glad for her black veil, feeling as though that barrier made it easier to bear their sympathies.

Still, though, the anguish would catch her off-guard, making her nearly bend double from the surprise of it. She had never considered a life without Marie, hadn't thought such a thing was possible.

But she knew, somehow, that they must go on. For each other, for Rose, for any hope of the future. And she had been told, by one who ought to know, that life was worth the living, despite it all. Despite her broken marriage with a man she had loved so much she had fled him in terror. Despite death, heartbreak, and war, deprivations and separations. Life must go on.

Chapter Sixteen

When the end of August rolled around, Adeline was perfectly happy to get out of the city with its stifling heat, endless waves of tourism, and constant demands. They took her Rav-4 on Friday afternoon, buckling Jude in the back and tucking his bag of snacks beside him. Adrian loaded everything, not even allowing her to carry her makeup bag this time.

"Wait," she said as they were turning out of the drive. He braked. "Did I get the stuff I copied from your dad's box?"

"It's right beside your bag," he affirmed.

"Good." She settled back for the not-too-arduous drive out to the island, which charmed her immediately. There were shops and restaurants and vacationers, but it still had a peaceful feeling.

They turned in at the cottage, which had an excellent view of the ocean and was cute to boot. It was wood, weathered white, with a tiny cupola that made it look like a birdhouse. She could see the excitement in Jude's eyes. They had been on the island approximately thirty minutes when they were setting out for the beach. Walking the long plank boardwalk, Jude ran out in front of them, cute as a button in his navy-blue trunks and light blue shirt.

Adeline wore a loose black cover-up with a print of dark green leaves and an oversized straw hat which she had to put her hand on for the first ten minutes to keep it from blowing off. Laughing, and seeing she wasn't letting go of it, Adrian helped her down from the boardwalk, retaining her hand through the sliding sand until it was more packed by the ocean. Her breath caught, looking at him. His whole face changed when he smiled. It was always attractive, but it was otherworldly with his black eyes glittering, his carefully sculpted lips lifting. Have mercy.

"Jude and I have a pact," he said, while he was still walking with her.

"That terrifies me."

"We're going to throw you into the ocean."

"Oh, no," she said, disbelieving. "You wouldn't harm a mother."

Before she could even get the words out, he had swung her up into his arms, causing her to squeal. "Adrian, my hat!"

He was unmoved on that front. He took her out until the water splashed around his ankles. Jude, catching sight, came puddling back through the water, giggling, saying, "Daddy, throw her, throw her!"

"Jude! I thought we were friends!" Adeline exclaimed, trying to retain control of her hat. It wasn't every day a girl found perfect retro headgear.

He laughed with delight, splashing around them.

"How far do you think I could throw her?" Adrian questioned.

"Ten feet," Jude said, apparently having thought the matter over. "Then throw me!"

Adrian laughed softly, walking out farther with her. Her arm clamped tightly around his neck. "Adrian," she said lowly, with caution.

"I won't let go," he said for her ears only.

She knew that. That wasn't the problem. Being surrounded on all sides by water and totally unable to control the situation was the problem. Her hand tightened on his bicep. He ducked her just a little until her toes touched the water. "Adrian!"

"All right," he conceded. "That's enough for today. And tomorrow, when you walk out here on your own, you can remember you were already all the way out here," he said, quite reasonably.

"O-Okay, but I wasn't actually serious about learning to swim, Adrian."

"You already know how to swim," he said as they exited the ocean. "It's just your fear we have to overcome." He sat her down on her towel as gently as a feather, handing her a bottle of water and leaving her mind whirling. And then he was off, tossing his kid in the ocean, terrifying her. If he wanted to risk sharks and drowning, that was his business.

They lunched on sandwiches they had picked up from Jude's favorite shop in Charleston. Jude chattered like a happy little boy, making Adrian's eyes smile.

When a thundercloud rolled in, they hastily gathered up their stuff and headed back to the house. Adrian got the brunt of it, since he had to carry Jude, who had fallen asleep against him.

The first large pebbles of rain had started to fall when they made it to the back door. Adeline used the keypad and let them in. The air swirled around them, along with the quiet coziness of the house, the echoes of their laughter on the beach, and the rain pelting the tin roof, creating a lethal stew.

She turned back Jude's covers for him, and Adrian lay the limp boy in bed. His hair was only slightly damp and jet black against the white sheets. Adeline stood out in the hall by the utility closet, waiting to ask if she needed to find him another blanket, when Adrian came out, closing the door softly behind him.

"Does he need a blanket?" she whispered, opening the white slatted doors.

"No, he's fine," he whispered. He helped her throw the wet towels from her bag into the washing machine, and then they stepped back into the hall.

There was still some daylight streaking through the windows of the bedroom across the hall. She realized that his attention was arrested on her, and she went still herself, her heart flying. He took a step toward her, his hand slipping to her back, pulling her gently against him. His other hand touched her face to tip it softly, expertly, up to his. His thumb stroked across her cheekbone. His dark eyes were very serious as they roved her face, totally absorbed, his desire evident. And she melted into him, her hand slipping up into his feather soft hair, her lips surrendering to the give and take of which his were so fully capable. His hand slid from her cheek to finger one of her curls, before he slipped it around to her back, getting a good grip on the fabric.

It was slow at first and then hotter than blazes in no time flat. If she'd ever wondered how she'd been so stupid four and a half months ago, how she possibly could've let herself go for a little passion, she wasn't wondering it now. But she was remembering where it led perfectly well. It was just like before. She was hungrily getting as close as she could, wanting more.

But she wasn't ready. At least, she had told herself she wasn't ready and set that boundary. Boundaries were good. Boundaries kept a wayward soul in line. She feathered her fingers across his jaw. *Stop that, Adeline.*

She broke away suddenly, leaving him a little out of breath and probably confused. If he would just stand there, and then she could back away slowly, maybe she wouldn't toss her life into confusion again. Maybe she could maintain her fragile hold on sanity. His eyes followed her as she backed away, holding hers and trying to reason it all out. "I can't do this, Adrian," she said softly, just before fleeing.

Their bedroom at the cottage had a really big bed with cute beachy furnishings. From her refuge there, Adeline had heard Adrian working in the kitchen and taking a phone call. Her mind tried to focus on the old documents she was holding, but she was attuned to his every movement, trying to catch what he was saying. Jude must've gotten up from his nap because she heard them playing a board game.

She went out when she adjudged it to be time for supper, not wanting to be a bad sport. It was extremely awkward. Adrian wouldn't really look at her, and she couldn't seem to make conversation in light of that daunting fact.

He told her to go on and get a shower, that he would clean up. For once, she didn't argue.

When he finally came in, he nodded to her once and headed straight for the shower. She wallowed in misery. When he got out, he said nothing. It kind of reminded her of his moodiness on the honeymoon. She wasn't sure what emotion it was springing from. She did know she probably shouldn't have kissed him silly and then run.

He lay down beside her, reaching for his light.

"Goodnight," she said.

"'Night."

She pressed her lips together, turning on her side. They had been laying there maybe fifteen minutes when he got up. She thought he was going to the bathroom and then realized after a while that he was, instead, standing by the window, arms crossed, looking out, probably thinking she was already asleep.

She sat up, able to see him in the blue light coming in through the blinds. "Adrian, are you mad at me?" she asked softly.

He stilled, turning to look at her. "No," he said, sounding truly surprised. "Of course not."

She hesitated, studying him closely. He was maybe hiding something, but his tone convinced her that he was not, in fact, angry. "About earlier..."

His jaw flexed. "I'm sorry. You had your line drawn, and I crossed it."

She shook her head. "No, it's... It's fine. So why won't you lie down?"

He looked a little wry, and she was surprised to see the slightest smile on his face, even if it was a slightly grim one. "It's not always easy, Adeline. To lie there next to you, night after night."

When his meaning took hold, warmth spread through her body. So she wasn't the creep who was all hung up on him: he was attracted, too. "But you... You acted like this on our honeymoon," she protested.

"Because I wanted to sleep with you," he exclaimed, in a rush, probably without his own permission. He looked kind of put out.

"Oh." She cleared her throat. There was a dignified beat of silence. "Thank you for that clarification," she offered formally.

He nodded sharply, turning his face to the side, giving her an excellent view of his profile.

She began to grow amused. Here he was, all agitated, and she had been thinking he was mad. She wondered how many of the little nit-picky nothings that had stirred up between them would've been soothed by... She bit her lip, wondering if her resolve was wrong.

"Adrian..."

He looked up, glancing her way. She hesitated. She couldn't talk to him with him standing like that. He walked toward her, mind-reader, sitting on the bed beside her but keeping his hands to himself. She smiled slightly, biting her lip before saying, "Look, I... I think we can safely say that, whatever problems we might have, chemistry isn't one of them."

He smiled a bit.

"But we...never talked about that night, Adrian."

"Are you ready to?" he asked softly.

She lifted a shoulder, hesitating. "It all happened so fast," she whispered.

"I know." His eyes, deep and caring, roved her face. She knew he had to be excellent at his job.

"And after, I just felt so...bewildered," she said.

The remorse on his face was swift, and slightly pain-ful. "Adeline..."

"No," she said, catching his hand. "Not by you." He was shaking his head, and she said, "I mean that, Adrian. I think we both know that what happened between us was kind of..." Her voice faded.

"Amazing," he supplied softly.

"Yeah," she said, color blooming in her cheeks. "And you were...great—I mean lovely. Well, that, too," she said, laughing nervously.

He smiled, pressing her hand where she still held his. "I mean that...doing what we did...a one-night stand... It should've felt wrong." She moistened her lips, afraid to admit the next. "But it didn't," she whispered. "I mean it *was* wrong, and the consequences were pretty thorough—I don't mean the baby, you know that."

"I know," he said, squeezing her hand again.

"But it felt...right, and natural, and...I was so confused," she whispered. "I mean, shouldn't it feel...dirty?"

He studied her, obviously unable to answer that one. She probably sounded like a lunatic. He looked like he wanted to say something, but something held him back. "It wasn't dirty, Adeline," he said softly. "Not to me."

She studied his features. "Were *you* ready for it?" she asked, deciding that while they were being candid...

He gave a laugh-sigh, shaking his head. "I have no idea. But that doesn't worry me. Psychiatrists are supposed to be crazy."

She smiled, though she bit her lip. "Adrian, when I asked if you were okay with it—I mean, not... Why didn't you say something?"

"Because it was the right decision," he said. "You made the right call. There was no way you were ready for it emotionally. We hadn't even been dating, and all of the sudden you were pregnant. You didn't know me. Sex clouds everything. I tell that to my clients all the time. It would've gotten in the way, covered up some stuff that shouldn't be covered, made things more confusing." Apparently he was perfectly comfortable with using the big S word. That made one of them.

"Adrian, if you want..."

"No," he said, shaking his head. "When we...make love again, it'll be when you feel perfectly ready. Not before."

She nodded, looking down again at her tiny bump. She looked back up at Adrian, and he, after holding her eyes, gently lay his hand against it, covering it almost entirely, stroking his thumb caressingly. He whispered, "I've been wanting to do that."

She swallowed, blinking rapidly. Gah, hormones.

"Have you felt it move yet?" he whispered.

"I think so."

"You know, we could find out what it is in two weeks."

"We could. If we wanted to," she said, giving a warning look that was belied by the twinkle in her eyes.

"We do."

"We'll see."

Chapter Seventeen

Things kind of shifted between them after that night. She couldn't say exactly what it was, but it was different. On Saturday morning, they took Jude to the beach again, and Adeline could almost palpably feel the understanding that had been reached between them. It was a step in the right direction.

Jude was interested in "teaching Adeline to swim," so she let him hold her hand and walk out with her until the water splashed around her ankles.

"Are you afraid of drowning or sharks?" he asked, trying to get to the root of the problem.

"Um, both," she said.

"There are no sharks," he said. "I checked."

"Thank you," she said, looking at Adrian. "That was very brave." Adrian's eyes were twinkling as he stood behind them.

"Come a little farther," Jude said encouragingly. At her hesitance, he said, "Daddy will hold your other hand, won't you, Daddy?"

"Sure I will, buddy," Adrian said, winking.

She sent him a warning look as he threaded his fingers through hers. They got her out to her knees before she realized it, and then Jude was too short. He was perfectly content to ride on his father's hip and encourage Adeline from there. She stumbled, and Adrian wrapped an arm around her waist. "You're doing great," he said.

She shot him another look, wondering if she'd put on enough sunscreen. Not that either of the Ravenels had to worry about it, but *she* could fry in about five minutes.

"Try swimming a little," Adrian said, letting her go and putting Jude on his shoulders.

She was still clinging to his arm. "Adrian..."

"You used to love to swim, I bet, before the accident," he said, cutting her off. "Maybe the summer you were eighteen? You'd go with friends and your sister, spend all day on the lake..."

She looked up at him, moistening her lips. He couldn't know how much that boating accident in college dictated her actions. She had told him that drinking on board had led to the death of one of the guys in the group. What she hadn't told him was that it had been her boyfriend. Not the love of her life, or even a serious or long-standing thing. But it had shaken her to her core and led her to do some pretty reckless things in the days and weeks following. And after, she had never wanted to feel that way again.

But that was precisely the way she had felt after her night with Adrian. She studied his features. Maybe he did know. Not the details, of course, but that there was something deep there. She met his eyes. Yes, he did. There was understanding in his dark eyes.

She swallowed, looking out at the water. She was going to be a mother, for heaven's sake. She had to conquer this. She let go of his arm, finger by finger, and lifted her feet, pushing off. She swam with a butterfly stroke about ten feet and then back, to Jude's delight. He clapped and celebrated, and Adrian smiled.

"All right, all right," she said, returning to them. "Enough for today."

They went to The Obstinate Daughter for a light lunch, where Jude tried, and was impressed by, the famous Geechie Frites. They took him to Beardcat's afterward, where he discovered a new obsession in gelato.

Then they went back to the beach for a while, and Adeline sat under an umbrella with her binder of documents. She had started a promising letter last night that had begun, *My Dearest Sir* but had been too distracted to read it.

She pulled it out now and let herself be taken back through the years.

My Dear Sir,

It seems an age since last we met. You know of my troubles. You know what this war has stolen from me. I beg that you will not repeat the entreaties which give me more pain than I can say. I must also ask that you burn this letter upon its receipt, as I know perfectly well I ought not to be writing to you.

Nonetheless, may God keep you safe on the battlefield.

SRH

Adeline swallowed, feeling her pain and desperation cry out through the years, as palpable as if it had been yesterday. It would be of no help to her restoration of the house, but Harris was perfectly correct. She wanted to know who Shannon was writing to.

And why she had never sent the letter.

They decided to grill out for supper that night, and to tell Jude then.

Adeline wore a black sundress, since the breeze made the color bearable, and the boys were a little more dressed up, too. They sat on the deck overlooking the ocean on the wooden picnic table poised for a perfect view.

They had finished eating and Jude, sitting on the side next to Adrian, was too smart not to know something was up. It was making him a little nervy.

"Hey, buddy, we have something to tell you," Adrian said, hands clasped between his knees.

Jude looked up, all attention and big eyes and cute chin. Adeline smiled gently. She felt Adrian reach for her hand and was glad, unsure why she was so nervous. Jude was still watching intently, eyes darting between them.

"Adeline is going to have a baby, Jude."

His brows drew together.

"You know what that means?" Adrian said, bringing Jude onto his lap.

Jude went willingly, shaking his head no. "It means you're going to be a big brother."

Adeline injected enthusiasm into her smile. "A great big brother," she agreed.

Jude looked between them. "Really?" he asked softly.

"Yep," Adrian said, brushing a strand of hair out of his eyes where the wind had been playing with it.

Jude's eyes glittered. "I always wanted to be a big brother, Daddy!" he said softly, too shy to be enthusiastic out loud.

"I know," he said, kissing the top of his hair.

"Like you and Uncle Harris!"

"Just like, but it might be a girl, you know." Jude's enthusiasm suffered a slight set-back, but he was willing to take on the duty. With noble forbearance, which almost made Adeline laugh.

"But it might be a boy," Adeline said. "You never know."

Jude agreed to it, seeming to decide that was a brighter way to look at things. One had to be optimistic, after all.

Chapter Eighteen

One year and four months later

A ribbon blew in the wind on the end of the long stick as Rose squealed, running through the lawn while Shannon chased her. "Oh, you little fiend, I'll never catch you!" she exclaimed, feigning exhaustion. Rose giggled and squealed, still running. She and Shannon had, by chance, both donned lavender dresses. The picture they made, Rose's red hair spilling down her back, and Shannon's caught up primly, was so lovely that even Mr. Ravenel, who had many cares and troubles brought on by the war, stopped for a moment and watched them from the window of his study.

At three years of age, Rose was a determined and restless child. She was quiet, but for her own purposes—most of them, Shannon had found from experience, diabolical. She had learned that she must gently discipline her. Shannon's father did not interfere, but he did question whether Shannon thought she had been any different. Nothing was too good for his Rose, and he thought her still too young for much correction, a fact oddly at variance with Shannon's childhood recollections.

"Come to me, dearest," Shannon said, putting a note of firmness in her voice.

Rose came, slipping her little gloved hand in Shannon's. "We go in? No!"

"It *is* warm today, but the wind is picking up, and you've only just gotten over your sore throat."

Rose frowned and stayed where she was. And yet, when Shannon looked at her, she saw an angel. Long, waving hair, skin of a porcelain, eyes more like Marie's every day, and her father's stubborn chin. It was, indeed, difficult to deny the sprite anything.

"Come," Shannon said with gentle authority, and they walked into the house hand in hand, one of them pouting.

Shannon took her upstairs to the nursery, where she waved off Rose's attendants and removed her gloves and scarf herself. "Now, you must take your nap," she said, softening her voice to create the peace and stillness conducive to rest. She sat next to her, stroking Rose's hair as she lay in her little bed.

When at last Rose submitted, she left Mammy to watch her, and, her smile slipping, she walked down the hall to her room, where she closed the door and lay her hands and forehead against it for a moment. It was her anniversary, a thought which had come to her the moment her eyes had fluttered open that morning. She had not had the leisure to think, for her morning had been devoted, as she wished it to be, to her niece. But now she was alone, and she needed peace and reflection.

She turned, walking to her chair, which was beside a window, and picked up her Bible. She read until she felt peaceful, even if happiness was far from her. She ached for him with a strength which brought the prick of unshed tears to her eyes, and she never ceased to worry for him, all of which must, of course, be unspoken. But as the war intensified and turned more dreadful by day, it seemed that the news they were able to obtain from the North grew ever sparer.

She brushed the tears from her cheeks and looked out the window upon the gray day and contemplated her promise to Marie. In that moment, it had seemed impossible, the problems between her and John Thomas insurmountable. It was only as she began, slowly, to find strength over the course of the last year that she realized matters never had been truly hopeless. Or, at least, they hadn't been until she had left.

Now if she did try to reconcile, the possibility of which seemed a forlorn dream, would he have her? She had once believed that he would never consent to a true divorce, but the war might have changed him. He wouldn't be the first, although it would be difficult to imagine. And even if he did not divorce her, would he prefer to live separately?

She exhaled, looking out over the beautiful lawn, knowing she must not carry the weight of it. The burden was too difficult to bear, the guilt and misery. And yet, no matter the peace within, which she had come to realize was life's greatest gift, she had learned that grief could and still did occur. It might not swamp her, unhinge her, but it did keep her in her chamber all the afternoon, until it was time to change and go down to dinner at three o'clock with her father.

It was just the three of them now at Santarella from among the family. But she smiled genuinely at her father as she entered the dining room, and he got up to hold her chair. They had, despite the sadness which must always be with them, managed to develop pleasant routines, especially at Santarella. They had decided to stay on the island for Christmas since there was nothing of a season in Charleston now, and since Rose seemed to thrive where she had plenty of ground to roam, animals to menace, and wonders to explore. Frederick, too, liked the thought of them there, of his child being raised in his ancestral home. And they, very naturally, did whatever they could to give him pleasure.

And Shannon was glad today not to be in the house where she had married John Thomas. As she sat with her father, her mind drifted back, across the years, to their wedding day. She hadn't allowed the groom to see her before the wedding, but he had sent her a note. And then after the wedding, they had gone into the music room. He had kissed her, a little deeper than ever before. But his touch had been reverent. He thought always of her and was piercingly gentle. His eyes had glowed with love and pride and disbelief.

"Shannon?"

She looked up at her father, lifting her brows pleasantly.

"I asked whether Rose's cough has gone away?"

"Oh, yes," she said, putting down her untouched glass of wine, which her fingers had clasped tightly. "I didn't hear so much as a whisper of it this morning."

"Excellent," he said, and proceeded to read to her a newspaper article about the activities of the Federal blockading squadron off Charleston's coast. "And despite this," he said, finishing, "we are unconquered."

"Yes," Shannon agreed. "And yet, more and more of the islands are falling. Mrs. Christian refuses to come to Ridgecrest with her husband now, fearing that they might be trapped. And the Federals do hate Charleston so that there is no telling what they might do if we *were* trapped." There had been an assault on Charleston in April which had been summarily vanquished by the Confederates, and the attacking regiments had withdrawn back to Port Royal and Hilton Head Island. But they had come with words of vengeance, and no one could quite forget that. They were living in the cradle of secession, and they would pay for it dearly, Shannon feared.

"Well, if our boys in the field and at sea can stand firm, the least we can do is not abandon the lands they are trying to protect," Mr. Ravenel said in his decisive manner.

"Yes."

Her father looked at her with his sharp, clear eyes. "I trust *you* are not falling ill, Shannon?" he asked.

She lifted her brows, and then smiled. "Oh, no, Papa, merely a little tired."

"Hmm." He then proceeded to talk about the obstructions and torpedoes which had been placed in the harbor to protect them, perhaps thinking that she might be a little frightened.

"Dahlgren is a most determined man, Papa," she said of the Union commander of the South Atlantic Blockading Squadron. When her father looked at her, silver brows lifted haughtily, she said, "I have met him. The people must not think he will be weak and inept like his predecessors."

"What sort of man is he?" he asked, surprised.

"An ordnance expert. Joh... He was thought to be very talented. I know little more. He has a great many modern ideas."

"Hmm," he said, looking at her with his brows lifted. "Well, I am heartily tired of his bombardments. I thought you and the child would run mad from the shelling."

Shannon smiled. "Did I indeed appear so?"

He shook his head, looking at her. "No, you are changed, Shannon." He studied her for a long moment. "Marie's death..." His voice softened. "You have become the matriarch of our family, Shannon, and I was never prouder, even, I think, on your wedding day."

Shannon got up, kissing his cheek. Emotion clogged her throat for a moment, but she managed to say, mischief in her voice, "One thing you will be glad to hear, Papa."

"Yes?"

"Admiral Dahlgren suffers miserably from seasickness."

They were smiling and laughing together when the blue wood-paneled door was opened, and John Tilman said, his eyes a little wary, "Mr. Christian's here, sir. He's wantin' to speak with you."

Shannon met her father's eyes, and, after wiping his mouth with his napkin, he got up. Shannon naturally followed as the butler led the way. "I put them in the study," he said, and before they could ask who accompanied Mr. Christian, John Tilman opened the door, and Shannon saw Mr. Christian and his son, Seymour. The latter must be home on furlough, she supposed, even if it seemed impossible that he was indeed standing in the room, looking as handsome as ever with dark hair and eyes, although he was thinner and a trifle weather-beaten.

"*Seymour*," her father said, going forward wreathed in smiles. "This is quite a surprise! How on earth did you manage it?"

He smiled, shaking his elder's hand, and said, "My adroit manners, no doubt, sir."

Shannon smiled along with the rest of them and studied his face. He did seem changed, the reckless glint gone, replaced by fatigue. But she stayed rooted several feet away, nonetheless.

Seymour lifted his head from talking to her father and seemed to notice her. "Shannon," he said. "That is, Mrs. Haley." She smiled with difficulty, forcing herself by sheer will to go forward and extend her hand. "It is so good to see you," he said, and something about the way he looked at her told her he did not for a moment see her as any man's wife.

"And you. I am glad you are well, sir."

Feeling her father's eyes upon them, Shannon retracted her hand.

"Listen, Ravenel," the elder Mr. Christian said, "I dearly wish this were a social call, but I come bearing bad tidings." He waited only a moment before saying, "It would seem that our forces outside of Savannah have been heavily attacked. Two of our ships have gone down."

Shannon's lips parted, and she could feel the blood draining from her face as she met her father's eyes. He did not seem to be able to speak for several moments. Finally, though, he looked back at their neighbor. "There is no word as to the casualties?"

"No, my friend."

"Then we must return to Charleston to see what news we can obtain."

The carriage took them along the rather desolate streets of Charleston. The people walked without spirit, their money thin, their hopes low, and their grief unabated as tales of new battles were carried to them every day.

Shannon sat with Rose on her lap, both ensconced in warm coats, mittens, and hats, and her father sat across from them, staring out the window, deeply in thought. Even to Rose their mood had been communicated, and she had sat silently for most of the journey from Santarella, though now she began to grow restless as they made their way in the direction of the Battery. "Aunt Shannon, can we play in the garden?" she asked tentatively.

"No, my love, but you shall share my tea in the dining room," she promised.

Rose's eyes lit. "And Grandpapa, too?"

Shannon looked across the carriage at her father, whose eyes softened, and she answered, "Grandpapa must go to the government offices, but you will certainly see him tonight when you come down from the nursery." With this, she was content, and she relapsed into silence, which was not broken by either of the adults.

Mr. Ravenel deposited his daughter and granddaughter safely at home and went off to see what news he could find.

It was hours later, after he had returned and the evening shadows were beginning to fall, that Shannon heard a commotion in the foyer. She stepped out to see her friend, Elizabeth Middleton, apparently in great distress, an almost frantic look in her eyes as she was requesting from the butler in a voice quite unlike her own to see Mrs. Haley.

"Dearest," Shannon said, going forward in grave concern, "I am here. Whatever is the matter?"

Elizabeth turned desperate blue eyes upon her and said, voice shaking, "Shannon, is Frederick hurt? We have only just heard, and I..." She swallowed with difficulty, searching Shannon's face.

Shannon studied her for a long moment, regarding her carefully. "No. That is to say, *yes*, he is injured, and is being sent home. But not fatally, my dear Elizabeth, I promise you!" As she continued to search her friend's face, Shannon's lips slowly parted in sudden realization as the truth crashed upon her all at once. She could not speak, could only stare at Elizabeth, who had looked away, wiping tears of relief.

"Elizabeth," she whispered in wonder.

Elizabeth swallowed, her lip trembling, and looked back at Shannon. Regarding her friend as though she had never seen her, Shannon said, taking her arm, "Come with me." She took her into the small parlor, where she forced her to the sofa and sat next to her. "Elizabeth, how long?" she breathed.

Elizabeth dabbed her eyes with her handkerchief. She shook her head miserably.

"Elizabeth, how long have you felt this way?"

Elizabeth met her eyes, hesitating another long moment. "As long as I have been out in society," she said.

Shannon drew a breath, feeling dizzy. "But you never said!" As fresh realizations dawned upon her, she whispered, "He is the reason you never married?"

Elizabeth turned her face away until Shannon could only see her lovely profile, upon which the ravages of emotion were writ. She picked slowly at the lace-edged handkerchief which she held against her skirt, her lower lip between her teeth.

"Why didn't you say?"

"How could I say?" Elizabeth asked, looking back at her. "It was settled amongst your family between him and Marie before ever he came back from his grand tour, and what sort of woman would I have been had I made the attempt to cut Marie out?"

Shannon eyes filled with tears. "Oh, Elizabeth," she whispered, reaching to cover her hand. "You mustn't look so hopeless. Perhaps..."

She shook her head. "Even now it does not feel proper. I only pray that I have kept it hidden, that he doesn't know. That *she* didn't. To set my sights now upon her husband..."

Shannon's blinders fell away and, finally, her eyes distant, another piece of her final scene with Marie at last made sense. "But she did know," she whispered.

Elizabeth looked at her with shocked horror, almost starting to rise, but apparently not finding the strength and falling back. "*What?* Oh, Shannon, no!"

"Yes, she did," she whispered, remembering, almost as though she were back in that room. "She said, on her last breath, 'Tell Elizabeth...' And then she was gone, and I never knew what she wanted me to say to you."

Elizabeth blanched, covering her mouth.

"The words seemed so unfathomable at the time, but of course it makes perfect sense now. She had said so little about Frederick, but she was thinking of his fu—"

"Shannon, *no!*" Elizabeth said, starting up, tears in her eyes. "Do not say such a thing! That I was the last thing on her mind, a woman in love with her own husband, and at such a precious moment..! She might have meant to say, 'Tell Elizabeth that she may go to the devil!' and rightly so!"

Shannon was almost startled into laughing, but she shook her head, grasping Elizabeth's arms, "No, my dear friend, no! There was nothing but kindness and peace in her, and love, in that moment." The thought made tears start to her eyes and fall down her cheeks. She and Elizabeth merely looked at one another for a long time, tears falling silently, and yet...

At length, Shannon whispered, "Elizabeth... Oh, my dear friend. You must not let this slip through your fingers. You must *tell* him."

Elizabeth was shaking her head.

"You *must*! Elizabeth," she said emotionally, "listen to me! I tell you that there is no pain like regret. Until now, you have had pain, but you have not had to regret your actions. But you will if you are not brave enough to speak what is in your heart." Elizabeth held her eyes, expression arrested. Shannon pressed, "Do not tell me it was easy, watching him marry Marie, watching her carry his children." Elizabeth turned her face away, and she added as a clincher, "What if he were to marry again?"

Elizabeth looked at her, but she shook her head. "We run ahead of ourselves, Shannon."

"By that, you mean that *I* do."

"Yes." She wiped her eyes with the back of her hand. "What is his injury? You haven't told me that."

"A severely broken arm and a minorly broken leg. There was a blast on the deck, and he was struck by something. He is to be brought to the hospital, where I think he will have better care. Until we may properly care for him, of course. Now, the question is: will you tell him, or shall I?"

Elizabeth's eyes widened at her audacity. "For heaven's sake, let me do this in my own way, Shannon!"

Shannon smiled. "Good. I shall."

Chapter Nineteen

"**A**m I in a private room?"

Shannon looked up from her vigil in Frederick's room, surprised at his first spoken words since he had been in Charleston. He had been heavily sedated, and she had been left to sit with him. To study the cuts on his handsome face, the swelling in his right arm, the bruising of his neck. "Brother-mine," she said, slipping her hand into his good one and smiling sweetly. "How are you feeling?"

"Like I've been hit by a large flying object," he rasped. "Answer me, Shannon."

"Yes."

"Shannon, how could you?" he exclaimed. "It will look as though I think myself above the rest."

"Hush, that is not your concern, as it was not your choice," she said firmly, and he was too weak to protest, merely sighing in displeasure. After recruiting his strength, he looked at her quickly. "Shannon, the girl—"

"She is quite well," she said, smiling reassuringly. "And if you think we have regaled her with tales of her Papa's injuries, you are fair and far off. She doesn't know you are in Charleston, and she won't until you are well enough to receive her."

He sighed in relief. "Oh, thank you. Yes, that is right. Her sore throat?"

"Gone. She is well, and as spirited as ever her papa was."

"A proper South Carolinian," he said, smiling in relief, eyes growing heavy. He seemed to find comfort from holding her hand, so she left it.

"Yes," she agreed softly, thinking he might go off to sleep again. But he was studying her, seeming to try to divine her emotions. She knew—somehow—that he was thinking about John Thomas.

"I haven't heard anything from him, you know," he said wistfully, almost dreamily as though the drug were having its effect again. "Have you?"

She blinked. "No," she said faintly.

"He couldn't be dead, though," he said, drifting off to sleep. "He couldn't be, and I not know it."

She brushed away a tear with her other hand. "No. I imagine not."

As the days progressed and Elizabeth's idea of handling matters in her own way seemed to be letting Frederick reach the age of perhaps eighty, having remarried and fathered dozens more children, Shannon realized she must take matters into her own hands.

She waited two weeks until Dr. Eisley pronounced him stable enough to be transferred to Ravenel House, and she gave him time to settle in and to reacquaint himself with his daughter. Then one sunny day, she waited in his doorway until Emma took Rose away. She went into his bedchamber once they had made their way down the hall.

"Is she not an excellent child?" he asked, still weak but beaming.

"Indeed, she is. And so beautiful," Shannon murmured.

He laughed, punctiliously kissing the hand she extended to him. She stood by his bed, studying him for a moment, and said, "Frederick, there is something about which I must speak with you."

He lifted his brows, seemingly interested. "Yes?"

She swallowed, finding it more difficult than she had imagined now the moment had come. His interest turned to worry, his brows drawing together. She swallowed again. "It is only... That is... Frederick, Elizabeth...has feelings for you. Warm feelings."

His brows drew together in confusion. "*Which* Elizabeth?"

Not a promising start. "*My* Elizabeth. Middleton," she said in frustration.

His brows lifted, and he choked on the drink she had brought him. "What? Nonsense! Shannon! Why, no man in Charleston—in the country, for that matter, for she might have had anyone—has ever been good enough for her! Do you expect me to believe..?" His voice trailed off as the force of his words dawned on him, and he stared at her in disbelief. "How? I haven't seen her since—"

"She always has," she said softly.

"Good God! Me?"

"That is what I said. And if you tell her I told you, she will murder me, and my death will be upon your head," she told him seriously.

"She did not send you as her emissary?" he asked, still staring at her closely.

"No, Frederick. I told her that she must tell you, for if this war and these past years have taught me—us—anything, it is that time is precious." She swallowed.

He looked at her in sympathy and pressed her hand. Though she might struggle, she was glad to see that his eyes did not instantly well up. There had been a time when anything remotely melancholy had made his losses unbearable. There had also been some foolishness about never marrying again, and that was what worried her. But it had been so long, and that was what gave her hope.

"What, then?" he asked gently. "Am I to pretend I don't know when the Middletons call?"

"Yes, that is precisely what you must do. I will tell her at the appropriate time that I have told you, but I merely wanted you to be thinking of it, of her, if you can."

He looked at her, seemingly lost in consideration, his mind obviously whirling.

Elizabeth performed admirably. One would never have known that Frederick was anything other than her childhood friend from her behavior, and, to her credit, she did not betray a moment's awkwardness. Shannon realized that the situation in their world wouldn't generally be thought conducive to love. The number of bodies buried, battles fought, and homelands ravaged was long past counting. And, of course, Frederick knew he must return to war as soon as he was healed. As that day seemed to Shannon to be fast-approaching—too fast, in any event, to permit any real courtship—she said to Elizabeth one day several weeks later, "I have told him."

"Told who what, Shannon?" Elizabeth asked, looking dubiously at some not-very-successful confections which had been made without sugar.

"Frederick."

Elizabeth's eyes snapped to her face. She did not flinch or move. After a moment, she said, in the voice of a person who could kill with no remorse, "I thought we had an agreement, Shannon, that if you did so I should—"

"Put an end to my existence," Shannon agreed, eyes fixed on her face apologetically.

The first shock leaving her, Elizabeth said with difficulty, looking away, "How could you, Shannon?"

Shannon rose, lifting her skirts and hoops, and pleaded, as she reached for Elizabeth's hand, "For your own good, I promise you, my dear friend."

"Shannon, he is a widower. He has been married to a woman he deeply respected and...I must suppose, loved. He lost her and their child. We are at war. What if he doesn't feel the same? Indeed, he has given me no indication that he could."

"What if he might?" Shannon whispered, the proposition seeming to echo within the room. Shannon saw that she had silenced her friend and then pursued, "Now, I will tell him that I have—"

Elizabeth drew a breath and then, looking firmly at her, said, "No." She rose. "I am going up to him this moment and apologizing for the awkward situation in which he has been placed. I need no further assistance from you, thank you, Shannon, and if you follow me—proprieties be damned—I *shall* find a way to murder you!"

She swept off, and Shannon watched her, eyes twinkling.

"Enter," called his voice.

Miss Middleton turned the handle and stepped across the threshold, her shoes and dress making soft clacks and rustles. Captain Ravenel looked at her and then looked behind her as though he expected to see Shannon follow. She closed the door behind her.

He looked mildly surprised, lifting his dark brows. "Elizabeth." He seemed to sit up a bit.

She cleared her throat. "I am told…" She suddenly found it much more difficult than she had thought it would be with his handsome face staring at her, the door closed, and the room quite improperly devoid of anyone but the two of them. "That is, Shannon tells me that…that she has told you something which..." She took a deep breath, summoning every austere ancestor in her history as she straightened her shoulders. "Frederick, Shannon and I are friends. I believe you and I, too, have been friends. And it is my earnest wish that you might not be made to feel uncomfortable. Therefore, I beg that you will forget it."

She found it very difficult to meet his eyes, but when she had forced herself to do so, he was looking at her in quite a different way from what she had expected. Almost anxious. After a time, he said softly, "Elizabeth... Why on earth would I wish to forget it?"

She looked at him closely, searching his face.

"You... I cannot believe it still, but...I promise you that the very last thing I could feel is uncomfortable," he said.

Cautious, she studied him. Slowly, his good hand lifted, and she realized he wanted her to take it. Her heart was thrumming loudly, her blood rushing. Breathless, she walked forward and let her fingers touch his, and she looked at their hands for a long moment. When she lifted her head, she saw that his dark eyes were serious, and deadly in earnest. He brought her hand slowly to his lips and kissed it.

"Frederick..." she whispered.

He swallowed, and she watched his Adam's apple move down and then up. "Elizabeth," he rasped back. Time seemed to still and lengthen all at once.

Shannon watched the progression of the courtship across the spring with the anxiety of a mother hen—encouraging, helping the couple over the little troubled moments, and generally exasperating them very much. One day when Mr. Middleton called, Frederick had asked permission to court his daughter, such as a courtship could be under the circumstances. The anxiety in their long-time friend's brow belied his inner worry that his daughter might be widowed. However, he was extremely fond of Frederick, and he consented. Had it been before the war, he would have done so with joy, for it was an excellent alliance, just the kind of match Elizabeth ought to make.

Frederick's health began to improve, his leg healing until he was able to hobble down the stairs. As the couple's shyness left them, Shannon watched as Frederick's eyes began to light for the first time since the tragedy, and it was not difficult for anyone to see that Frederick and Elizabeth were drawn to one another strongly. And slowly, over the course of a spring which saw the Confederate armies and people pushed almost beyond the limits of human endurance, it became obvious that the spark which had awakened in Frederick had flamed into a love.

And so it was in April, four months after Frederick's injury had brought him home, that Frederick, finding Shannon one evening by the fireplace in the library, shyly asked if she would mind if he gave Elizabeth their mother's ring.

Looking up quickly, Shannon breathed, "Oh, Frederick!"

He smiled softly, taking her hand and sitting next to her. "Do you think I've run mad?"

She smiled. "Of *course* I don't, dearest. The ring—yes, of course. It is right that you should give it to her." She blinked away tears at the poignancy. Marie—how far they had come since that dreadful day—her mother—and the forward progression of time that seemed to be the only thing which was certain in this life besides God's love.

Frederick was looking at her, and he said after a time, "Do you... Shannon, you...you know I could never forget her."

Tears flowed down her cheeks as he gripped her hand. "Yes. Oh, Frederick, yes!"

His voice was not quite steady. "We thought to make a family together, but...Rose is all I have left of her. And I... never dreamed my life would take this course. But I love Elizabeth—it is strange to me even now to say it, and to realize how deeply. I can't...fathom it, but I know that I want for us to be a family, and I don't want to wait until after the war, or until it is too late."

Shannon embraced him fiercely. "No," she whispered. "Don't wait until it is too late."

Chapter Twenty

S hannon fastened the crown of wildflowers in Elizabeth's hair, pushing aside thoughts of the last time the two of them had been together in a room preparing for a wedding. There was a sparkle in her brother's eyes that she hadn't seen in a very long time; ever, if she were honest.

They were at Elizabeth's family plantation, where Frederick and Elizabeth would be married in the formal parlor. A breakfast would follow in the gardens, however sparse and sometimes strange the food might of necessity be. But they had managed to scrape together all that was required and even to make a lovely showing amidst their deprivation. Elizabeth looked beautiful, as did her bridesmaid, and Frederick would, of course, be handsome in his uniform.

"Mama mourns that my dress did not come from Paris," Elizabeth said with a fiendish look in her eye. "Not only that, but it is *made over*, Shannon."

"I know. You wore it to the Talbot Dinner in 1858," Shannon agreed.

Elizabeth gasped. "Is it so obvious?"

"Not at all," she said enviously, brushing a petal from her own blue pagoda sleeve before it reached Elizabeth's cream silk and stained it.

"Oh, I say, what does it matter? This foolish blockade!" From the look in her eyes, one might think she felt kindly even toward the blockade on this day.

Arthur wasn't able to return home for his sister's wedding, and the couple would have a honeymoon of only two days before Frederick must leave. But they seemed strangely hopeful for the future amidst all of the trials and suffering.

"Oh, here is this," Elizabeth said, handing her maid a small bunch of flowers. "A posy for Miss Rose." Shannon smiled.

"Yes, ma'am." The maid took it and left the room.

When all of the others, including Elizabeth's young sister, had slipped out, leaving only the two ladies, Elizabeth caught Shannon's arm, looking at her measuringly for a moment before saying, "Is there anything you...wish to tell me?"

Shannon's fair brows lifted, and she felt rather like an animal pinned by a huntress. "Em, no."

Elizabeth studied her calmly. "Only, my mother asked if there were anything... And I couldn't bring myself to ask her."

The duties of a friend were sometimes nearly sacrificial, but, seeing the unaccustomed anxiety in her friend's eyes, she forced herself to speak. Shannon gathered her courage. "You may...bleed," she began kindly.

"No, I know all of that," Elizabeth said, shaking her head, her blue eyes searching Shannon's. "I heard some of the slave girls talking once. I mean... That is, when they say I am the ice queen, they are entirely correct. I haven't the faintest notion of... How do I please him?"

Shannon's features softened. "You please him by being Elizabeth Middleton," she said lovingly. "That is plain enough for all to see."

Her friend's eyes welled, but she said, "Shannon." It was almost a plea.

Shannon sighed and, after a hesitation, looked at the door and, seeing it ajar, went to close it. And then she went back to her friend and whispered some very specific advice that the decent guests below stairs would be stunned to hear pouring from the lips of one of its own daughters.

"Aunt Shannon, is it a *boy* rabbit?"

Shannon, sitting in the nursery at Ravenel House, and trying not to laugh, took one of her niece's wood-carved animals from her and said, "You know, I don't believe it is."

"Then she shall be Shannon."

"Thank you," answered Aunt Shannon gravely, even if her voice quivered. She watched while Rose played, dirtying her white pantaloons, but quite unconcerned, innocent of battles or killing or leave-takings. And yet, she had already lost a mother and a sister. And gained a new mother.

The wedding had gone off splendidly, and the two had stayed at Middleton Place for their brief honeymoon, where they were now. Had it been earlier in the war, with Frederick's rank, many of his fellow officers would have been able to have come and a longer furlough would have been granted, but things were too desperate for that now.

Shannon wondered what the next year would bring. It would include a holocaust of Charleston, if the quotations she had read from some prominent Northerners were to be believed.

Shannon looked again at Rose, fearful, but not for herself. The thought of her niece in danger made her wish to fly away with her, but where could they go that they would be safe? And she knew her mind to be fevered on that point anyway, not entirely rational where a child was concerned.

She brushed back Rose's hair with her hand, selfishly wishing she could have longer with her. But Elizabeth would join them tomorrow, and for that Shannon was deeply grateful. Her friend would be a solace. But handing Rose over to her care would not be easy, even though it was right and natural. Rose was not her child: she was Frederick's, and now she was Elizabeth's.

"Why you cry?"

Shannon looked up, surprised, and smiled. "Some dust from your pantaloons, merely, dearest," she said, holding her tightly.

Rose kissed her on the cheek. "Aunt Shannon, will Miss Mid'ton be my mama?"

Shannon studied her. That was a complicated question, but it really came down to one word that her niece could understand and that was also the barest truth. "Yes."

There was a knock at the door frame, and Shannon looked up, seeing her father. She lifted her brows. "Grandpapa," she said sweetly. "What brings you to this part of the house?"

He bent to receive Rose's effusive embraces, kissing her cheek. "I would like to speak with you, my dear, if you have a moment?"

Shannon was surprised but agreed and went off to find Alice or Emma to sit with Rose. She then followed her father to the library. That he was troubled, there was no doubt, and she almost began to feel like a naughty child, checking her conscience and growing worried.

He stood in front of the fireplace, looking austere for a few moments before saying, "I have just received a proposition which I believe you will find interesting." His jaw worked. "I was paid a morning call by my old friend, George Christian. He proposes an alliance between our families."

Shannon's brows drew together as she watched him.

"He tells me that, when the war is over, and your husband consummates the divorce, his son, Seymour, will still be willing to marry you, considering your high standing in the community, in order to salvage your reputation."

She stood staring, her lips parted, unsure what to think, and whether he was angry with her.

At length, he said, with barely-suppressed fury, "To think that I should live to be so insulted. And by one of our own!"

"Oh, Papa," she whispered. "I am sorry that you have been put in such a position." She swallowed.

"As though any daughter of *mine* could need rescuing by any son of *his*! What right had he, I ask you, to presume to speak of your marriage or divorce? Of a subsequent marriage while you are still wed to another! I tell you truly, Shannon, I was within a hairsbreadth of knocking him to the floor."

She turned her face away, wiping the tear which tracked down her face, wondering how many more insults her family would be forced to endure for her sake.

"Did you and Mr. Christian...fall out?" she asked weakly.

"You may lay your life on it."

After a few moments passed, she felt him looking at her for the first time. "I've upset you," he said, sighing. "And I wouldn't have done so had it not occurred to me... Shannon, I've stewed over it all the morning long, but I..." He studied her closely. "I never imagined... Is that what you would wish?"

"No!" she almost yelled. Collecting herself, she said, "No, Papa. I am, as you said, still married."

He studied her closely, and Shannon thought that he saw too much. She turned her face away, and, swallowing the painful lump in her throat, she let the silence draw out. She pressed her lips together, feeling a single tear trickle down her left cheek. She nodded. "Forgive me, Papa, you must excuse me." And then she left the room.

Chapter Twenty-One

The paint job turned out really well, and Adeline praised her crew to the skies. They had never pulled off such excellent work without her, and it was gratifying. The crew from Williamsburg was set to arrive and restore the paint on the crest in the library, which put her on edge.

As did a phone call to her mom, to tell her about the baby. She could tell her mom was kind of stunned. She didn't seem to be sure if they had married because of the baby or if Adeline and Adrian had gone all loopy in love. But she was definitely kind of quiet. *Well, honey, that's great. A baby is always a blessing.* And there was more hesitance. It wasn't exactly a dream reaction to the first grandchild. It actually kind of left her with a big, gaping hole, but she'd get over that. Her dad's reaction was similar, but she thought that came more from worry than anything, and she was more easily able to bear that.

During the days, she was restoring and recovering the chairs to the dining table herself and meeting with architects about possible structural damage in the basement. She heard Jane and Jude coming and going but saw little of them, since he had a full summer schedule of fun to complete before he went back to school. She and Adrian hosted dinner for his best friend, a local pediatrician known to Jude as Mr. John, and his family. If Adeline sometimes felt she didn't fit in with this lifestyle, at least everyone was being nice.

One night, she was sitting in the living room and reading still more documents from the box when Harris called. Jude was already in bed, and Adrian was sitting across the room, glasses on, going through a file. Since it was too early for taxes, she could only assume it was for work. Whatever it was had him pretty intent.

"Hey, Harris," she said, in a friendly spirit.

Adrian looked up, studying her for a minute before glancing down at his phone and then back at his file.

"Hey. Y'all have fun on Sullivan's Island?" Was that the slightest bit of humor she detected in his voice? She glanced up at Adrian. How often did he talk to his brother? What had he said?

"Yeah, Jude loved it. Kind of a last hoorah before school, poor guy."

"He should come spend some time with me in Savannah before he goes back."

"I'll tell Adrian," she said, getting the distinct impression that Adrian was no longer actually reading his file, whatever he *seemed* to be doing.

"Listen, I've been reading the documents before I go to bed. Picture me, the studious scholar by my lamp, and you have a pretty good impression of my life."

She laughed. "Hardly, I imagine. Have you found something?" He was reading the documents and letters out of order, she knew, and might have gotten further than she. She sat up.

"Yes, I did, but there'll be a forfeit for the information," he said, sounding smug.

"A forfeit? Not fair."

"You and Adrian have to come to Sunday supper at Mom and Dad's."

She laughed again. She covered the mouthpiece of her phone, still smiling and said, "Harris has information he'll only give me if we go to your parents' on Sunday."

He studied her, taking his time. "Sure, but not this Sunday. Jude has choir."

"You have a deal," she said, going back to her conversation. "We may have to put it off a couple of weeks, though."

"All right. But you can't back out. I can't take the laser focus anymore. All we talk about is you and Adrian anyway." That, she imagined, was perfectly true.

"We won't back out."

"Okay, so I was reading this letter from Frederick Ravenel's new wife to Shannon. Have you figured out why Shannon wasn't living in her father's house anymore?"

"No, it's driving me nuts. That's why I'm reading right now. What did she say?"

"I think she must've been nervous to usurp Shannon's role as mistress."

"Anybody would've been," Adeline said, eyes twinkling.

"She was asking what she thought about a particular print for the wallpaper in the ladies' sitting room."

"*She* covered the silk?" Adeline demanded.

"Sorry. Were you able to tell what the paper over it looked like?"

"No, the layer of paint on top had ruined it."

"She talks about a delicate floral print with irises and violets, and the occasional pink peony. God, I hate myself for remembering that."

She laughed. "Wow. That's super helpful. I'm going to save the silk or die trying, but I'll definitely incorporate that somewhere. What do you think about one of the bedrooms?"

"Yeah, I wouldn't put it downstairs. Historical accuracy only goes so far."

"Hey, it'll be classy," she said, but she had been thinking the same thing.

They talked for another minute about Post-Civil War Ravenel drama, something he said making her toss her head back and laugh. Adrian put aside his folder and crossed his arms, looking up at the TV, where the news was on.

She wrapped up the conversation in the next few minutes and lay aside her folder, stacking it in the box. It was all a little haphazard in there, but then, so was her life. She stood, putting the box in its corner and pulling down the cuff of her cute sweatpants.

She said goodnight, received similar well wishes from Adrian, and went up to bed. She kept thinking he would come in, but she ended up falling asleep before he did, and she didn't hear him when he finally did lie down. She fell asleep worrying what joint custody looked like, dreamed of running in a sourceless panic on foot from South Carolina to North Carolina, and awoke in the middle of the night, hearing a low mumble.

Her eyes flickered open and she leaned up a little. They hadn't closed the curtains well enough, and she could see Adrian by the window seat buttoning up his shirt, still on the phone. "Yeah. I'll be there in a minute. Thanks. Bye." He pocketed his phone and looked over at her, seeing that she was awake. "Sorry," he said, drawing a hand through his hair and sitting to tie his shoes.

"Adrian, what's wrong?" she asked, sitting up fully.

He glanced up and back down. She saw now, as her eyes cleared, that his hair was ruffled, and his hands were shaking very slightly. "Uh... One of my patients tried to commit suicide. I'm needed at the hospital."

She drew in a breath, straightening and watching him. "Oh, Adrian," she whispered. "Can I do anything?"

He looked up, swallowing. His nose and eyes were a little red. "No, it's... Sorry. If Jude needs anything, he'll probably come in here."

"Yeah, okay. Don't worry about him," she said meeting his eyes. "I got him."

He swallowed, and she saw his vulnerability. He looked younger and wearier all at once.

"Is he going to be okay?" she whispered.

"Physically, I think so." He was getting his prescription pad and tablet out of a drawer and laying it on the dresser. "I thought we were making progress—not that I ever delude myself in these situations. He's only seventeen."

"Oh, Adrian," she said, seeing a dozen lives he led that she knew nothing of. The very slip from *client,* his personal choice for respect, to *patient,* showed his protectiveness. Was he this caught up in the details of all of his patients' lives? Probably. Would he get this upset in this situation with all of them? She didn't think so. She thought he saw a troubled boy and saw Jude. "You go on. We're fine."

He reached for her, anchoring her jaw with his hand and kissing her square on the lips. "Sorry," he said, and then pressed a lingering, sweet kiss on her cheek, as he had originally intended, as though to make up for it.

She stroked his arm, and he leaned up, going toward the door.

He didn't come in until dawn. Groggy, Adeline sat up, blinking away the sleep. She saw that he must've been in the room a few minutes because he had already dressed for work. "Hey," she said softly.

"Hey," he said, stopping on his way to the closet, turning back a little.

"Do you have to go to work?"

"Yeah," he said, reaching for a tie and going to the mirror. "Maybe you can get a nap today. Sorry I keep waking you up."

"You're the one who's had like two hours," she said.

He shrugged.

"How is he?"

"Sedated," he said in his clinical tone. "We've got to get him through this before there'll be any real progress. If there is any."

She nodded softly.

"I'll probably be getting home pretty late," he said, finishing the knot and reaching for his coat.

"'Kay," she said. She winced. "Today is my doctor's appointment, so..."

He looked up, expression arrested, like he was afraid he had hurt her. "Crap. I completely forgot."

"No biggie. You're covered up—"

"No, I'll be there."

"Adrian. You're spread about as thin as melted butter."

"I'm not letting you go alone."

"But—"

"Adeline." He stopped beside her, meeting her eyes. "Do you imagine anything is more important to me than my family?" His eyes were serious. She swallowed. She might at one time. But she wouldn't again.

"Sorry," she whispered, almost tearing up.

"*Adeline*," he said, sitting on the bed beside her, eyes concerned. "What is it?" He stroked her arm, looking like he was running the past few weeks through his mind.

"Nothing. You're sweet."

His hand slid down her arm, his thumb making gentle strokes. His eyes flickered over her features. "I think it's rising levels of estrogen, progesterone, and hCG causing changes in your neurotransmitters," he said softly.

She choked on a soft laugh, eyes widening. "Adrian!"

His brows lifted in a look of surprise. "What?"

She shook her head. "Nothing," she said, trailing a hand down his chest.

She retracted her hand speedily, embarrassed. There was nothing she'd love better than to explore the particularly pleasing way his chest gave on to his abs, ripple after ripple, as she had once before, the slow trail of her fingers igniting a flame in him. As it was, she was a little embarrassed to be emotional in front of him. "Nothing," she kind of mumbled.

He seemed to take this as more evidence of her emotional state. Never mind. Just a puddle of goo over here. He didn't touch her, seemed to restrain himself from doing so. "So it's at four?" he said, clearing his throat.

"Yep."

"Meet you there?"

"Sounds good."

Adeline turned into the parking garage, looking for Adrian's car. She had spent all day at Drayton Hall, discussing the wallpaper with their curatorial team and also being given access to some of their archives for research. Adrian's name had opened doors to her. Apparently he was pretty involved in the Charleston community and certain charities, and it seemed like he had been just about everybody's doctor at some point or other. She was surprised at how open people were about their family members, but then, Adrian had a way of soothing the stigma.

She saw him leaning on his car and pulled in beside him. He came over and opened her door, handing her a milkshake. "Oh, the famous hospital milkshake," she said, taking it with a smile. "Jude always gets these from you, but I never do."

He just smiled, waiting.

"Oh," she said, taking her first sip as she got out. "It *is* good."

"Told you."

She drank it speedily and was soon sitting in the cold exam room, padded bra in place this time. The nurse came in and took some measurements, chatting them up while she rubbed the goop on Adeline. "Y'all burning up in this heat?"

"Yeah, it's pretty intense," Adeline said.

"You'll be having this one in the dead of winter though," she said. "Just think about how nice and cold it'll be. Aw, there's your little one."

Adeline looked at the monitor and saw, after just a moment, little bitty feet. It turned, giving them a good glimpse of its face, and Adrian said softly, "Did you feel that?"

"Oh, yes," she said, smiling.

The nurse was smiling, looking between them. "Everything looks perfect to me. Do you want to know what it is?"

Adeline nibbled her lip. "I'm not sure..."

Adrian said at the same time, "Yes." He looked at the monitor for another moment. "I think I already know, but I want to make sure."

The nurse laughed. "All right, Mom, step out in the hall, and I'll send Dad out to you."

Adeline gave him a stink eye. "I don't know how I feel about you having that kind of power."

The look he gave her said maybe she shouldn't be so hippie about it then. She grabbed her purse, giving him one last look before going out.

Adeline waited about three minutes, hearing the low murmurs of their voices as they talked.

He opened the door, looking like a tall drink of water, with a smug/triumphant look on his face. "I'm assuming you were right," she said, eyes twinkling despite herself. He looked like Jude had when he'd caught a fish on Sullivan's Island.

"Of course I was," he said, looking down at her, lips curving slightly.

She gave him another look, the suspense almost killing her. He knew what they were having, whether their lives would be changed by a son or daughter. Whatever it was had pleased him, and she was kind of sad that she wasn't sharing that moment, but she was also thinking about the moment she'd look for herself. "You can't tell anyone. Not even Jude. It'll get back to me."

"I won't." His lips were twitching now, and she could tell he was thinking of all of the ways he would hold this over her head. So the gentleman had a mischievous streak, did he?

"Adrian, I'm going to have to put you in time out," she said.

"I wish you would," he said provocatively, a demon in his eyes.

She gasped, reaching out to whack him hard with her cardigan. She held his eyes, matching the quiet amusement in his own. He laughed, offering his hand. She took it. She liked the touch, the husbandly feel about it. The safe way it made her feel.

She thought suddenly of his wife. He had never been sure whether she had Bipolar Disorder, but she had definitely refused any medication. And maybe she had just been unhappy. Adrian had never let much drop, but from what she'd gathered from Harris, life had been tough, to say the least. And she had a feeling Harris didn't even know the half of it.

But how could she possibly not have felt secure with him? What could have made her throw her child into her Mercedes and drive through a storm at ninety miles per hour away from him? It had to be something little short of an emotional collapse. And she knew, sometimes when Adrian's eyes looked distant, or vulnerable, that he was wondering it, too.

She was overseeing the sanding of the floors upstairs when her phone buzzed. She pulled it out of her pocket, seeing Harris's name. Odd, since he was at work.

"Hey, Harris," she said, closing the door on the room and going out onto the balcony. The water glistened in the distance, a sailboat rolling by on the horizon.

"Hey, Adeline. What's up?"

"Oh, you know… Scraping a hundred years' worth of funk off floors. Pretty glamorous."

He laughed. "I can't top that. But anyway... I don't have long to talk, but I got a call back from that title abstractor I gave your property description to." A long silence. "The long and short of it is: he's found it. He's found Santarella."

Chapter Twenty-Two

The spring and summer had been almost unendurable. The news of the Battle of the Wilderness in Virginia was followed closely by word that the Federal armies were driving toward Atlanta. The struggle was as bloody as ever it had been, and the people of Charleston were hungry. So many of their friends' sons had fallen that it seemed impossible, if such were the case across the entire South, that there could be much left of their armies at all. And then, of course, Atlanta did fall, and the enemy was hot on the trail toward Savannah, a stone's throw away from Charleston.

Shannon had resumed her work at the hospital after settling Rose with her new step-mother. The temperatures of the summer had been boiling, making life, such as it was, almost unendurable for the wounded and sick men and for ladies in black gowns and corsets. Such was Shannon's exhaustion that her father had insisted that she depart with Elizabeth and Rose for a rest at Santarella. And looking at her haggard expression in the mirror, she found it difficult to argue with him.

Elizabeth's mother agreed to take Shannon's place as a nurse for the autumn before Shannon had even known she was to leave the city. Her father and Elizabeth's mother had worked everything out between them so neatly that there was nothing left for Shannon to say, even if she hated to leave the poor men. But as she could scarcely say so without insulting Mrs. Middleton, she held her tongue and left for the island.

She felt so guilty for resting that she could not at first enjoy herself. But at length, the cool breezes washing over her began to renew her mind, and her spirits lifted. To be with her niece again was heaven, and to have Elizabeth with her, too, was an unexpected joy in her life.

Elizabeth had set the Ravenel household in better order than ever Shannon had done, instituting a few changes, but not enough to insult. She tenderly cared for Shannon when she would return from the hospital at night, so exhausted she could scarcely move. Elizabeth's bond with Rose grew by day. Rose was a passionate child with decided opinions and a deep capacity to love, and she decided to love Elizabeth from the first day and never, Shannon thought, looked back. Just when Shannon would think, with a rueful smile, that she had been entirely deposed, however, Rose would sidle up to her caressingly and look at her as a girl could only look at her aunt. And so, happily, there were no uncomfortable tensions in the household, and Mr. Ravenel packed his ladies off to Santarella with peace about them and promised to join them at Christmas.

Two days after their arrival, when Shannon sat with Elizabeth in the dining room at three o'clock for their dinner, Shannon looked at her sister-in-law and said, "I will ask you again, who was that Negro woman?"

Elizabeth looked at her, still holding her spoon, and remained silent. It had long been common for some of the less well-circumstanced of Charleston to come outside to watch as the gentry left for their plantations either on the Ashley River or in the Sea Islands after the first killing frost. There had been one woman, in her forties or fifties, who had been walking down the street, not one of the onlookers, but appearing as though she had just come from one of the hospitals, for she wore a blood-stained apron. Shannon first noticed her for the beauty of her features but soon realized that the woman had stopped and was looking at them closely with a soft smile, almost as though she knew them.

Shannon had remarked upon it, at which time Elizabeth had grown decidedly cagey and finally silenced Shannon by glancing at Rose. That had, naturally, piqued her interest all the more, but Elizabeth had evaded her all of yesterday, wrapping herself in household matters.

Now Elizabeth feigned surprise and said, "Why, dear?"

Shannon gave her a scathing look, and Elizabeth sighed. Gathering herself, she said, "She is Mr. Ravenel's mistress."

Shannon blinked. "My father?"

Looking down at her soup, Elizabeth nodded. Shannon felt surprise but did not look as though she were about to shatter, as Elizabeth had feared. "Since my mother's death, or..?"

"She has been for decades, apparently," Elizabeth said softly, meeting her eyes at length.

Shannon absorbed that for a moment, finally saying, "Well. I suppose that explains a great deal. How do you know?"

"I believe it is common knowledge amongst the men of Charleston. I heard my father and another gentleman speak of it one night. And, indeed, Shannon, I do not think it is an uncommon thing."

Shannon took a moment to think, mostly of her mother. What had been her thoughts? Had they reached some sort of agreement? For Shannon didn't imagine for a moment that her mother had been unaware. She had possessed the sharp eye of an eagle. She ached for her and wondered what her own feelings would have been in such a circumstance.

John Thomas had never given her a moment's worry in that direction, and, though she knew many men conducted their affairs discreetly without such indiscretions ever coming to the ears of their wives, Shannon knew, as one simply did, that she could place her trust in him.

During their estrangement, though? Would he not have had a perfect right, given the utter finality of Shannon's words? Heat shot through her, paralyzing her, until she couldn't speak.

Elizabeth covered her hand. "I knew it would upset you, Shannon, and that is why I did not speak of it. But you know, my dear, that there are all sorts of marriages, and people have many and varied reasons for doing the things that they do."

Shannon shook her head, coming to earth. "Oh, no. No, it hasn't upset me. Tell me, is she a Free Negro?" she asked softly.

"Yes. She lives in a house he provides for her. That is all I know."

Shannon thought the matter over prosaically, deciding not to fall prey to any righteous indignation on her mother's behalf. She had long ago ceased to try to understand the mystery of her parents' marriage and its inner workings. They had found a way to carry on, which was more, when she thought about it, than Shannon had.

"You know, I have never known him, since my return to South Carolina, to spend a night away from home," she embarrassed Elizabeth very much by saying. "I think that is very sacrificial of him, don't you?"

Elizabeth choked. "I vow, Shannon, there is no saying what next will come from your mouth—"

"Well, you can't expect me to pretend I am a simpering miss, when *I* was the one you asked when you wished to know how to—"

"I had thought you were the Virgin Daughter of Charleston?" Elizabeth intervened hastily.

Putting down her glass, Shannon said, "Now, you begin to sound like Mar—" Her mouth snapped shut, and she met Elizabeth's eyes.

"Like Marie," Elizabeth agreed softly. "I remember she used to tease you for it."

After an awkward moment had passed, Shannon said, "Forgive me, Elizabeth, I hadn't meant anything by it."

"Shannon!" she exclaimed. "She was your cousin as well as Frederick's wife. Naturally she is often in your thoughts, and I promise you, I wouldn't wish it otherwise. And so please, when she comes to your mind, do not banish her. Not for my sake."

Shannon studied her, the blue light from the old wood paneling reflecting in the late afternoon sunlight off of Elizabeth's blue eyes, dark brown hair, and her beautiful features, and said, "Rose is very lucky to have you, my sweet friend."

Elizabeth smiled and said softly, "I hope so." After a moment, she said, "Frederick and I intend to raise Rose as a family, the three of us—"

"And perhaps someday others," Shannon interjected.

Elizabeth flushed. "Indeed, I hope so. But I will not encourage Rose in the belief that her mother never existed, and..." She hesitated.

Shannon's brows drew together. "Yes, my friend?"

Elizabeth picked at a loose thread on her wide sleeve. "We intend to raise her Catholic."

Shannon almost choked. "What?"

"Frederick wishes to honor Marie's last wishes regarding her child."

"Do you mean to tell me that my brother intends to follow the decrees of the Pope?"

"He intends to convert, once the war is over, and so do I," Elizabeth said firmly.

Shannon said, astonished, "But you are an Episcopalian!"

"It is his wish, Shannon. He had decided it long before he ever thought of me, while he was away, and he explained his feelings to me before we were engaged so that I could make my decision."

Shannon sat aghast at the loyalty her brother engendered from women. "I declare, Frederick made a Protestant of his Catholic wife and a Catholic of his Protestant wife, and both of you were happy to oblige him! I don't know what he has done to—"

"Oh, Shannon, spare me such dramatics!" Elizabeth said long-sufferingly. More seriously, she added, "If you think I made the decision lightly, without a great deal of thought, merely because I was infatuated with your brother, you are fair and far off. And," she said gently, "did you not give up your own denominational affiliation for your husband?"

Shannon blinked, struck by the truth of it. She might make an argument that Elizabeth's change was far more drastic, but she didn't. After a long silence, she said with hesitation, "In the spirit of honesty, I must say that I believed John Thomas's faith to be far superior to mine. It was a part of him. While mine was...merely in my mental reserves." She swallowed. "I didn't join the church, though. He never asked me to, though he must have wished it."

Elizabeth pressed her hand. They had never talked about Shannon's marriage, and her new sister-in-law knew very little of it, or of John Thomas. She simply supported Shannon and asked no questions, for which Shannon was more grateful than she could say. "I remember that about him," Elizabeth said softly. "His air of quiet assurance." At length, she added, "But I also remember that he loved you. And he was too much like Frederick ever to have forced you to do something you did not wish."

Shannon's brows drew together. "But I did wish it," she said in confusion. "I loved his church. Why did I resist it, when it would have given him such pleasure?"

Elizabeth merely shook her head and commiserated with her in sympathy. Finally, she said, "You know, Shannon, I think there was so much between you that was different that perhaps you didn't quite know how to let go of any piece without losing yourself entirely."

Shannon stared into the distance. "I don't think I knew who I was at all," she said softly.

Chapter Twenty-Three

The two ladies sat in the great paneled library, surrounded by books from across the world. The mail had been brought to them, and Elizabeth sat reading a rare letter which had made it through the Confederate post from Frederick. Shannon gave her attention to a missive from her Aunt Coraline, who was beginning to heal and to take an interest in her granddaughter. Shannon sought to encourage this initiative, promising, after discussing it with Elizabeth, to bring Rose for a visit as soon as circumstances should permit.

Shannon looked out the many-paned window and could see the grounds stretching into the horizon. Beyond that, of course, was the sea. They had discussed taking Rose for a walk later in the day, but it was questionable if the weather would permit it. The day was gray and overcast, and as afternoon came, it seemed to warm only marginally.

"Shannon, do you—" Elizabeth had started to speak, but just then, with no warning whatsoever and as unexpected as a thief in the night, John Tilman ran in, shouting, "Miss Shannon, Miss Elizabeth, Yankees on the island!"

Shannon bolted to her feet, hands clutching her skirts, mouth open in utter shock as she stared at the butler in speechless horror. Elizabeth said, "John! What are they doing? Are they—?"

"Headin' for Santarella, ma'am, Harry says. Lookin' fierce as demons. We've got to get you ladies and Miss Rose hid."

Both were trembling, Elizabeth exclaiming, "How? How on earth did they break the lines with no warn— John! Bring Miss Rose down immediately!"

"Yes, ma'am."

"Wait!" The word from Shannon made them halt and look at her. She swallowed, knowing their world was about to change, and also that they would be shocked by what she was about to say. "Bring a pair of clothes belonging to one of the little Negro boys for us to change Miss Rose into."

Elizabeth stared at her before her meaning hit, and the blood drained from her face. "Oh, Shannon," she whispered, holding her eyes, seemingly unable to move. Shannon held her eyes, inclining her head. Elizabeth swallowed and then nodded, looking at John, who returned with a protesting Rose moments later. Shannon and Elizabeth undressed her quickly, with trembling hands, slipping her into little breeches and a shirt, and Shannon tied her hair back into a queue, telling her that she would pretend to be a boy, and her name would be Robert. "Won't that be amusing?" Elizabeth asked.

Rose giggled, willing to be charmed out of the sulks, and Elizabeth said, "Now, there are some men coming, love, but

I don't want you to be afraid. Aunt Shannon and I will take care of you," she said, voice breaking.

"Mama is sad?"

"No, dearest." Elizabeth handed Rose off to Mammy, who looked utterly shaken. Turning a circle around the room and looking at all of the furnishings and priceless ornaments in anguish, she said, "Shannon, we had no warning! What can we save? What, that will not be plundered?"

Phoebe ran in, her hand on the door frame as she steadied herself, saying, "We're putting the china and the silver in the cellar, ma'am."

Shannon nodded, trying to stay calm, to keep her presence of mind. "Good, that is good." Her voice shook. Reaching up, she pulled her necklace from within her dress with trembling hands and undid the clasp. She handed the North Star to Phoebe. "Put it somewhere you think safe, Phoebe. Don't risk yourself." Phoebe's dark, beautiful eyes met Shannon's, and, for once, as her own hand closed over the necklace, she reached up with her other to cover Shannon's, which couldn't quite let go.

They all spent the next ten minutes furiously hiding items away in a frenzy which upset Rose, but they had no choice. Shannon could only think of the fact that her father wasn't there, and that they were entirely unprotected, except by the male slaves—and would they have any authority with the soldiers? Oh, goodness, one heard such stories: heirlooms thrown on piles and burned, necklaces ripped from ladies' necks. And these had not been against the people of Charleston, who were more hated than all of the South combined.

She prayed within herself for strength, for courage and protection, and barely had the words left her heart when they heard hoofbeats thundering. There were so many of them that the crystal candlesticks rattled on the mantle, the very floor beneath them trembling. Elizabeth reached for Shannon's hand, looking behind her and seeing Mammy clutching Rose to her breast and keeping her quiet.

Suddenly, there were a hundred men on the lawn, firing guns in the air, cracking whips above them and screaming, "Rebels! *Damned Rebels*!" And any chance that they would be in the magnanimous mold of some Federal officers they knew of faded.

Shannon's hand tightened on Elizabeth's just before they heard an authoritative voice yell, "Everyone who is in the house, slave or white, remove yourselves to the portico immediately!"

Shannon swallowed and then, after she glanced at Elizabeth, they started forward with steps of courage, Elizabeth telling Mammy to stay behind them. "Yes, ma'am," she answered softly.

John Tilman tried to stand in front of them, but as the ladies stepped onto the porch, surrounded by the four columns, their chins in the air, the leader, an officer in blue with a harsh face, said, "All Negros are to assemble down the stairs and stand to my left. Your liberators have arrived." They did so, heads bent, Mammy handing Rose reluctantly to Elizabeth.

Just then, some of the men produced two tree saws and, one on either end, they started hacking away at the three-hundred-year-old trees. A scream left Shannon's lips, but the man produced a gun and fired it into the air, screaming, "Silence! Anyone who moves or speaks will be shot!" Removing his hat and holding it to his chest, he dismounted, replacing his hat on his head and walking forward.

"Is this the home of Captain Frederick Ravenel?" he demanded.

"Yes," Shannon answered, still above him on the porch, her feet holding her firmly. There was no use in lying, she thought. *Ravenel* was emblazoned on everything in the house which could be printed.

"Who are you?"

"I am his sister," Shannon answered, "and this is his young son."

"This other white lady?"

"My nephew's governess."

He stalked forward, eyes narrowed. "Indeed?" Stopping before Elizabeth, he suddenly jerked up her left hand. "A married governess?" he demanded. "I hear tell that the Captain was recently remarried. Are you certain, Miss Ravenel, that you are not mistaken?"

Elizabeth stared forward, not deigning to look at the man, and Shannon pressed her lips together.

The man turned to his company and announced, "Behold, the wife, child, and sister of Captain Frederick Ravenel, who sank the *Washington*, and the *Iroquois,* and who is responsible for the deaths of countless of our brethren! Behold the women of the Rebel Land, who reap the benefits of slave labor, who live in the cradle of rebellion, where the very heart of this war which has claimed tens of thousands, *hundreds* of thousands of lives, started! Let it be upon their heads!" A massive oak crashed to the ground, and Shannon's eyes slipped closed, a tear slipping down her cheek, as the men began giving a poor imitation of the Rebel Yell, firing off their guns, and letting their horses rear and whinny.

The officer forced Shannon and Elizabeth down the stairs and out onto the lawn.

Shannon caught out of the corner of her eye movement coming down from near the slave cabins and realized that it was Phoebe. What on earth had taken her down there? She was running, trying to get back to the house, the chaos and pandemonium obviously frightening her. Before Shannon even registered this thought, she heard a gun fire, its shot echoing and registering, and a scream left her lips. Phoebe fell, and Shannon screamed ferociously, starting to run to her, but Elizabeth, tears running down her face, grasped her and held her back with an iron grip. Shannon struggled, still screaming and trying to get to her, but she didn't still until she heard Elizabeth whisper, her head buried against her neck, "Don't, Shannon, she's dead. Shannon, didn't you see where it hit? She's dead, and they'll do the same to you. I'm so sorry. You can't move."

Shannon cried out but remembered suddenly, somehow, Rose. She knew she must obey whatever she was told, no matter what they did. The leader had not fired the shot—it was uncertain who had—but he said in sharp accents, "Let that be a lesson to you! *Do not move* until you are told to move!"

The men were scattering about the plantation, beginning to plunder it. They rounded up hundreds of slaves, confining them to one area. And then the slave cabins began to burn. Next were the outbuildings, and all of the animals were rounded up and tied together.

"I hereby declare that this island and all of its lands are confiscated by the Federal government, the *rightful* government," the man said as another tree fell with a thunderous noise, shaking the ground.

Shannon's eyes looked in speechless horror across the plundered land, her mind contemplating only one thought, over and over: *Phoebe. Phoebe. Phoebe.*

Rose sobbed against Elizabeth's leg, and Elizabeth stroked her head, trying to cover her within her skirts as best she could to keep her from coming to their notice.

And then, the thing happened that they knew must surely happen unless some miracle prevented it. Torches were thrown through the windows of the manor, the windows broken, and flames began to lick the walls. Elizabeth's eyes closed, her teeth biting her lip hard, and it wasn't long before flames were shooting in the air, stretching toward the sky, engulfing the house entirely as the roof caved in and crashed. Rose wailed, and Shannon squeezed Elizabeth's hand and looked at her comfortingly. It was unthinkable, but they must keep their wits about them.

"Move forward!" the man screamed, and all Shannon could think of, as they numbly did so, was her father. This would kill him. Frederick, too. Not the house, not the confiscation of all of their lands and slaves. But the women being subjected to terror and them not there, not even aware. Oh, dear God, it would be more than they could bear, she thought, praying for protection.

They forced them, more or less, to the center of the lawn, where the man said loudly and fluently over the plunder, "Strip to your chemises!"

Elizabeth and Shannon looked at each other, each beginning to tremble almost violently.

"Strip, or be shot!"

They began unbuttoning one another's gowns, although they could hardly manage it with hands which were shaking so badly. *Rose. Not in front of Rose*, Shannon thought. It was strange, but it was her only thought.

"We are going to give you the punishment common to traitorous whores," the man said, motioning for another of the men to come forward.

When they were standing in nothing but their shifts, trembling from the cold, Elizabeth summoned the courage to plead in a hoarse voice, "Sir, we are not whores. We have kept ourselves only to our husbands!"

"Your razor, Thibodeaux!"

Shannon's eyes shifted to the man who had produced a razor which looked freshly sharpened.

"Unbind your hair!"

They did so, breathing hectically.

"Go down to your knees!"

Again, they obeyed. What choice had they? And then Shannon felt her hair jerked back and knew. They were going to shave their heads. She closed her eyes, tears escaping the corners, and it began, her hair falling in large lumps to the ground. Tears fell silently down Shannon's face while Elizabeth stared stoically ahead, her eyes fixed on the distant horizon. Shannon's lip trembled, and here and there they cut her, until finally they were bald.

"Stand up!" the man ordered at last. They did so, with less fear now, seeming to agree by tacit consent not to be afraid of these men anymore. *Do you think my Father could not send ten-thousand angels?* she wondered. And her spine straightened. Her God was far more powerful than anything which could be done to them.

As soon as they rose, her house burning behind her, her servant and impossibly dear friend dead on the lawn, Shannon said in a loud voice, halting those before her, her eyes taking on an other-worldly, defiant hue, "'If I forget you, Jerusalem, may my right hand forget its skill. May my tongue cling to the roof of my mouth if I do not remember you, if I do not consider Jerusalem my highest joy. Remember, Lord, what the Edomites did on the day Jerusalem fell. 'Tear it down,' they cried, 'tear it down to its foundations!' Daughter Babylon, doomed to destruction, happy is the one who repays you according to what you have done to us!'"

Silence reigned suddenly. A few of the men fell back. Even the leader seemed momentarily stunned. Then he jerked Shannon's hands up behind her and forced her to walk. "We are leaving the island," he said, regaining his confidence and ordering all the rest to follow.

They walked them for a mile or more toward a boat, where they forced them aboard, beginning to row them away from the lands which they knew they might never see again, and certainly not as their own, away from the towering flames. Her courage not leaving her, Shannon watched them with what occurred to one of the men as the look of a tigress intent on kill, impervious to all feelings.

"Do you know," she asked in a strong, blank voice, "whose wife you have assaulted?"

The men looked at her, still a little frightened of her. "John Thomas Haley," she said in the same voice.

As recognition struck them, their faces paled, even the leader's.

"That was his servant, lately *in his employ*, whom you slaughtered. A most highly regarded member of his household. And I am his wife, who came to my family in Charleston. And I hope, with all my soul, that he disembowels you for what you have done to us."

The oars, continued to hit the waters, making rushing noises, but otherwise, there was utter silence on the boat. The men exchanged glances. No one spoke a word until they neared their enemy, and they sent Shannon, Elizabeth, and the child to walk back through Confederate lines and into Charleston in their shifts with nothing covering their heads. A humiliation, apparently, appropriate for daughters of Charleston. Only they didn't look so sure of it as they walked away.

Chapter Twenty-Four

Adeline walked across the field in her waders. The island was unnamed and not easily accessible, but it wasn't too far outside of Charleston. She imagined at one time it might simply have been called Santarella, since the plantation had apparently taken up the greater part of it. Now it was owned by the federal government and was part of a nature preserve.

She had driven as far as she could and then got out of her car. She knew, of course. Harris had told her. But nothing could stop the grief that twisted her heart as she approached. And she knew it couldn't even begin to compare with Shannon's the first time she had seen it, if she ever had.

She caught glimpses of a brick foundation of what might have once been a flanker and stopped, her eyes roving over it numbly as she guessed where the other buildings would have been. Then she turned and looked at the view it must have commanded. The grass was high, of course, and nothing was kept as it would've been. But she could picture it.

The gentle lawn that stretched for a mile. The trees that would've lined the driveway. The pristine outbuildings. The tiny glimpse of the ocean in the distance that one had only to mount one's horse and fly toward to escape. And then she turned and pictured the house.

She knew it had been brick and thought it might have been Palladian style from contemporaries' comparisons with Drayton Hall. She was almost unable to contain her sorrow. She tried to remind herself that some of the damage could have happened in the century and a half since the war, but she couldn't believe all of it had.

She heard a vehicle and turned, seeing a black Land Rover. She blinked in surprise, and for a minute, she was afraid something was wrong. She hadn't told Adrian she was coming out here, and he should be at work.

He got out and closed the door, walking toward her in dress shoes that were scarcely snake-proof. She sniffed, wiping away the stray tear that had fallen. "Adrian," she said as he neared. "What is it?"

"Harris called me," he said, stopping and slipping his hands in his pockets. He looked good, handsome...a breath of fresh air on the island. "I can't believe he let you come out here alone." She wasn't sure if he was afraid for her safety, or— "Obviously, he doesn't know you yet, or he'd know."

She gave a soft laugh, choking on her tears. "I'm okay, Adrian, I promise."

His eyes lifted, and he looked around him. She felt the weight press in even on him. The significance. The loss. "What must it have been like?" he said, scanning out across the sweeping view.

She shook her head. "I can't even imagine."

He made a slow turn, had to have noticed how level everything was. How there weren't even many trees. "They didn't leave a thing, did they?" he said almost numbly.

She shook her head, pressing her lips together to keep them from trembling. "Some of it could have burned later, I suppose. But why would someone do that?" she questioned hoarsely. "How could you destroy beauty, whatever your differences?"

Adrian turned quickly, his attention now focused on her, which was embarrassing since tears were flowing freely down her face. "Oh, Adeline," he said softly, stepping up to her and taking her into an embrace. And she clung to him.

"I'm sorry," she whispered. "I'm really out of control."

His hand slid up and down her back. "They survived, though," he said softly. She looked up at him. His eyes roved her face. "That's the beautiful thing about the human spirit. They went on with their lives... And their blood still runs through my veins." He looked down and put his hand gently on the baby. "And his or hers. I can promise you that would mean more to them than all of the houses in the world."

She breathed emotionally. "Adrian, if you want me to stop crying, you're going to have to stop talking like that."

He smiled a little. She always felt like a heroine when she drew one out of him. This was good. It distracted her from all of that lost history. He tucked her hair behind her ear. "We can look around for stuff if you want."

She swallowed. "Yeah, okay. Everything's so grown up, though, if there *is* anything it's long buried."

Her prediction proved true after they had walked around for about fifteen minutes, hand in hand since the ground was uneven. Images of slaves working the land came to her, the stark, ugly reality against the beautiful setting. She had seen images in her books during grad school showing what rice cultivation had looked like. Back-breaking, soul-wearying work. What must it have felt like, to walk off this island free?

Her eyes skimmed to a tree that would've stood to the left of the house. "That's probably three-hundred years old," she whispered, as if her voice would disturb it. It was a live oak, its massive limbs long and twisted.

Without saying anything, he started walking that way. It had a deep keyhole, like a magical tree in a fairytale. Her fingers skimmed the bark as she wondered if Ravenels past had played in this tree, if they had affixed a swing to it or broken limbs falling out of it. There was some inde-scribable romance to the tree. She turned and looked at Adrian, who was looking up at the soaring and sloping branches. "Adrian..."

"Yeah."

She bit her lip. "Will you stick your arm down in this?"

He looked down at her. "What?" he demanded.

"I want to know what's in it."

He looked at it. "Why would anything be in it?"

"Well, if I had something to hide, and your Aunt Shannon almost always did…"

"Why don't you?"

"I'm pregnant."

He gave her a grim look, holding her eyes as he ran his arm down in it.

"Nothing?" she asked when he'd been feeling around for a second.

He had paused and was looking like he was reaching for something. Her heart sped. He came out with a dirty hand and something in his palm. He opened it and held the item out. It was a corroded silver necklace.

"A Star of David," he said, looking stunned.

She breathed a sigh of shock. "I…found one just like it in Shannon's room. Was anyone in your family Jewish, Adrian? Harris had thought it must belong to a little girl who stayed with your grandfather's family during the war, but… I don't see… I think it must be older."

He shook his head. "We've been Catholic for centuries."

"You've been Catholic since Marie Ravenel's death. You were originally Huguenots who became Presbyterian," she said absently. "Adrian, what are we going to do?"

"I'm going to take you back to your car, and we're going to drive back to Charleston," he said, reaching for her hand.

Chapter Twenty-Five

They sat in the small parlor at Ravenel House, Shannon in the window seat and Elizabeth in one of the wing chairs, both wearing gray knit caps.

Between the march on the island and the walk back into Charleston, it had been five miles in the cold, in their shifts, struggling between them to carry Rose, who screamed in terror. Elizabeth had had blood running down the side of her face where they had cut her. Shannon had wanted to stop by a creek to clean her up, but Elizabeth had shaken her head. Shannon knew well the signs that it was almost more than her friend could bear, but they had borne it, had made it to the Confederate soldiers, to whom Shannon had told their story. Their outrage had been palpable, but it was nothing to her father's.

He couldn't believe his eyes when they had been delivered to him, did not for quite some time recognize them. And why would he? They were bald and undressed, save the sheets the Confederates had given them to wrap around themselves. They had nothing more, poor men. The cry that had left her father's otherwise very closely-guarded lips as he had bolted to his feet, Shannon would never forget.

Shannon thought it had taken two weeks for him even to comprehend that the island had been confiscated, that his ancestral home stood in ashes, and that his hundreds of slaves were taken. Or *freed*, she supposed. Yes, by heaven, freed. She blinked in surprise.

Shannon did worry for them. Many of the field slaves only spoke Gullah. How would they manage? And the house servants—they were unaccustomed to living rough. Shannon did not fool herself, as did many of her neighbors. She knew most of the slaves pined for freedom and would never return of their own volition. But the house servants, some of them, were family—John Tilman, Mammy, Abigail, and Rebecca. Would they wish to return? *Phoebe*.

It felt as though an arrow struck through Shannon's chest as the thought arose, and she closed her eyes. Such kindness and goodness in her soul, and more dignity in her little finger than most could muster in a lifetime. That was the hardest: the death of another person she didn't know how to live without.

What had she been doing? Hiding Shannon's necklace? Warning the slaves? Shannon's mind continually turned to all they had been through together: from Shannon's earliest days as a bride among strangers, to breaking through Confederate lines to return to the South, to the weary days at the hospital. And Marie's death. *Phoebe. Phoebe. Phoebe.*

Her spirit mourned for her, something all who knew the Ravenels understood, for the word *Phoebe* was synonymous with Ravenel House and Miss Shannon. Shannon had been the one to tell Phoebe's aunt, the cook, upon her return, and she had, most unusually, embraced the slave as they wept together.

Everyone knew Charleston would fall. It might be days, or a matter of weeks, but the city couldn't hold out much longer. Some of the citizens fled up to Columbia, and even more did so once the story of what had happened to the Ravenel ladies became known.

And it had become known. The story spread like wildfire, the flame catching in a sudden gust and igniting. It started in Charleston, of course, and then moved throughout the South, causing no small degree of mania and furor. Shannon and Elizabeth were horrified to find that their names were printed in every last Southern newspaper still in operation. And they were invited by President Davis to Richmond to be honored, which they had to assume was more of a formality than a reality given that no one could think of a safe route to Virginia anymore.

And then it was only a matter of time before the Northern press had caught on. From what they could reason, it seemed that the Northern Democrats and Copperheads picked up on the story when the officer of the company was recalled suddenly back to Washington, Then they had gained all of the details after that from contacts in the South. Hotly opposed to the war and wanting to compromise with Southerners on the issue of slavery, the Democrats were using it as fodder to the claim that the Republican president and military were executing a barbaric war. If the news the Ravenels received from President Davis was correct, the matter was even argued on the floor of Congress.

They could not keep what had happened from Frederick, of course. They could only imagine that, if he had access to any newspapers, he might either be reading a softened or aggrandized version of the truth. There was no certainty whatsoever that their letters would reach him with the postal services all but defunct, but they did write to tell him what had happened, even if they softened the horror of it themselves.

Shannon devoted most of her time to her niece, who suffered from terrible nightmares. She had at first been able to sleep only if Elizabeth and Shannon had been with her, unable to let them out of her sight. A kitchen maid had been assigned to her, but she did not want her. She wanted Emma and Alice if anyone was to wait on her, and at night, she wanted Mammy, but of course, they were not there. In caring for her and trying to help her to forget, Shannon and Elizabeth managed to keep their minds occupied.

And then, inevitably, weeks passed. One day, when Elizabeth was helping Shannon to dress, she paused, catching sight of herself in the mirror, and began to laugh.

"What?" Shannon asked, fingers on her corset as she looked over her shoulder.

"We look *hideous!*" she exclaimed, still laughing.

Shannon looked at the mirror, taking in the sight of them, and her lips twitched. "So we do," she agreed.

And somehow, it was easier after that. Christmas could not be a celebration with what had happened to Phoebe, with the Confederacy dying, and with no word from Frederick in three months. But as a new year began, they swore that not all would be doom and gloom, for the sake of Rose and for Shannon's father and Elizabeth's parents, who could scarcely bear what had happened.

They read together daily, taking refuge in Shakespeare. They devised inventive recipes from the meager foods they were able to obtain and began trying to teach Rose to read. With a household staff of only six, they were forced to labors for which, as fate would have it, Shannon's sojourn in Massachusetts had given her some degree of preparation. She knew that Mrs. Haley would have taken on the labor of a dozen servants without batting an eye, but it exhausted Shannon, and she couldn't pretend otherwise.

In the middle of January, she went back to the hospital against her family's wishes, but she had to do something. To alleviate suffering, to remember that there were many less fortunate than she. She worked even on Sundays because the casualty toll from Virginia was so overwhelming. It was heart-breaking to see what had become of the Army, to look into men's eyes and see no evidence of a soul, not the slightest vestige of hope.

One night, she was brought home with blue circles under her eyes and coughing still from the cold she had taken after the seizure of Santarella. Elizabeth and Mr. Ravenel issued an ultimatum: either they would find someone to take her place and she would stay home, or they would lock her in her room.

This might make her laugh, but as the laughing turned into a coughing fit, she knew it would be unwise to continue. Her father seemed to worry so much and to bring so many doctors to her that she suspected him of thinking she had gone into a decline from which she wouldn't recover. That frightened her a little, for, having been assured that her life was of worth, she wanted to go on living. And so she stayed home, recruiting her energy and wondering what Providence had in store for her.

Her mind turned, inevitably and often, to the future. It was there now, on a gray February day as she sat in the parlor with Elizabeth. She was so lost in her thoughts that she didn't realize Elizabeth had risen until she sat down next to her in the window embrasure, their skirts billowing around them.

Shannon looked at her and, seeing that her friend was studying her, turned away so Elizabeth couldn't see her face.

"You're thinking," Elizabeth said. "And plotting. I know well that look from our days in school."

Shannon looked at her.

Elizabeth took her hand. "What?" she asked gently.

She swallowed. It was difficult to speak of, but, at length, she said, "It...has been more than three years since my rift with John Thomas. I know we have not spoken of it, but... My regret is...significant." She paused for a moment, pressing her lips together. "I...swore an oath to Marie, of which I have never told anyone, that if God ever granted me a second chance…" Her voice cracked. She cleared her throat. "I would set things to rights with my husband."

"Shannon," Elizabeth whispered in awe, lips parted, eyes alight. "Do you mean to do it? Are you going to try to return to him? I mean if—when—you can?"

Shannon took a shaking breath, almost afraid to say the words aloud, terrified at the leap of faith, of rejection, of the possibility that he might not be amenable. Three years and a war—good heavens, one only had to look at her to know it was possible he was an entirely different person. Perhaps he was bitter, resentful, or too angry ever to love her again.

And even if he might (because of the leadings of his conscience) have her back, did her promise to Marie mean she might have to take a man, one who could never fully forgive her, on sufferance? For she didn't delude herself into thinking that forgiving her would be easy. There was more to pardon than just that night, just that choice. And her pride rebelled at the thought. She couldn't pretend otherwise.

But dear God, how she ached for him. Longed to see him, to touch him, to talk with him. Her heart nearly burst with the thought. He could not be dead. She would have heard, somehow, wouldn't she, or at least known it in her soul? And oh, sweet heaven, the joy and relief to have his safety confirmed! To see his face, even if he rejected her utterly. She thought she could bear a great deal to have that pleasure once more.

She moistened her lips and said to her sister-in-law with a calm belied by her racing heart, "Yes. If he will have me."

"But how will you contact him, Shannon? *That* is the question."

Shannon was, three days later, heartily regretting her confidences to Elizabeth. Her friend had, five years ago, formed a fancy for Shannon's husband which, she said, could only be brought about by the sure knowledge that he loved her friend so much. One could trust a heart like John Thomas's, she had told Shannon in the window seat, causing an ache to spread in Shannon's chest. It was true, and she had thrown it away, for an argument, many arguments, a cause. For fear.

"Elizabeth, I do not think he will have me," she said softly.

"Nonsense, of course he will. He loved you."

"Note the tense of your verb, my dear."

Elizabeth flicked her hand. "The war is almost at a close. I can feel it. All of us can. Do you think he'll return to Massachusetts from wherever he is immediately? Where *is* he? Never mind, you don't know."

"He is a Commodore, a successful and famous war hero, and I am the wife who betrayed and humiliated him," Shannon said, biting her tongue as she pricked her finger with her needle. She was mending Rose's gown, torn in one of her more interesting adventures. That it had involved a chandelier, there was no need for Frederick ever to know.

"The wife he loved."

"Who left him." Did Elizabeth not comprehend the gravity of that statement? How shocking, un-heard-of, and scandalizing what she had done was? Yes, Elizabeth was no fool: she must understand. But she couldn't know that the depth of the betrayal reached far beyond any act or what the public knew; it would have reached to his very heart, to the thing between them that he had thought couldn't be broken. Because Elizabeth would never do such a thing to Frederick.

Elizabeth, not pretending interest in anything other than her overwhelming obsession, tipped her blue eyes up to the intricately molded ceiling. "He is a religious man, is he not, as we discussed? He would not divorce you, I think. Therefore, he must have you back."

"I don't *know*, Elizabeth," she answered. "And do you think I would *want* him on such terms?"

"Hmm," Elizabeth said, unperturbed by the distress in her friend's voice. "Well, not everything in life is easy, Shannon," she said, as if Shannon had passed a breezy existence. "If you must earn his respect and trust back, you simply must earn it."

Shannon opened her lips to tell her friend that if she spoke of his having her back as a foregone conclusion just once more, she would find a heavy weapon. But just then, her intentions were halted, and the words died on her tongue as the parlor doors were opened. She could not believe her eyes as Frederick materialized in the threshold, thin and bedraggled, but those were his eyes, brown and warm, which she recognized.

Elizabeth turned her head, unaware, but when she saw, her lips parted, and her breath left her body in a rush. "Frederick, my *love!*" she cried. And she was on her feet running to him. He caught her against him, and they stood there, of a height, clinging to one another, foreheads touching. He looked miserable, whispering, "Elizabeth." Elizabeth cried, and Frederick stroked his hand over her short hair, tears running down his face.

Shannon stood to excuse herself, but Frederick, noticing, caught her arm, eyes lingering on her hair, now about two inches long. And she realized she wasn't interrupting the joyous reunion of lovers. There could be no joy for Frederick, not until he accepted what had happened to them. "Shannon." He squeezed her hand as he pressed a kiss to Elizabeth's temple. "My girls. Tell me what happened," he pleaded, voice shaking. "Everything."

Shannon met Elizabeth's eyes and nodded once. Taking the hand that was around her waist, Elizabeth kissed it and said, "The house was burned, my dear. The slaves and lands confiscated." She held his eyes. "And yes. Phoebe was shot, and our heads were shaved, which..." She cleared her throat. "Which we have since discovered has been a traditional punishment for women traitors in wars past."

A noise emanated from Frederick's throat. It took him several moments to recover, but when he was able to speak, he looked at Elizabeth, touching the small of her back. He whispered, "And you were forced to strip to your chemise?" He pressed Shannon's hand, which he was still holding, hard.

Seeing that Elizabeth was embarrassed, Shannon said softly, because it seemed to bring the men comfort, "We were not defiled, Frederick." She couldn't say that it felt almost as much a violation as though they had been. Perhaps more. It was a curious feeling, one she knew she could never explain, for she didn't understand it herself.

Just then, before Frederick could respond, there was a noise at the door, and they looked up to see Rose. She was in a white dress, her blue sash all askew, her nose dirtied with something she had been playing in or eating, and her red hair, once trailing down her back, barely reached her chin. When he saw that, Frederick utterly stilled, the blood draining from his face. He looked as though he might faint, and Elizabeth and Shannon, each grabbing an arm, rushed to explain. "No! Frederick, she was playing with my sewing scissors—she thought she ought to have a crop, too!" Elizabeth said.

"Yes, and a fine mess she made of it," Shannon added, infusing levity in her voice. "You've never *seen* such jagged edges, so that we were forced to make it very short." She winked at her niece, who wrinkled her nose at this unexpected behavior in her aunt.

"Papa will *not* make me sit in the corner," Rose said defiantly. "He has only just got home!"

Lip trembling, Frederick went to his knee, and she went to him. "No, I will not," he said, folding her against him. Pulling her away, he lifted her chin with his finger, saying, "I heard that my girl was very brave at Santarella."

"I was," she confirmed. "I wanted to *bite* that man."

"Which man?" Frederick demanded.

"Never mind that," Elizabeth interjected quickly.

"Yes, indeed," Shannon said, reaching for Rose and taking her hand. "Come, dearest, let us find Grandpapa and tell him that your papa is home." Rose was agreeable, always fond of delivering a secret, and Shannon was able to shut the door behind them to give Frederick and Elizabeth privacy.

But her father had heard already of Frederick's arrival, and, though he was glad, of course, there was also a contemplative look behind his eyes. Shannon held them, feeling the soft, small hand in hers that gave her more fear than anything else. "You're thinking that the Navy has been disbanded?" she asked softly.

He nodded, looking grave. Rose looked between them, trying to understand. Seeming to recall his granddaughter, Mr. Ravenel said, "We shall see what Rose's papa has to say at dinner."

It was strange to see Frederick dressed in his pre-war civilian clothes, but that was how he came down to dinner, clean and cagey, with a smile which sought to cover pain. When his father remarked upon the lack of uniform, Frederick smiled tightly and said, "It is a mere relic now. An artifact from a failed rebellion."

"You have been disbanded, then?"

Frederick nodded once, eyes across the table on Elizabeth. She held his eyes.

The silence which fell over the room was deafening. It was odd to be gathering like this, the ladies in their formal gowns, the gentlemen in their elegant, if old, evening suits and waistcoats, the elegance of the dining room breath-taking.

It seemed a trifle frivolous after the war, even if there was nothing frivolous about the meager meal before them.

"How long before Charleston falls?" Mr. Ravenel asked, looking as though his wine had turned sour in his mouth.

Frederick looked at him. "Columbia fell this morning, and is now in flames. Charleston..." His voice broke, and he said, clearing his throat, "It is only a matter of how fast the Federals can make it here. The Confederate defenders are evacuating the city right now."

Elizabeth paled. "All of those people, the refugees from Charleston in Columbia..." She swallowed. "Ought we to leave, to go somewhere in the interior of South Carolina?"

Frederick reached across the table for her hand, curling his fingers around it. "No, my love," he said gently. "There is nowhere we can go and not encounter their armies. We must stay and ask for God's protection—and their mercy."

A tear rolled down Elizabeth's cheek, and Shannon's heart sank. More destruction, more killing—it seemed inevitable. And *what* were they doing in Richmond, she would like to know? Did they care that the South's finest jewel was about to fall, that its people were endangered? Could they not strike a bargain with the Union and save Charleston, the Confederacy's last hold-out? God in heaven, must its people suffer even more? The war had been doomed for months now, only she must assume the politicians were too afraid to risk their own necks to capitulate. When Jefferson Davis had said it was better that the city be reduced to *a heap of ruins* than surrender, he had meant it. And they weren't very far from that, between the fire, and the bombardments, and the armies pouring across the lines.

"What about the slaves?" Shannon asked softly.

Frederick looked at her. "They won't be returned, Shannon."

"No, I mean the *family*—John Tilman and the rest. Will they be able to return, if they wish to?"

"I couldn't say," he said, looking surprised, but then as though he should have thought of that. "They are with the Federals, and so we are all at their mercy."

Shannon lay her hand on Frederick's, for she was sitting beside him, and he looked at her, smiling sadly. "We'll stand firm," she said. "We are Charlestonians, are we not?" She might grow more and more conflicted about the war and its causes, but that would always be true, wherever she went, whatever she became. "It is our way."

Chapter Twenty-Six

Charleston fell on the 18th of February, when the mayor surrendered the city to the Union General, and the 55th Massachusetts marched in, a Colored Regiment. That such a fact was taken as an affront by the citizens of the city was a gross understatement. Shannon, while hearing the reports of that regiment and the others spilling within the city, felt what she couldn't say aloud: that there was some degree of justice in it. One couldn't see the other side without being at least a little changed. And her time with John Thomas had changed her a great deal.

Middleton Place was burned, with only one of its flankers surviving in poor condition. Its lands, and that of many other plantations along the Ashley River, were confiscated. They waited daily for Frederick's arrest, but the Federals were too busy securing the forts and quelling violence and unrest within the city. Charleston did not fall gently, and Shannon could almost wish, for its own sake, that it had.

She watched from the window of her red chamber upstairs as blue uniforms marched down the Battery. With spring's first blush had come the fall, at long last, of Fort Sumter. They ran the American flag up among the rubble on the same day they received belated news that Lee had surrendered at a place called Appomattox. Lincoln was shot that night.

Shannon thought about the late President now as she watched below her, her arms crossed. She remembered the dinner at the Executive Mansion, and how he had charmed her out of her dislike. She felt it deeply for the man's family. She knew well what such a loss meant, how it changed everything one knew. Her mother's absence was still the same gaping hole it had been when Shannon had arrived, frightened, in Charleston that first night. And it always would be, unless they could forget her, and they couldn't, of course.

She swallowed, thinking of her family's plight. They had hosted the Middletons to dinner the night before, and Shannon had overheard the men whispering, trying to keep their concerns of how they would survive from the ladies. With their lands confiscated, they had no means of sustenance. With their slaves freed, it would be difficult to cultivate the lands in any event. She thought of Frederick's family. Already he had lost so much, his future ripped away along with his ancestral home. Somehow, she saw herself as separate from it, but the thought of them suffering made her insides churn. They were all already much too thin, and they had lost enough.

And that was why, one day, as they were sitting in the large parlor, the ladies mending various articles at the table, that Shannon said casually to Frederick, "Brother-mine, if one *did* wish to make one's case to have the lands returned, where would one go?"

He was seated behind them on the sofa, his hand pulling absently through Rose's hair as she slept. They did not take care with their voices, for the child had learned to sleep through bombardments and now slept like the dead. "To the General, or one of the Admirals. I'd imagine they've been given authority to sign." He yawned, covering it with his other hand. "Probably no use in it, though."

"Hmm," Shannon said.

"Shannon, I don't think this *can* have been caused by her leaping from the banister," Elizabeth said, engrossed in Rose's mending. She picked at a large hole in her stocking. "What on earth..?"

"Best not to ask, dearest," Shannon said sagely, knowing the Middletons had always been far more circumspect than the Ravenels, and that Elizabeth was destined to be stunned a thousand times over.

They continued sewing, the time passing quietly. At length, Shannon realized Frederick was watching them, a smile hovering about his lips, and said, "What, Frederick?" Elizabeth looked up, her face innocently inquiring.

He gave the first laugh and the first true smile that they had seen in the two months he had been home. "You look like two boys," he said, shoulders shaking.

They both exclaimed loudly in protest, Elizabeth saying, "Oh, how could you, and when we've just managed to accomplish a true crop!"

"I can't think *how* we should punish him!" Shannon agreed, protesting loudly with her sister-in-law, and enjoying, for the first time in so long, unexpected merriment.

It was a week later before Shannon managed to gather her courage. Her arguments had taken some time to form, but she had decided what she must do. She dressed in one of her day gowns, a plain gray creation from before the war with narrower hoops than the rest, since she fancied that now to be the style in places where ladies had leisure to think of styles. She wore a cape in case the wind didn't settle, and a hat which concealed her cropped hair.

She had very nearly made it to the door when Elizabeth, coming down the stairs, lifted her brows. "Where are you off to, dearest?"

Shannon hesitated only a moment. "Word has been sent from the hospital that Mrs. Netherton was called away, and that they will need me today."

"That will be the baby, I daresay."

"Hmm?"

"Her daughter was expecting her confinement soon?"

"Oh! Yes, indeed, I imagine that is correct."

Elizabeth came further down, her hand on the banister, studying Shannon. "Are you certain you feel well enough?

Your papa would not like me to let you go unless I was assured of that."

Shannon smiled, heart hammering. "Quite certain."

Elizabeth let her go, imagining a carriage from the hospital waiting outside. But instead, Shannon found, with great difficulty, a hired carriage that took her to the docks. Most all of the quays were now ragged and rotted, and she saw very little commerce taking place. Instead, figures lurked in the shadows and made her question the wisdom of her solitary expedition.

She paid for passage on a boat too shallow to trigger any lingering mines that had not been cleared out. The owner agreed to approach the Union ship on which he knew there was an admiral. They did so under a white flag in case the Federals suspected any threat of hostility. She had chosen the Navy because she felt much more on her own territory among them. She was not so unwise as to believe that most Army men were cut from the same cloth as those at Santarella. But she was still enough shaken that she shied away from their camps nonetheless.

As she was taken away from the harbor, she looked back over her shoulder at the shattered city. Then she returned her attention to the ship, gathering her courage, unsure of whether to use her real name. Would the Admiral feel guilt for what had been done to her and help her? Or enmity for her family's betrayal of the Union? It depended every bit on personality in any situation involving a great deal of authority centered in one person, as she had ample cause to know.

With the letter she had written out in her own hand-writing, they let her come aboard. She was encouraged to think it was the workings of the Divine, and so she didn't question it, and merely let them pull her up in their boat. As she first stepped aboard the ship, the men stopped and stared as though they hadn't seen a woman in months. And perhaps they hadn't.

The underling officer took her into some inner offices, where men were sitting at desks and going about their work, much as though they were on land. She found matters clean, if lacking a feminine touch, and the man with her so far had been courteous.

"If you'll wait here, ma'am, I'll speak with Captain Short."

She nodded, taking the chair he indicated and folding her gloved hands, trying to pretend the men weren't surreptitiously watching her.

Captain Short was less civil. He was a stoic-looking man, who at long last emerged and asked her to state her case. He watched her in growing suspicion as she spoke, even if the kinder officer seemed, somehow, after everything, to stand in awe of her gentility and to think that she ought to be heard. The young man did not say so, of course—that would've been insubordinate—but she could tell as much from the sympathetic look on his face.

"You wish to speak with the Admiral?" Short repeated, as though he didn't quite believe what he had heard.

"Immediately, if at all possible," she said pleasantly, with a smile.

The man looked aghast, curling his lip.

The other officer cleared his throat. "With your permission, Captain, I will take this to the Admiral and ask what he wishes to be done." Shannon bestowed a beaming smile upon the man, though she had little hope that his endeavors would succeed. The Captain agreed to it reluctantly, and the other man went off with victory in his step.

Shannon sat back down, feeling the eyes of every man nearby upon her again. How many were there in the room? Good heavens, at least thirty. Apparently, all had found her words, her person, and perhaps her audacity, fascinating.

The kind officer returned after being away a seemingly inordinate amount of time, looking a little crestfallen. "Well?" Short barked. The other men in the area continued about their activities, chattering, writing, or looking at her longer than was strictly polite, and they seemed to pay Short no heed. A good sign: perhaps his bark was worse than his bite.

The other man cleared his throat. "If you please, ma'am, the Admiral requests that you write your case down, and it shall be considered along with all the rest."

Shannon felt her hopes sinking. "There are others?" she asked, careful not to let any emotion show.

He smiled in sympathy. "Many. And frankly, ma'am, we are still awaiting word from Washington on what is to be done with abandoned lands."

"Abandoned?" Shannon demanded, before she could think better of it. If abandonment meant being marched off the island in one's shift while everything one ever owned burned, the Yankees had a much different conception of the word than she. She was within an inch of telling the man so. But he was her only ally, and she must remember it. She bit her tongue and cleared her throat. "If you might ask the Admiral if I could have only five minutes of his time," Shannon said, knowing this was her only chance.

The Captain was outraged. "If you think, ma'am, that I am going to allow a Rebel woman within ten feet of Admiral Haley, when all she might have on her mind is assassination, you are indulging in a dream!"

His voice had trailed off on the end, for Shannon had paled, and her lips had parted. It seemed as though her heart stopped, and all of time stood still. "Admiral..." She blinked. "*John Thomas* Haley?" Her voice was a mere reed, thread and weak.

Captain Short and the other officer exchanged looks, Short moving so that he stood between Shannon and the door. "Yes."

She gripped the post which was beside her. Oh, good heavens, she could not faint on a ship full of hostile men. She took a breath, trying to fill her lungs, and said in an odd voice, lifting her chin, "Ask..." She swallowed. "Ask Admiral Haley, then, if he will see his wife." She met the Captain's eyes.

Silence descended as surely as a bombardment. No one pretended now not to gape at her, and someone at one of the desks dropped something. The young officer stared at her, mouth ajar, and Short blinked. Meeting her eyes for a long moment, he turned, without a word, and went to do as she asked.

The seconds he was gone were the longest, she felt, of her life. They seemed to stretch out infinitely across the ocean, but she was in too much of a whirl of emotion to have a single rational thought.

At last, the man returned and, meeting her eyes again, he said, swallowing, "Yes, Mrs. Haley. He will see his wife." He gulped again.

She held his eyes a moment, as though seeking courage, and then she followed him, while stares followed her, through the door. They walked a few more paces in a hallway, and then she stared at the door where the Captain was leading her, feeling as though she might faint or be ill or perhaps dissolve into nothingness.

The officer opened the door, and then, somehow, she was across the threshold. He was standing, his cheeks pale, looking directly at her. She saw him, saw his blonde hair, his handsome face upon which time had wrought changes which she couldn't quite discern. She saw his long frame, taller than she remembered, his hands curled slightly, as though from nerves, and his plain blue eyes, which were fastened on her.

She could see him *breathing*. If she had been closer she might even have heard his heart beating. And then, studying him, long and slowly, to her horror, she *did* dissolve. Into tears, right in front of him. It was not something she could control, but she felt it rising nonetheless, softly at first, and then into sobs which shook her to her core. She covered her mouth and tried at least to be silent.

"Shannon..." She heard her name rasped, heard a world of time and agony, and then he closed the distance between them, touching her arms first and then enclosing her in an embrace while emotion shook her. She felt his arms around her, and his chest, but her mind could not fathom it. She cried silently, sobs wracking her body, until she was capable of commanding herself again.

"You are alive," she whispered when she first could speak.

He ran a hand across his mouth, a hand which he couldn't hide was not quite steady, and looked at her. The years rolled back and then drew up, tallying themselves into a horrifying quantity. She could smell him, his scent, and she hadn't realized how she had missed it until that moment. She saw on his hand that he still wore his wedding ring. Her heart surely stopped.

He still studied her, seeming not to know what to say, or not to be able to speak at all. Finally, he managed in a dazed whisper, eyes cataloguing her features, "I am sorry for what happened. We heard— you probably know that. I'm so sorry."

She shook her head, lip trembling. "It was not your fault. Of course it wasn't."

He shook his head slowly, looking away, and then stepped backwards, putting some distance between them. It was a bit dark in the room, and she could not entirely make out his expression at this distance. She noticed then that they must be in his quarters, a well-appointed room that was as neat as he always was. Her chest ached. "I cannot believe... Please know that I had no knowledge it would be you," she said, making him look up at her quickly. She flushed. "I meant that I would not presume to impose..." Her voice trailed off under his stare, which she had always found too searching.

He cleared his throat. After a moment's silence, he said, as though striving for a semblance of normalcy but failing when everything in him was in turmoil, "Your family... Frederick made it through the war?"

"Yes," she said, nodding, turning her head to dry her eyes with her handkerchief. "Yes, he is well."

He nodded once, a little unsteady on his feet, too. He looked back at her as though there were something he wanted to say, or perhaps a thousand things, but didn't know where to begin. And he searched her as though she were a mystery he could not fathom. Realizing that she had no right to put him through such misery, she said, "Please, I did not mean to... I will go. It was wrong of me to come here."

He took a step as she did, lifting his hand and saying, "Wait. Wasn't there something you needed? Forgive me, my head is not clear. I cannot remember."

She hesitated, looking at him. She ought not to have cried and set him at a disadvantage, but she had not meant to, and she certainly had not wished to. He ought to have railed at her, or demanded answers, or *something*. But she had caught him unaware and thrown him off his balance. "It doesn't matter," she said, shaking her head, attempting to smile, but it was a travesty that fell miserably short.

"No," he said. "Tell me."

Her heart nearly stopped again. He was looking at her in such a way. It reminded her of...something. "I..." Good heavens, now *she* couldn't think. "It is my family. And my sister-in-law's. They are suffering, and their lands have been confiscated." What would have been a noble purpose with any other felt suddenly wrong, and she had to force herself to say, "You...must use your own discretion, but I had come to ask that an order be signed to the effect that their lands be returned to them."

He held her eyes for a moment as though thinking. She thought perhaps he meant to deny her without answering. Certainly, it was what she felt she deserved. But instead, he turned and walked to his desk, where he sat and took two pieces of paper on which he wrote something. She watched as he did so, the tilt of his head so familiar, that it took her right back to their house in Washington as she stood one night in the threshold of his study watching him. She clasped her hands tightly, tears threatening again. Finally, he looked up, holding her eyes for a long moment before coming around the desk and extending the papers toward her.

She took them, holding them out from her for a moment, still studying him. She brought the papers against her bodice, not speaking, watching him. Finally, he said, his voice sounding as though it had not been used for awhile, "You are not alone?"

She nodded.

"Surely you did not travel the streets of Charleston—this Charleston—alone?"

"I had no choice," she said in a soft voice.

He looked chagrined. "Then you will have an escort home," he said. She lifted her hand, but before she could protest, he had slipped out of the room.

He was gone only a minute or so and returned with the kind young man. "Lieutenant Simmons will take care of you," he said softly, still looking at her.

She moistened her lips and held his eyes another moment before turning to go with Simmons. She was quiet as she did so, looking over her shoulder to find him still looking at her with such an expression she couldn't fathom his feelings. Simmons escorted her out with great punctiliousness and stayed with her all the way through the boat ride, in which she thought they tarried a bit more than was necessary. A messenger had gone on ahead of them, she assumed, to secure a conveyance for them. But instead, when they made it to the wharves, Simmons asked her to wait a few minutes. And it wasn't long then until she saw, riding up on the cobblestones, masterful Union Cavalry in their greatest pomp and circumstance. Their blue and gold uniforms were shining, their swords at their hips, and an officer led a horse with a lady's saddle.

Shannon blinked in surprise. She looked up, meeting the eyes of the bearded man she assumed to be a captain from his shoulder boards. He and Simmons greeted one another, and the Captain said, smiling at her in a charming way, "Admiral Haley requests a guard for a lady?"

"Yes, sir," Lieutenant Simmons said.

"We are happy to be of service," he said.

Simmons took her hand and helped her to mount the side-saddle, averting his eyes. She wasn't wearing her habit, of course, but she managed to arrange her skirts modestly as her heart pounded in her throat. If head-shaving was used as a message in war, this could only be taken as the same. Shannon just didn't know to which side it was directed and what, precisely, that message was.

The men gathered around her, five on either side, and formed a military escort as they traversed the streets of Charleston. People in the streets gaped, and she did not doubt for a moment that she was recognized. She lifted her chin, perfecting her posture and holding her reins with care, for the horse was a powerful beast.

She felt like a medieval queen arriving in London, victorious after war. As word spread, people ran out to look at the lady being escorted by the Yankees. Somehow, Shannon became convinced that the intended message was to his own people, that she was a person worthy of respect, undeserving of the violence inflicted upon her. But there was something more, too, which she couldn't quite reason out yet. Her mind was spinning too much with the surreal discoveries of the day to think of it.

As they drew up before Ravenel House, her father and Frederick came out on the balcony. When Frederick recognized her, he looked so startled that Shannon was afraid he might run out and demand an explanation. But he stopped in the middle of the balcony, two paces in front of her equally stunned father, and stood stock still. Shannon looked down, rather hoping the men wouldn't notice them. But they did, of course, a couple of them tipping their hats to them. The Ravenel men didn't move or speak. The Captain dismounted to help Shannon down, escorting her right up to the door, where he waited until a maid opened the door and then departed.

Shannon stepped into the silence of the foyer, trying to catch her breath, feeling Rebecca's eyes upon her. But she didn't have long to recover. Her father and Frederick came down the stairs immediately, a hundred questions on their tongues.

"Shannon, what on earth?" Frederick demanded, advancing on her. He caught her arms, eyes wild. "What did they want with you? Did they—"

She caught his shoulders, saying calmly, "He is here, Frederick." She held his eyes to convey her message. "John Thomas is in Charleston."

Chapter Twenty-Seven

Shannon sat alone in the small parlor, staring at the papers on which John Thomas had written out orders that John Ravenel and Williams Middleton were to be reinvested with all rights of ownership in the lands they had held before the late conflict between the states. Her fingers glided over his signature as she wondered what it would cost him.

She ought not to have asked it of him, she thought, looking up and into nothingness, out the window and into the rainy spring day. People would say that he had acted unfairly, or with nepotism, or even, with the shocking language being thrown about, traitorously. He had known all of that and still he had done it. She swallowed, looking back down at the papers.

She hadn't told any of her family that she had them. They knew why she had gone, but they had been too shocked by the subsequent occurrences, especially that she had chanced to encounter John Thomas, to think to ask whether she had been successful. She supposed they assumed she had not.

Her mind seemed continually to spin. She was on the brink of two decisions, and one of them, she felt, had only one answer. It was time for her to choose, once and for all.

She stood, crossing the beautifully ornamented room to the fireplace, where a low flame burned. Kneeling as best she could, she put the papers in, letting their corners catch and then consume.

God would provide for her family and Elizabeth's family. He always had. It was time to leave matters in His hands. Probably their lands would be returned to them eventually, in a better day, along with everyone else's. But Shannon would not be responsible for the downfall of a brilliant career.

She had just risen when Elizabeth came in. "Shannon," her sister-in-law said sunnily, "did you hear? Arthur is to return home tomorrow. We've finally gotten word!"

Shannon's expression changed, and she rushed to embrace her, saying with real delight, "Oh, my dear friend, such wonderful news!"

Elizabeth held up the letter, reading over it with shining eyes. "And Seymour Christian."

"Do not speak to me of Seymour Christian."

"Very well, I shan't," Elizabeth said, taking her arm and forcing her to sit with her on the dainty sofa. "Now, Shannon, we shall talk."

"No, we shan't."

"Very well, then, *I* shall talk. You have scarcely spoken two words of it, but Shannon...the *coincidence!* You can't tell

me your wheels aren't spinning, for I can see that they are."
Elizabeth clasped her hands against her old and frayed pink
skirt and fixed her eyes on Shannon's face.

Shannon swallowed. "Perhaps I should like to keep my
own counsel."

"No, you would like to convince yourself that he *wouldn't*
wish you to return to him—"

"Well, what proof have I to think he does?" Shannon
demanded. "Nothing! He said not a word on the subject,
and I believe it would be very forward to presume upon...
upon old feelings when three and a half years have passed!
When I had told him that our marriage was finished. When
I have no notion of his feelings toward me; when they might,
in fact, be the very opposite of benign."

"Shannon, he has revealed his feelings for all the world to
see!" Elizabeth exclaimed in great exasperation. "Frederick
and I have decided it. *That* was his meaning."

Shannon looked at her, biting her lip. She felt the prick
of unshed tears. "Do you truly think so, Elizabeth?"

Elizabeth rose, taking her hand, and came closer on the
sofa, looking at her earnestly. "Yes. I do. I can't know, of
course, for certain, but, my dear friend, you will never know
unless you ask."

Shannon straightened her shoulders, realizing that great
courage would be called for. More courage than it had taken
to marry him, and more than it had taken to leave him.

Gathering herself, Shannon stood outside the door to her father's library where she knew him to be, and, with a pounding heart but steady hand, she reached to open the door.

She found him standing in front of the windows, hands clasped behind his back. Shannon lay her hand against her bodice and said, "Papa?"

"Shannon," he answered, not turning around.

She stepped into the room, well-aware that something was on his mind. He never broke his concentration when that was the case, was fiercely intent until a resolution was reached. She looked around her at the bookshelves, at the view through the windows, at his desk where she had found him sitting and grieving her mother, seemingly so long ago.

"Shannon, I have been thinking," he said softly, but with clarity.

"Yes, Papa?"

"On your marriage."

She studied him from behind.

"'What God hath joined together, let no man put asunder,'" he quoted. He looked over his shoulder at her and then turned to look at her fully. He shook his head. "Perhaps I am that man." She watched him, not moving. "I never meant it so. I meant only to support my daughter, but, Shannon, I cannot support this any longer."

"What?" she breathed.

He paused only a beat before saying, "You must return to him, Shannon."

She blinked.

"The war is finished. He must provide for you, whether he thinks it best to send you to his people, or to keep you with him. But you must place yourself under his protection, rather than mine."

Her lips parted. "Do you mean to say," she asked in utter shock, "that if I wish to remain in this house, I would not be welcome?"

After a pause, he nodded once.

As she stood staring at him in amazement, he added, "If you return to him, and he will not have you, that would be another matter. But a marriage is sacred, Shannon, and I'll no longer stand in the way of yours. I gave you to him five years ago, and I meant it to be final. And final it is still."

She blinked, stunned, a trembling beginning deep within her.

"You'll find a way," he told her, some degree of compassion in his eyes that she didn't wish to acknowledge. "People usually do."

"I suppose I am to leave this instant?" she demanded, her temper flaring.

"Shannon, be reasonable," he said with irritation. "Of course not. Suitable arrangements will be made, and in a few days—"

She had been gathering her skirts in her hands for flight, and she said, "Well, I choose *not* to wait a few days! If my presence is unwelcome, I choose to leave at once. and if and when you try to stop me, you may remember that this was your decision. If you imagine I will stay for one moment in a house where I am not wanted, you have never known me at all!"

With that, she left, slamming the door behind her.

It was nearly nightfall by the time Shannon made it to the ship. Her rage aside, she had made her decision. However, she would have arrived with a bit more preparation and circumspection had her father not enraged her.

She clasped her valise in her hand as she was handed onto the ship, wondering where she would go if he refused her. He was not ungentlemanly, so he would provide her with lodging until morning, but having her back as a wife was quite another matter.

And so the moment she stepped aboard the ship she would always consider the bravest of her life. She was treated quite differently this time. The men still gawked, but they went right away to deliver her message and returned to her after only the briefest interlude.

What must they think of her, Shannon wondered as she walked past man after man, gripping the strap of her case tightly. A woman who had left her husband, a renowned Northern hero, and who now came aboard a ship at nightfall with a valise in hand. The officer opened the door for her, and, swallowing, she stepped across his threshold for the second time.

John Thomas was standing at attention, still shaken from last time, let alone from this new development. Shannon aboard the ship with a valise? What could she mean by it?

He was not looking very certain or poised when the door opened and Simmons showed her in, saying something to her that John Thomas could not hear. She was wearing a gown too fine for travelling aboard ships, as though she had been caught in the middle of dinner. She was still so beautiful it knocked the very breath from him. Time had passed, of course. She was twenty-five to his twenty-nine. He could not tell if that had caused the subtle changes in her or something else. Certainly, she was thinner. He swallowed.

He became aware of Simmons closing the door, and he cleared his throat, wondering why he should feel like a youth, thrown off his course, unsure. Only, it had been so long. She was looking at him, one foot, he thought, slightly in front of the other, the bag held so tightly in her hands that her fingers had turned white. Her lips were parted as though she wanted to speak, but her blue eyes were uncertain.

She swallowed.

He didn't know what to say, was uncertain he could speak if he tried. And she looked terrified.

"John Thomas," she said, her voice cracking. She cleared it, lifting her chin as though preparing herself for courage. "I know that you... That a great deal of time has passed. And that you don't know me anymore." She pressed her lips together. "I know...that my actions were unforgivable... And I should never wish to presume..."

His lips parted slowly. He watched her without moving, feeling waves of hot and cold wash over him, dizzying him, until he felt as though the room were spinning.

One of her hands released the bag, fluttered up to her neck, and then trembled as it rested against her chest, as though to still her heart. "I beg you will send me away if..." Her voice faded. "If..." And then, she looked him in the eye squarely and said, "Will you have me back for your wife?"

Chapter Twenty-Eight

Adeline was just getting off the phone with her carpet supplier in England on Friday when the phone buzzed again. She walked out of the room, where the sander was screeching, and into the currently vacated kitchen. Looking at the screen, she saw that it was her secretary in Charlotte.

"Hey, Janice," she said, opening the fridge and pulling out one of Adrian's expensive bottles of water.

"Hey, girl. How're you doing?"

"Great," she said, hoping it didn't sound forced.

"I found your wedding pictures on the photographer's Facebook page. Y'all were stunning."

She smiled. "Adrian and his son photograph well."

"Not just them. I like the black and white one of your hands—you know, fingers intertwined, ocean in the distance..."

One of her favorites, too. She had only looked at them once. Hadn't even been confident she should hire a professional photographer. She wasn't sure what that said about her future. "Yeah, they were taken by Adrian's cousin. She's great." She kind of let the conversation fall into a lull, wondering why Janice was calling.

"Listen, Addy, I've got big news." Adeline's pulse quickened. She'd had about enough big news, but this sounded good. "You know those pictures we posted of Ravenel-Thompson House?"

"Yep." She always posted her current project on her website with permission from the owners. It was the key way to generate new jobs. Adrian had signed the release last week, glancing up at her once. She hadn't been able to make eye contact.

"We've had like a thousand views on the website. Three requests for bids on smaller projects. But..." Janice took a deep breath. I got a call from John Thierry." Adeline's ears tuned in. "He's bought Carrington Place. He and his wife, Nancy, want to restore it. They want a bid from Miller Restorations. But 'Charleston' and 'Ravenel' pretty much have sealed the deal. I think the bid's just a formality, Adeline."

Adeline's jaw hung open. Carrington Place was once the largest plantation in Asheville and had pretty much been in ruins since the 1930's. She couldn't count the number of times she had passed it, wishing someone with the money would buy it and restore it. Its white columns had often tortured her dreams. Yeah, that was pretty nerdy, but it's who she was. "Janice...are you serious?"

"Yep. Right there in your mama and daddy's backyard. It'll probably be a three-year job. I can't even imagine what the commission would be."

Adeline sank into a kitchen chair, fingers over her mouth. She breathed for a few seconds. "Janice, I can't..." The sentence died away.

"I told him you were on a job until October, maybe November. He said that was no problem. He's looking for investors, needs a few months anyway. I didn't mention your ties to Charleston or the baby."

Adeline bit her lip, looking out the window. "When does he want his bid by?"

"February 15th."

Her heart pounded, and she felt a little dizzy. "Um... Wow. Thanks, Janice. I... You know I have to think..."

"Yeah. Of course. And take care of yourself, girl."

"I will." She wrapped up the conversation, her mind whirling. Because in the end, it came down to a straight-forward choice: jump in with both feet with Adrian, saying no to the job when they'd never discussed forever, or leave it on the backburner, keeping the means of support for herself open in case it didn't work out.

Adrian drank his tea by the door, looking across his parents' garden to the table where Adeline sat next to his dad. Harris stood over them as they looked at a binder of old family documents in page protectors that his dad had stumbled upon in the basement. Jude was sitting on his dad's lap, eyes bored, but content, his belly full and the ice cream maker humming in the background.

His mom came out on the brick pavement with him, handing him a glass of tea. She met his eyes before looking briefly to the party at the table and then away, her arms crossed. "Does this mean you're no longer snubbing me?" he asked, taking a sip of the tea.

She gave him a cold look. "Honestly, Adrian."

"What? You haven't called in three weeks, haven't been to see Jude in longer—"

"I'm worried about you," she snapped. "Not angry."

He studied her, saw she was laboring under unusually strong, if refined emotion, and held his tongue. After a silence had passed, she said, as if it had been simmering under a lid, "I fear for your happiness, your...state of mind. This is not you, Adrian. Having a baby with a girl who—though perhaps I'm mistaken—wasn't even your girlfriend. Marrying women you hardly know... Harris I might have believed it of, but not you."

"Mom, that's not fair," he said.

"No, it wasn't," she conceded. "Don't tell him I said that." He wondered at her, asking him to keep confidences even as she railed at him. "And then making some foolish bargain..." She looked across the way at Adeline. "To...to agree with her that you would part ways if it doesn't work—"

"I hope Harris's clients find him more discreet," he said grimly, jaw clenching.

"Don't mind that," she said. She looked up, studying him for a long moment. "This is not who you are." Her eyes roved his face, deep emotion on her own. She hesitated before speaking. "Do you miss her so much?" she whispered.

He looked away. He was silent for a long time. Didn't know really how to touch that one. Finally, he said, "This has nothing to do with Lauren, Mom."

She surveyed him again before looking across the garden, her eyes resting on Adeline. "Well, I must say, she's nothing like Lauren."

"No," he said softly. "She's not."

"Listen, Adrian, I'm sure she's a lovely girl," she said, acting like she hadn't been speaking of her like she was some floozie three seconds ago. "But how on earth could you be so reckless?"

"Mom." He crossed his arms. "Not that it's any concern of yours—"

"Everything is a mother's concern," she said, her earrings bobbing.

He bit the side of his jaw. "I'm doing the best I can with the situation. I *must* support her—I want to. And I refuse to be anything less to this baby than a real father."

She sniffed. "This has nothing to do with the baby, Adrian," she said softly. "You know we'll love it just as we love Jude."

He held her eyes, the tension leaving his body. "You better," he said softly. She met his smile briefly. "And just so you know, I want it to work with Adeline, Mom," he added quietly. His eyes trailed across the way to where she was sitting, pretty in a floral sundress. "Very much," he added softly.

Adeline had been distracted since he'd gotten home Friday. He'd asked her if she was feeling okay and had received a belated, but affirmative, *"Oh, yeah! I'm great!"* He'd watched her after that, trying to think what could be on her mind. Saturday they'd barely seen each other—she'd worked all day. This morning, she had gone to mass with them, which he knew made her a little uncomfortable. He'd asked if she wanted to talk about it, about doing something else, but she had shaken her head. *"No, this is best for Jude."* She held his eyes and nodded to seal the deal.

"Meaning..?"

"He's been raised Catholic. This is his church."

He had studied her, hesitated a minute. *"And the baby?"*

Her eyes shifted. *"Um...can we talk about that...later?"*

He was stressing her out. He had immediately retracted the statement. But it had been on his mind nevertheless. Still, that she was thinking of Jude meant more to him than he had said.

He kept an eye on her during the course of the evening, but he really didn't think she was ill, except for a little tired. Vanilla ice cream helped him to recover from talking about his sex life with his mom, and by eight o'clock, they were driving back to Charleston.

Jude, worn out, was fast asleep in the backseat. Adeline was sitting beside Adrian, looking out the window.

"What is it, Adeline," he said softly.

She looked over at him, seemingly surprised. The tension in her shoulders lessened. "Nothing, sorry. Janice—my secretary—called to talk about potential jobs once I finish with Ravenel-Thompson."

He held her eyes before looking back at the road. "Jobs you're going to take?" he asked.

There was an awkward silence. "Isn't that a little up in the air right now?" she answered softly.

His jaw clenched.

She put her hand on her forehead. "Sorry. Wow. No pressure, huh?"

He looked over at her again. He could see she really was stressed out, something that, if he wasn't mistaken, rarely happened to her. She'd even taken the marriage and the baby in her stride. He shook his head. "No, I'm sorry. You were being honest about the situation."

"I still think it's more organic if we don't talk about it, though."

He didn't even know what that meant. Okay, he did. She wanted to let things develop naturally, and he got that. But there was only so much a man could take. He was becoming the king of forbearance. He couldn't even brush her hand getting silverware without thinking he had crossed some boundary. And wanting more. Couldn't see her beautiful legs propped on the coffee table without remembering. Couldn't watch her laughing with his brother or the crew without wishing there weren't barriers between them.

He looked over at her. "Listen, Adeline, at the risk of sounding like a sexist pig—"

"Which obviously you are," she said.

He cracked a smile. "You should just think about you and the baby." He looked at her to see how that went over. She seemed to be characteristically mild. "I know you want to finish the house, and that's great. But don't worry about the future, or me, or...all the rest." She was looking at him, listening. "It'll come together, okay?" He lay his open hand on the console, and she placed hers in it. "Right now, I just want the two of you to be healthy and safe."

"Which we are," she said softly, seeming to find comfort in the notion.

"Which you are," he agreed, turning his head to smile softly at her.

She smiled back, sleepily putting her head against the headrest. She looked down, touching her middle briefly. "Want to try again?" she said, almost in a whisper.

"Sure," he said, giving his hand. She placed it on the curve, covering it with her hand. He felt a flutter and looked at her quickly. She smiled at him, absently stroking his hand with her thumb. He glanced over at her as she lay her head back and closed her eyes. His chest tightened, but fear pooled in his stomach.

THE END

Many thanks to...

Hannah Cowan Jones, Pamela Cowan, Dana Womack, and Beverly Crouch, first readers and editors extraordinaire. It's pretty cool to have two English teachers, a History teacher, and a Historian on your side! Thank you for making this book ten times better.

Tara Mayberry, for your expertise and diligence in formatting and for making the most beautiful book covers!

My family and friends, for your continual support. My readers, for your enthusiasm and kindness. And my Savior, for Your steadfast love.

TARA

Books by Tara Cowan

The Torn Asunder Series

Southern Rain

Northern Fire

Charleston Tides (Available Autumn 2020)

About the Author

TARA COWAN has been writing novels since she was seventeen. She is the author of the *Torn Asunder Series*, including *Southern Rain* and *Northern Fire*. A huge lover of all things history, she loves to travel, watch British dramas, read good fiction, and spend time with her family. An attorney, Tara lives in Tennessee and is busy writing her next novel.

Tara holds a Bachelor of Science Degree in Political Science, with minors in English and History, from Tennessee Tech University and a Doctor of Jurisprudence from the University of Tennessee College of Law.

To connect with Tara, visit her blog at
www.teaandrebellion.com,
follow her on Instagram @teaandrebellion_,
or find her on Facebook or Twitter.

www.ingramcontent.com/pod-product-compliance
Lightning Source LLC
Chambersburg PA
CBHW030313200626
46816CB00006BA/1768